SERIOUS

MAGGIE GIBSON

POOLBEG

Acknowledgements

Thanks to the usual suspects!

Published 1997 by
Poolbeg Press Ltd,
123 Baldoyle Industrial Estate,
Dublin 13, Ireland

© Maggie Gibson 1997

The moral right of the author has been asserted.

A catalogue record for this book is available from the British Library.

ISBN 1 85371 775 4

Cover photography by Telegraph Colour Library
Cover design by Poolbeg Group Services Ltd
Set by Poolbeg Group Services Ltd in New Baskerville 11/14
Printed and bound in Great Britain by
Cox & Wyman Ltd, Reading, Berks.

For
Anna Egan

Chapter One

"There's a nutter outside," Xin said. "A real weirdo."

"Define weirdo," said Grace, intrigued to know what she of the Geisha make-up and shaved temples would consider weird.

For once the pint-sized Ninja seemed lost for words. She shrugged "Well . . . not yer common or garden nutter, and she's goin' on abou' a murder."

"A murder! Didn't you tell her to go to the guards?"

Xin opened her mouth to speak just as the said weirdo sailed into the room.

"Run along, dear," the weirdo said to Xin, and shot her hand across the desk towards Grace. "Poppy Dalglish-Stuart, how do you do?"

Her hand-shake was firm and her deep voice had an Anglo-Irish accent but Xin's description hadn't done her justice.

The strong aroma of either Patchouli or very

1

good quality cannabis had wafted into the room ahead of her. Grace looked her up and down. She could well understand Xin's reaction. She was at least six feet tall, pushing past fifty, and she obviously hadn't noticed that the flower children had disbanded after Woodstock. Every time she moved, she either jangled or tinkled as her numerous bangles and bells knocked and jostled against her angular body. She was dressed in a long Indian print multi-coloured caftan over which she wore a brown woollen man's cardigan onto which had been stitched little mirrors and coloured beads. Her feet were shod in sandals and she wore brightly coloured odd socks.

Grace thought that thirty odd years ago this woman would have been beautiful, but now she had a haggish appearance accentuated by too much kohl settling into the lines round her eyes, a slightly heavy hand with the blusher brush and long plaited salt and pepper hair with two streaks of orange at the temples.

Xin wore a look of outrage. As a Shadow Warrior, a living weapon, she didn't take kindly to being told to "run along" and was about to give the ageing hippy a mouthful when she saw Grace's warning look and beat a hasty, and to her mind, tactical, retreat.

"So, are you going to look into my sister's

murder or not?" the older woman demanded impatiently.

"Have you been to see the gardai?"

Poppy Dalglish-Stuart inhaled deeply on a foul smelling roll-up cigarette "Of course I have, but they won't listen to me, the fools! Emmet O'Connell has murdered my sister Carenza and the gardai won't do anything about it." She said it with a note of high dudgeon and then sat down and waited for Grace to react.

"When and where did this happen?" Grace asked, more than somewhat bemused.

Poppy cast her large black-rimmed eyes to the ceiling and sighed. "I don't know where or when, my dear . . . that's why I need you. I just know that he did it."

"I'm sorry Ms Stuart I . . ."

"*Dalglish*-Stuart," the woman snapped.

Grace was beginning to lose patience with her already. "I'm sorry, I don't understand. What makes you think that this Emmet O'Connell has murdered your sister?"

"Because he has done it before, he poisoned my cousin Anabell. He seems to have a habit of murdering his wives."

"Oh, I see," said Grace. "And when was this?"

Poppy slowly turned to face Grace and pursed her lips. "Don't patronise me, young woman. I made a complaint to the gardai at that time too and was ignored. I warned them that he would do it again. God knows I tried to warn Carenza, but she wouldn't listen, silly woman."

Grace didn't move. "Go on, dear. Check it out. See Sergeant McEvoy at Harcourt Terrace. He'll tell you."

Grace was still silent, she detested being addressed as *dear*, and didn't know what to make of this geriatric flower-child.

After a moments thought she said "Would you excuse me Ms *Dalglish*-Stuart," stressing the first part of the name. "I'll be back shortly. Would you like a cup of tea?" The black eyes just glared at her. "Well perhaps not then," she said and left the room.

Xin was sitting smugly at her desk, smirking.

"Get me Dermot McEvoy at Harcourt Terrace will you," Grace hissed. "And wipe that stupid smirk off your face."

Phoebe glided through the door of reception weighed down with shopping bags and slumped her elegant frame down on the settee.

"God, I'm knackered!" she said, kicking off her shoes, then she sniffed the air. "Who's smoking dope?"

"The nutter in the office," Xin said as she handed Grace the phone.

"Hello, Dermot."

"What do you want, Grace?" Dermot asked without preamble.

4

"I'm fine, Dermot, thanks for asking. And how are you?" she said.

Grace had worked with Inspector Dermot McEvoy for four years before she had resigned from the garda síochàna after ten years service. It had been a career move, though not of her choosing. Dermot and a very few others were alone in believing that she had been set up, and that the accusation of taking corrupt payments levelled against her had been malicious. Not that their faith was much consolation. She knew the sticking power of slung mud and that her career was dead in the water, so she had cut her losses and gone into partnership with Phoebe Lamplighter (high-class hooker, retired) and Phoebe's friend and mentor Mungo (a very large, black Vietnam veteran) in Sleuths, Investigation & Security Specialists.

Weighing in at ten and a half stone and five feet tall, Alice Mountjoy, aka Xin, was their receptionist and general factotum. Xin took pride in the fact that she was a qualified Ninja (her words) and had a bizarre style all her own.

Coincidentally she shared the Christian name of Alice with Grace's mother, but there any similarity ended. Alice de Rossa, though Grace loved her dearly, was a downtrodden mouse of a woman who wouldn't say boo to a goose and always took the least line of resistance. This wasn't surprising considering the fact that Paul de Rossa, Grace's father, was an overbearing control freak who gave the impression that his second daughter was a constant source of disappointment to him. He had expected her to follow him and her siblings into the medical profession, marry well and raise grandchildren, although not necessarily in that order. And the fact that Grace had achieved none of these aspirations led him to virtually ignore her.

But after initial reservations, Grace was beginning to realise that the eccentric partnership was working out much better than she had expected.

"Sorry Grace. How are you?" Dermot said at the other end of the line. "Now what do you want?"

"I've got a deranged woman here, who claims her sister's been murdered by her brother-in-law, and that he also killed her cousin Anabell six years ago. Says she made a complaint to you at the time but no action was taken."

"Anabell? Would that be Anabell O'Connell?"

"I think so. The woman's called . . ."

"Poppy Stuart?"

"Poppy Dalglish-Stuart, yes. Is she for real?"

Dermot snorted. "She's . . . shall we say, eccentric. I couldn't turn around that she wasn't behind me ranting on about Anabell O'Connell."

"Who was Anabell O'Connell?"

"Poppy Dalglish-Stuart came in six years ago

claiming that her cousin Anabell had been murdered by Dr Emmet O'Connell, the husband. I investigated the complaint and found that the cause of death on the cert was heart failure brought on by a congenital heart defect. Dr Brian Drummond, her GP, signed the cert. She'd been seen by him the day before she died and several times in the weeks leading up to her death, so no PM was needed. Dalglish-Stuart persisted, but there was little we could do because, by the time she made the complaint, Anabell O'Connell had been cremated, anyway everything was in order."

"D'you think she just has it in for the brother-in-law for some reason?"

"It looks that way," he said.

"OK Dermot, thanks, I'll talk to you soon."

While Grace was talking to Dermot, Xin had been filling Phoebe in about Sleuth's newest client and, as Grace replaced the receiver, Phoebe said, "Who's the basket case?" pointing at the closed office door.

"Shhhhhhh! she'll hear you. If you're so interested come in to the office and see for yourself."

When the two women entered the office the air was thick with cigarette smoke. Poppy was sitting by the desk where Grace had left her still puffing on her roll-up. Grace introduced Phoebe and they shook hands.

"I spoke with Dermot McEvoy and he told me the background. He seems to think that your cousin died of natural causes though. What exactly makes you think something has happened to your sister?"

"I told them it would happen and it has. He has done it again. He has killed Carenza, In the immortal words of Eliza Doolittle *'e done 'er in.*" She put on an exaggerated cockney accent.

"But what makes you think that Emmet O'Connell has actually killed your sister and, if she's dead, where's the body?"

Grace was watching Poppy closely. Her body language didn't suggest that she was lying and, for all her eccentric appearance, she seemed to be the full shilling. However she rapidly reassessed the situation when Poppy said, "Because she's missing, she was supposed to meet me three days ago but she failed to turn up, and he claims that he doesn't know where she is. He's lying of course. She's dead, and he did it. I cast Carenza's tarot the other day and I could see she was in imminent danger. She was crowned by the ten of swords and the three of swords was before her. The Ace . . ."

Grace interrupted, "Forgive me, Poppy, but tarot readings aren't exactly cast iron evidence. Is that the only reason you have to think that your brother-in-law could have killed your sister? Have you even reported her missing yet?"

"Yes of course. I reported her missing, and I want you to find her. That's what you do, isn't it? Find people." She was getting agitated and she waved her hands about scattering cigarette ash everywhere. Grace wasn't too keen to get involved. The woman was as mad as a hatter and didn't look as if she had two half-pennies to rub together.

Phoebe took the decision out of her hands, she said, "Trust us, Miss Dalglish-Stuart. We're professionals."

After Grace had reluctantly taken details from Poppy and she had departed, she rounded on Phoebe. "Don't you think we should discuss a case before we take it on?" she snapped." The woman's obviously crazy."

"For Christ's sake, Grace, we're not in this business for the good of our health," Phoebe snapped. "How are we supposed to pay the bills if you keep turning away work."

"Who's turning away work?" asked Mungo, who had just wandered in.

"Grace is. She's trying to reroute a perfectly good client to the gardai."

Mungo gave an exaggerated sigh, "You're not a cop any more, Grace. This is private enterprise."

"Well I just thought it would be a waste of our time, that's all," Grace said feebly.

Phoebe cast her beautiful eyes to heaven. "So

9

bloody what. If she wants to pay us for wasting our time, who are we to argue?"

* * *

Grace met Dermot for a pint in Smyth's a little after seven. "What else do you know about Poppy Dalglish-Stuart?" she asked.

Dermot took a long swallow of his Guinness. "You're not working for her, are you?" he said, furrowing his brow in disbelief.

"Against my better judgement."

"Poppy came in six years ago . . ." Dermot started.

Grace interrupted, "You told me that bit. What about her? Is she for real or what?"

"I'd say so. She's from a good old money ascendancy family."

"She has money! You wouldn't think so to look at her."

"Never presume, Grace. You should know that. Anyway she and her sister Carenza were orphaned when she was seven and went to live with their maternal aunt and uncle. A huge sum was placed in trust for them which they inherited when they were fifteen. Poppy was always eccentric apparently, and went off on the hippy trail when she was sixteen, not much interested in the money. When she got back she married some poor sod who couldn't cope with

10

her and he disappeared off the scene after she had two children. She and the kids use her family name and she's independently wealthy though, as you said, you wouldn't think so to look at her. She's interested in all things esoteric. And I think she paints."

"What about the kids?"

Dermot shook his head. "Never met them," he said. "I think they were away when she was making all the fuss six years ago." After a moment's silence he said, "Actually I quite liked the old biddy. Don't let her appearance deceive you, she's sharp as a needle."

"I've got to go and see Emmet O'Connell tomorrow."

"Lucky you," said Dermot.

"Why d'you say that?"

Dermot shrugged. "No particular reason, I just didn't take to the man, that's all. He's a bit of a cold fish."

"D'you think he could have killed his first wife?" Grace asked.

"I don't think so. Poppy strikes me as being a bit obsessive, and she's always been convinced that O'Connell did for Anabell, but I really can't see him being a murderer," Dermot said. "Though you'll never be able to convince Poppy Dalglish-Stuart of that. By the way, it's your round."

Chapter Two

Emmet and Carenza O'Connell lived in the leafy suburb of Grangetown which was on the very edge of the Harcourt Terrace garda district. Their home was an imposing creeper-covered detached house, hidden from the road by mature trees and shrubs and fronted by a well-kept expanse of lawn. A silver top-of-the-range BMW was parked to the right of the front door.

Grace just caught O'Connell before he left for morning surgery. She explained who she was and why she was there as diplomatically as she could, and he invited her in.

"I suppose this is down to the Dalglish-Stuart hag again," he said. He was a tall and distinguished looking man in his early fifties. Immaculately groomed and manicured, with what looked like a year-round tan. His hair was greying at the temples.

"Ms Dalglish-Stuart reported your wife missing, Dr O'Connell. Is that the case?

He was standing with his back to the fireplace and he stared at her for a moment before answering. "My wife has gone away, Miss de Rossa."

She stayed silent in the hope that he would elaborate. When he didn't, she said, "When did she leave?"

"Saturday or Sunday. Why?"

Grace ignored the question. "When do you expect her back?"

He shrugged. It was an elegant, almost Gallic gesture. "I don't."

"I beg your pardon?"

"Miss de Rossa, not that it is any of my sister-in-law's business or indeed yours, but I don't expect my wife back because the truth is she has left me."

"I see," said Grace. "Have you any idea where she might have gone?"

"None whatever." He was standing with his hands in his pockets looking down at the carpet.

"You said she left on Saturday or Sunday. Which day was it?"

He looked up and walked over to the french windows. He was standing with his back to her, looking across the garden. "I don't know which day. I was away at a medical conference in Cork. I didn't get back until Monday morning." He paused. "I found the house empty and a note on the kitchen table."

"What did it say?"

He didn't answer for a while.

"It said, 'I am leaving you for someone else.' What the hell do you think it would say? I checked her wardrobe and most of her clothes have gone as well as her jewellery."

"Do you know who she went away with?" He shook his head so she went on, "And she left no forwarding address?"

"No. I understand people don't usually leave a forwarding address in these circumstances," he said acidly.

Grace put her note-book away. "Perhaps you could let us know if you should hear from her, doctor. I know her sister is worried. It might put her mind at rest."

He nodded and started towards the door, opened it and invited Grace to leave. "If you'll excuse me, I have to be at the centre for surgery."

There was a smile on his lips but not in his eyes. Grace took the hint and walked out into the sunlight. He made straight for his car, nodded a farewell, and drove away leaving her standing on the gravel drive.

She drove straight to the Dalglish-Stuart household on Raglan Road. It was a big Victorian villa and looked the worse for wear with peeling paint and an overgrown front garden. She climbed the steep steps to the front door and rang the bell. After an interval the door creaked opened a crack and an ancient man in a tail coat, who strongly resembled Riff-raff from the Rocky Horror Show, appeared. He looked about one hundred and ten years old.

"Yes?" he said.

Grace stated her business and he opened the door wide, ushering her inside. She was anticipating something dimly lit and Gothic with cobwebs, but was agreeably surprised to find the hall bathed in light from a glass dome high above the curved mahogany staircase. The walls were pristine white, hung with brightly coloured abstract canvasses interspersed with the odd ancestral portrait. A profusion of healthy foliage was grouped in the lee of the banister. Riff-raff shambled away through a door to the left of the stairs and returned moments later and beckoned to her with an arthritic finger to follow him.

Poppy was sitting at the top of a long polished table eating her breakfast. She was dressed in a fairly tatty Indian print robe. Her hair was braided and decorated with beads. She still had the bag-lady look about her, which seemed bizarre in the grand surroundings of the dining-room. Though it was a little on the dusty side and had a lived-in air, Grace guessed that the dining suite alone must be worth more than the entire house on Baggot Street. Poppy invited Grace to join her, and moments later Riff-raff reappeared with a tray carrying a place setting and linen napkin which he set before her.

Grace was bemused and Poppy, seeing her expression, waited until the faithful Riff-Raff had left the room before saying conspiratorially, "He's been with the family since I was a gel. All this . . ." she made a gesture, sweeping her hand towards the beautifully set table, " . . . is Compton. He won't hear of doing things any other way." Grace smiled, warming to the odd woman.

Poppy went on, "Surprised? Expecting to find us living in a caravan?" Her tone was mocking but friendly as she poured tea into a Royal Worcester cup. She handed it to Grace. "Milk?" Grace nodded, still a little stunned.

"You went to see Emmet." It was a statement.

"Yes. How did you know?"

"He just phoned me. Though I guessed what he wanted and Compton told him I was not at home. I take it he denied my accusations."

"Well I didn't actually accuse him of anything at this stage. He claims that Carenza's left him. That she has a lover," Grace said.

"Rubbish! Although I've tried to persuade her to do just that until I'm blue in the face,"

16

said Poppy. Then before Grace could answer, "What are you going to do now?"

"We're going to check the ferries to see if she's left the country, and ask around her neighbours to see if they know anything or saw anything. D'you know if she had any close friends she might confide in?"

Poppy shook her head. "No. Emmet saw off any personal friends she had. He was very possessive, despite the fact that he was a swine to her."

"Then we'll monitor the situation, I'll go back in a couple of days and see what he says then, if Carenza still hasn't shown up."

Poppy gave a mirthless laugh. "I assure you she won't show up. She can't come back. He has killed her."

"Maybe she's taken your advice."

Poppy rubbed her chin between her index finger and thumb. "No. Carenza would never leave him, despite everything."

Grace drank some of her tea and Poppy offered her toast which she gratefully took. Her stomach was reminding her that she hadn't had time for breakfast earlier.

"Tell me about the Anabell business."

Poppy sat back in her chair and crossed her hands in her lap. "Well, what is there to tell? Emmet O'Connell suffocated her and made his partner Brian Drummond sign the death certificate saying that she'd died of a congenital heart defect."

"I didn't know Brian Drummond was O'Connell's partner," said Grace. "How did Carenza and O'Connell meet? Where did Anabell come into the equation? What did O'Connell get out of any of it?"

"One question at a time please!" Poppy threw up her hands.

"Sorry," said Grace.

"You must know that Carenza and I went to live with Anabell's parents, Aunt Dorcas and Uncle Willie, after we were orphaned." Grace nodded. "I was the same age as Anabell, Carenza, two years younger. Emmet O'Connell attended the same parties and social gatherings as our set. He was very dashing in those days, a little too slimy for my taste, mind you, but both Carenza and Anabell were smitten. Anyway, he started to escort Carenza about quite a bit to the Spring Show, the races, that kind of thing. Then, just before Anabell's twenty-first, he dumped Carenza and eloped with Anabell. My guess is that he got wind of her trust fund. She got control of it when she reached twenty-one and he didn't want to risk anyone else nabbing her."

"But I thought Carenza inherited when she was sixteen?"

"That's true, but Carenza was more prudent

than I, and hers was tied up in bonds and investments, so Anabell was a better bet for ready cash. You have to remember that Emmet O'Connell is a very ambitious man, and there was no old money in his family, he just appeared on the scene."

"Where from?"

Poppy shrugged. "I think one of the boys must have brought him home from Trinity, though I'm not sure about that." She stopped as if trying to recall events, then went on, "Carenza was devastated of course, but wouldn't hear a word against Emmet. I was in Tibet at the time, so I'm just relating those events as they were told to me, you understand." Grace nodded again, not wanting to stop Poppy's flow. "When I came home I couldn't believe how Carenza had deteriorated. She was painfully thin and pale and she had lost interest in everything. Our family GP had put her on Valium so she was in a continual stupor. Of course I soon took her off those awful things. As far as drugs were concerned at that time, I only believed in the organic kind. You know, the odd bit of hash. Things are vile in that direction now of course. Crack Cocaine, Ecstasy and those designer drugs, very unhealthy." She stared into space.

"Did Carenza remain single all those years?"

Poppy came back to reality. "Oh yes. She made friends with Anabell and Emmet. I think she was happy just to be near him, you know, crumbs from the table. I found it all very undignified."

"So what happened when Anabell died?"

"Anabell didn't just die, my girl. She was murdered."

Grace raised the palms of her hands. "Sorry, I meant murdered."

"Carenza was round there like a shot. He was playing the bereaved widower of course, but he didn't waste any time and they were married within two months of Anabell's funeral."

"Good grief!"

"I think the term is indecent haste, my dear."

"If O'Connell did murder Anabell, why wait so long? Why didn't he do it years before?"

"Now *that*, I don't know. But his two hundred thousand pounds inheritance came at the right time. The senior partner of the practice died and his share was up for grabs. Emmet had big plans for a state-of-the-art health centre. Maybe Anabell wouldn't give him the money."

"Do you know if he was a womaniser?"

Poppy threw back her head and laughed out loud. "A womaniser? He was always at it. I think Anabell knew but just turned a blind eye. "

"I wonder if he's seeing anyone at the moment?" said Grace, thinking aloud.

"I would put money on it," said Poppy. "And I'm not a betting woman."

Grace was inclined to agree with Poppy. She had taken an irrational dislike to Emmet O'Connell from the moment she had met him. This reaction troubled her until she realised, on the drive back to Baggot Street, that Emmet O'Connell was, in manner and attitude, the spitting image of her own father.

When she arrived back at the office, Xin said, "She's waitin' for you in the big office. She wouldn't take no for an answer."

"Who's *she*?" Grace asked, a little annoyed that Xin hadn't insisted that *she* stay in reception.

"That Kiera wan. She said she'd somethin' for yeh."

Phoebe, who had come into reception behind Grace, was just in time to hear the exchange. "Wow," she said. "Can I come and watch while you whack the bitch?"

Grace glared at her and, taking a deep breath, went in to see her former friend.

Kiera Lyons had been Grace's best friend until she and Andrew, Grace's husband of six years, had moved in together. The upshot of the situation, after much squabbling, was that Andrew and Kiera had bought out Grace's interest in the marital home, thus enabling Grace to buy into the partnership with Phoebe Lamplighter and Mungo. Kiera was now eight and a half months pregnant with Andrew's child.

She was sitting with her feet up on the leather sofa. Grace hadn't seen her for months and, although she was well aware of Kiera's condition, she was surprised at how big and bloated she looked. As Grace entered she heaved herself up.

"I expect you're wondering what I'm doing here?" she said.

"You could say that."

Kiera reached for her handbag and took out a cheque.

"I think this is yours," she said.

Grace looked at it. It was made out for the sum of one thousand pounds.

"What's this for?" she asked.

"It's the money Andrew charged you for the house conveyancing," she said. "Under the circumstances, I didn't think it was fair for him to charge you a fee, and I persuaded him that you should get it back."

After Andrew and Kiera had bought out Grace's interest in the house, in a fit of pique, he had deducted legal fees from Grace, much to her disgust. For just an instant she was tempted to tell Kiera to stuff it. But good sense prevailed and she decided that a thousand quid was a thousand quid, whoever it was from.

"Thanks," she said with the minimum of charm as she snapped the cheque from Kiera's fingers.

Kiera closed her eyes and swayed a little, and Grace noticed that her forehead was beaded with sweat.

"Are you OK?" she asked.

Kiera leaned against the desk and rubbed her swollen abdomen. "Fine," she said. "I had a Chinese takeaway last night and my guts have been giving me hell ever since. D'you mind if I sit down for a moment?"

Grace took her arm and led her to the sofa. "Sit here," she said. "Would you like a glass of water?"

Kiera nodded and Grace went out to reception, leaving the door open.

"Why isn't she screaming?" Phoebe asked, sounding disappointed. "Is she unconscious?"

"No, smart arse. But she's not very well. Get a glass of water, would you, Xin, and take it into her."

Just then from the inner room they heard a high-pitched roar and all three women rushed for the door. Kiera was writhing on the floor.

"I think the baby's coming. My waters have broken!" she yelled. "Oh God, the pain! Help me!"

Grace and Phoebe stood rooted to the spot, mouths agape, but Xin sprang into action.

"I'll get an amb'lance," she said galloping to the phone.

Phoebe retreated to reception. "I'll get Mungo."

By this time Kiera was crying with pain and Grace was still standing by the door.

"Help her, will yeh!" Xin yelled, snapping Grace from her paralysis. She hurried over to her one-time friend and helped her into a sitting position, leaning her back against the settee.

"How's the pain now?" she asked.

Tears squeezed out of Kiera's tightly closed eyes. She was rocking gently back and forward rubbing her swollen belly. "Not great," she said. "This shouldn't be happening. The baby's not due for another week. Why's this happening?"

Grace shrugged. "I suppose it's just decided to come early. I don't know."

Kiera convulsed with pain again. Grace felt very awkward. "Shouldn't you be breathing or something. You know, puff puff pant pant . . . that sort of thing," she ventured.

"No . . . It's, hoo haa, hoo haa, hee hee hee," Xin demonstrated with orchestrated panting.

"Are you sure?" Grace asked.

"Yeh. I helped me sister Madaline t'practise when she was havin' our Tristram. Of course there's . . ."

"Give it a rest," Kiera snapped when the contraction had passed. "And it's a bit late for a discussion on breathing techniques for the woman in labour. Where's the bloody ambulance? WHERE'S MY ANDREW?"

Xin looked down at her. "OK, OK. Don't get yer bleedin' knickers in a twist. How the hell should I know where yer friggin' Andrew is?" she said and re-dialled the emergency service.

Grace really didn't want to be involved in this, but an ugly monster of guilt climbed on to her shoulder.

"Eh . . .Would you like me to phone Andrew for you?" she asked. "Where is he anyway?"

Kiera sniffed. "He's at the Four Courts. You can't phone him." She started to weep. "And he so wanted to be at the birth. He said he wouldn't miss it for the world."

"Well I can leave a message, can't I?" Grace snarled as she snatched the phone from Xin. *P leeeese,* she thought, once again nauseated by her former friend. *Wanted to be present at the birth?* This didn't sound like the chauvinist, omnivorous, bristly, broad-snouted, extremely squeamish mammal she'd known and once loved.

"Is it really awful?" she asked, trying not to sound gleeful. Making every effort to sound sympathetic.

"What do *you* think?" Kiera gasped and convulsed in pain again.

A couple of minutes later Mungo and Phoebe reappeared carrying towels and a blanket.

"The amb'lance is on its way," Xin said as

Grace and Mungo managed to ease Kiera back onto the settee.

"How long have you been havin' the pains, honey?" Mungo said gently. Kiera looked alarmed at the sight of the huge bald black American.

Phoebe leaned over her and said, "This is Mungo, Kiera. He'll look after you."

"Is he a doctor?" Kiera groaned, though she looked past caring.

"No, but he delivered my son twelve years ago in the back of a New York taxi cab."

"I never knew that," said Grace.

"I know," Phoebe said as Kiera let out another moan which grew steadily into a scream, causing Grace to jump back.

"Oooh God . . . Fuck Andrew and his natural childbirth. Get me some fucking drugs . . . Get me something, anything, for the pain."

"How long have you been havin' the pains honey?" Mungo repeated.

Kiera gasped. "Since last night. I thought it was the sweet and sour pork and fried rice. I didn't . . ." The sentence was cut off again as she was shaken by another contraction.

Grace felt useless. "Shouldn't she be breathing or something?" she said again feebly. Phoebe and Mungo gave her withering looks.

After twenty minutes, when the ambulance still hadn't arrived, Xin went out to look for it.

Even to Grace's inexperienced eye it was obvious that Kiera was seriously in labour. Mungo was talking to her, trying to give her encouragement. She held on to Grace's hand with a vice-like grip, digging in her nails every time she had a contraction. Phoebe, bored with the whole affair, was sitting on the desk catching up with Princess Di's social life in *Hello!* magazine.

A commotion in reception announced Xin's return and she hurried into the office out of breath, followed by a hot and bothered paramedic and a nurse.

"There's been an accident an' the road's blocked. We had t'run all the way from bleedin' Merrion Square," she panted "How's yer woman?"

The paramedic and the nurse took over from Mungo, and Phoebe got interested again.

"Don't worry, pet. I'm Mary and I'm a midwife," said the nurse. "Let's see how you're doing. How far apart are the contractions?"

"Pretty close," Mungo said.

"Hmmmm. You're fully dilated," Mary said. "Too late to move you now, love. But don't worry. We'll have that baby outta there in no time."

"What! But I can't have my baby here," Kiera moaned.

"Baby has other ideas, love. It's nearly all

over bar the shouting at this stage," said Mary matter-of-factly. Kiera groaned and started to pant. "Give me a good push now, that's a good girl."

Kiera squeezed her eyes closed and her face turned scarlet with the effort. Grace realised she was holding her breath too, and exhaled.

"Good girl, good girl," Mary encouraged. "One more push now and we'll have the baby's head."

"I can't," Kiera wailed. "I can't do this anymore."

"Come on Kiera," Grace said. "It's nearly over. Come on. One more push."

"Yeah," Xin encouraged, leaning over Grace's shoulder. "Come on, Kiera. Come on. Give us a big push."

Kiera obliged, crushing the bones in Grace's hand in the process. Grace winced. She was glad she wasn't at the grizzly end.

"Good lady!" said the midwife. "Now don't push again for a minute." She carefully extracted the baby's head and eased out the shoulders, torso and legs. "You have a lovely baby girl."

Kiera smiled broadly, then started to weep, releasing Grace's bruised and battered hand. Grace and Mungo, grinning moronically, hugged each other and Grace was sure she saw the ghost of a tear in Mungo's eye. The baby joined in with the crying. Xin was jumping up and down hugging the bemused paramedic and Phoebe had gone back to *Hello!* magazine.

Shortly afterwards, when the midwife had cut the cord and made Kiera and the infant comfortable, and they had departed for Holles Street Maternity Hospital in the ambulance, the four Sleuths went in the opposite direction for a post delivery drink in Smyth's.

"I don't believe I nearly delivered my husband's lover's baby," Grace said as they pushed their way to the back of the bar.

"Hardly delivered!" Phoebe scoffed.

Grace held up her hand. It was black and blue and Kiera's nail marks looked livid red. "Look. I've got the bruises to prove it," she said, sounding grumpy.

Phoebe smirked. "I saw the gooey look on your face when the child was born. Don't try and tell me you're still bearing a grudge."

"It's more than a grudge," Grace snapped, trying to hide her embarrassment.

Phoebe laughed out loud. "Don't you think it's time you buried the hatchet in Kiera?"

"Don't you mean *with* Kiera."

"Whatever turns you on, Grace. But you're being a bit of a bloody dog in the manger when you don't want the bastard yourself. Why d'you have to be so bristly about it?"

"Because I can," Grace snapped adding. "Just mind your own business, will you?"

Mungo took her by the arm. "Give me a hand with the drinks, Grace."

When they were up at the bar he said, "Phoebe has a point about Kiera, you know." Grace shrugged, but Mungo persisted. "You don't want your ol' man anyway. Why d'you have to be so hostile?"

Grace glared at him. "I told you. Because I can," she said, and then she gave a sly smile. "Actually between you and me, I'm enjoying playing the betrayed wife." Mungo smirked and they carried the drinks back to Phoebe and Xin.

Later, when Mungo had gone back to the bar for another round, Xin said, "The Kiera wan said she wants t'call the snapper after you, Grace."

Phoebe took a fit of laughter. Grace looked horrified. "Oh dear. The mother-in-law from hell will be round next, trying to get you to be godmother."

"Not even in jest," Grace was still smarting.

The three women sat in silence.

Then Xin said, "It's a good job the sprog wasn't a boy."

"Why?"

She grinned, and her teeth looked yellow against the white pancake makeup. "She might've felt obliged t'call the poor little bugger bleedin' Mungo."

Chapter Three

Three days later Dermot McEvoy sat in his office working on the monthly crime figures. It was a job he detested. He much preferred being at the sharp end of police work. Rank had its disadvantages. The phone rang and he picked it up.

"There's a Miss Dalglish-Stuart to see you, sir."

Dermot cursed under his breath. Dippy Poppy wasting his time was the last thing he needed. He caught sight of Luke Ryan passing his open office door and called to him. Luke put his head around the door.

"Poppy Dalglish-Stuart's downstairs, go and talk to her, will you." He said it as causally as he could manage, without looking up from his paperwork.

"OK," said Luke, and was gone when Dermot looked up again. He was curious to meet Poppy

Dalglish-Stuart after the picture Dermot had painted of her.

However, Poppy Dalglish-Stuart wasn't sitting in the public office when Luke went out, but an attractive woman whom Luke judged to be in her late twenties. She stood when she saw him and thrust out her hand, taking his and shaking it firmly.

"Free Dalglish-Stuart," she said. Then as she noticed Luke's confused expression she added, "I know. I sound like a campaign or a T-shirt slogan don't I? I'm afraid my mother was a child of the sixties. Still, it could have been worse. My brother's called Whispering Wind."

"Good God!" said Luke before he could stop himself.

She started to laugh and her green eyes twinkled. "He goes by the name of Jack, now," she said. "Whispering Wind isn't a very appropriate name for an investment banker."

Luke was instantly captivated. Free Dalglish-Stuart was tall and slender and had spectacular cheek bones which were accentuated by her cropped raven-black hair. She was dressed in a sober, impeccably cut business suit and carried a briefcase. He cleared his throat. "Inspector McEvoy is tied up right now. How can I help you?"

"I need to talk to you about my Aunt Carenza," she said. "Is there somewhere private?"

Luke led her to an empty interview room and she sat on one of the hard chairs. He leaned against the edge of the table.

"You think that my mother is barking mad, don't you?" It was a statement in the true, very direct, Dalglish-Stuart style.

"Well," said Luke.

"Oh, it's OK. Most people do. Don't be embarrassed, Sergeant." Luke opened his mouth to speak but no sound came out. Free didn't seem to notice. "My mother is more sane than either you or I. And, whether you believe it or not, she *is* clairvoyant. If she says that Aunt Carenza's been killed, then you should believe her."

Luke shrugged. "What can I say? At the moment we have to assume that your aunt Carenza has gone off of her own free will. Either on her own or with someone else."

"Bullshit! Aunt Carenza was besotted with that creep. There's no way she'd even look at anyone else."

"Why would O'Connell murder your aunt anyway? What would be his motive?"

She looked up at him, surprised that he would even ask. "Money of course. What else?"

"But he hardly needs money."

"He always needs money. He's a greedy bastard. Mother says he's seeing someone else. Maybe the money's just part of it, maybe he can't afford a judicial separation."

Luke raised his eyebrows. That angle hadn't occurred to him.

"Does she have any idea who, or is this another tarot reading?" He hadn't intended to sound flippant, it just came out that way.

Her face turned to thunder and she snapped, "Well! I can see there's little point in talking to you." She stood up.

"Calm down," Luke said. "I hear what you're saying, but you have to appreciate tarot cards aren't really cast iron evidence."

"Sorry," she said, sitting down again. "I expect you've noticed I'm rather protective of my mother." She blushed.

"How come with a mother like yours you turned out so . . ." Luke couldn't find the word.

"Straight?" she said grinning.

"Well yes."

"I suppose Jack and I inherited more of our old man's genes. I think mother sometimes clutches her head and wails, *Where did I go wrong?* But I think she's come to terms with having produced an accountant and an investment banker by now."

"Inspector McEvoy said that your mother paints."

"Yes, among other things, but she has no sense of commerce, she thinks money's vulgar. Fortunately Jack took charge of her ever-dwindling portfolio before it was too late and restored the family fortunes."

"How well off is Carenza in her own right?"

"Absolutely bloody loaded. She was always the sensible one. Her little nest egg's been growing for over thirty years." She was silent for a moment before adding, "Unless Doctor Death's been dipping in over the last six years, that is."

"You really are serious about Carenza being dead, aren't you?"

"Deadly serious," she said.

After Free Dalglish-Stuart had gone, Luke went back to Dermot's office. "I was going to talk to O'Connell again, Dermot, there's still no trace of the wife."

Dermot tapped his pen on the blotter and looked steadily at Luke for a few moments before answering. "So what's to be gained by talking to him again?" he said. "He says she's left him. You've only Poppy Dalglish-Stuart's missing person report and her tarot card mumbo jumbo."

Luke exhaled noisily. "Well, for one, there's nothing to indicate that Carenza has a lover to go away with. Second to that, there's O'Connell's history."

"Just a minute Luke. What do you mean by 'O'Connell's history'? And before you cite Poppy's drivel again, remember he doesn't have a history officially. And Carenza was seen by the cleaning lady on the Saturday morning after he'd gone off to Cork. Anyway, how do you know that she hasn't just gone off on her own?"

"Point taken," said Luke. "But it's still procedure to talk to the husband anyway. I would point out that he doesn't seem very worried as yet and it's been over a week now."

Dermot gave a heavy sigh. "All right, talk to him, see what happened. But I still think that she'll probably turn up."

"I hope so too, Dermot, but I'm beginning to wonder if she will. There's no sign of her car yet either. That doesn't look too good, does it?"

Dermot looked up at his sergeant. He was puzzled by his sudden interest in Poppy Dalglish-Stuart. "Well the old biddy's really talked you round," he remarked. "But for what it's worth, I think it's all a waste of time. Still I suppose it can't do any harm."

Grace, prompted by Phoebe, had had the same thought. The two women arrived outside Emmet O'Connell's surgery about half an hour before Luke, though to call the huge complex a surgery was like calling Euro-Disney a fun fair. It comprised three long two-storey buildings forming a U shaped central space which was the car park. They followed the sign pointing towards reception, which was in the central block. On the way in, Grace noticed various other signs directing patients to the Well Woman Clinic, Pediatric and General Surgery. To the left of the main entrance was a blank door marked Accounts, and opposite it a glass door marked Creche.

"Wow," said Grace. "Big bucks."

"Hmmmm," agreed Phoebe.

They walked over to the reception desk. Phoebe flashed a smile at the receptionist and explained their business, but the dragon lady behind the glass snapped, "Take a number, you'll be called."

Phoebe patiently repeated herself and the dragon repeated the same message. Phoebe leaned towards the window, and gave the woman her best dazzling smile.

"Listen, lady, if you don't get Dr O'Connell right *now*, I'll stand on top of this desk, remove all of my clothes, and start screaming."

Phoebe's smile never faltered. The woman looked outraged and, cringing back from the glass, she reached for the phone.

Emmet O'Connell rose from behind his desk as the two women entered. He had the same insincere smile on his lips. "What can I do for you ladies?"

"We'd like to ask you some more questions about your wife's disappearance, doctor," said Grace.

37

O'Connell inclined his head. "Very well," he said stiffly.

"You'll forgive me for saying so, but you don't seem to be very worried about her," Grace started.

O'Connell leaned his elbows on the desk and formed his hands into a steeple.

"Miss de Rossa, my wife has done this before, many times, in fact, and I really think this is none of your business, and it is a complete waste of time to continue to search for her when she doesn't wish to be found."

Grace looked at him and thought, *smug bastard*.

"When did your wife do this before?" Phoebe asked.

O'Connell slowly shook his head. "Too many times to document or remember. She isn't the most stable of people. Definitely not a well woman." He looked at Grace. "I've suspected for some time that my wife has taken a lover, so you see I wasn't surprised when she left again."

"Yes, but when was the last time she went away without warning?" persisted Phoebe.

He turned to look at her for the first time and then addressed his answer to Grace which infuriated Phoebe.

"I think the last time was about four months ago. She came back after ten days."

"And she didn't say where she'd been?" Phoebe asked.

O'Connell inhaled deeply, suggesting patience was a great effort, and turned to Phoebe. "No. Not didn't. Wouldn't."

"Then we'd like to search your house, doctor," she said, chancing her arm." There may be some clue to your wife's whereabouts."

Grace thought O'Connell was going to explode, but he just managed to keep hold of his composure.

"How dare you!" he seethed. "Just who the hell do you think you are? Do you really think I would let a couple of tin-pot private detectives search *my* home on the word of a sick and unbalanced old harridan's ludicrous accusation?"

"Why not? What have you got to hide?" Grace asked.

O'Connell stood and stalked to the door, "I think you should leave now," he said, holding the door open. "And I shall be making a complaint to the gardai concerning your heavy handed tactics."

Grace looked over at Phoebe and shrugged. "I think he wants us to leave," she said. As they were passing him in the doorway, Grace smiled at him and said, "Thank you so much, Doctor, You've been a great help."

On the drive back to Baggot Street Phoebe said, "What do you think?"

"I think if I were Carenza, I'd be long gone. The man's insufferable."

"Very attractive though," said Phoebe after a meaningful pause. "I wonder if he could have killed her? It seems strange that there's no sign of her car."

"Yes, but I don't think you can go by that," Grace said. "If someone's determined enough, they can go missing without trace for years."

"Then how are we supposed to find her?" asked Phoebe.

"Well we've checked the ferries so, if she's left the country, it wasn't by that route. And her car's not at the airport so perhaps we should try an appeal in the press. I'll talk to Poppy about it."

"She'll think it's a waste of time. She's really convinced that O'Connell's done for Carenza," said Phoebe. "In fact I think she'd be a bit disappointed now if we find her alive."

Chapter Four

Grace leaned on Luke Ryan's doorbell. It was seven am. Twenty minutes earlier she'd been awoken by Pattie Doyle. Pattie was a former colleague who, aware of her interest in Carenza O'Connell, had phoned to inform her that Carenza had been found dead in Ballycoyle woods by an early morning jogger.

She heard Luke cursing on the other side of the door as he stubbed his toe in his hurry to stop the noise.

"Rise and shine, Sergeant!" said Grace, obscenely cheerful for that time of the morning. She pushed past him and went through to the kitchen to put the kettle on to boil.

Grace had been involved with Luke Ryan for a couple of months. Reluctantly so at first, stung as she was by the fact that he had initially agreed with the general consensus round the office that she had taken the shilling. She really hadn't been all that crazy about the idea of getting involved in any relationship after her marriage had broken down. But she had to admit that Luke was very attractive in a unconventional sort of way, and she found him fun and easy to be with. Though she wasn't sure he was the love of her life, she was enjoying the fact that there was someone who thought she was desirable and sexy. Also now that she had a partner again she was no longer a social leper and at last had some semblance of a social life other than the pub.

"Do you have to be so bloody jolly at this time of day?" he said. "What d'you want?"

"Well I'm glad you're so pleased to see me," she said.

He gave a sigh and kissed her on the tip of the nose.

"I'm pleased to see you. OK?" he said.

"Good. Because I just thought you'd like to know that Carenza O'Connell's turned up."

"Where?"

Grace followed Luke into the bedroom and sat on the end of the bed as he got dressed. "An early morning jogger found her in Ballycoyle woods about half an hour ago."

"Dead?"

"Dead," confirmed Grace gravely. "It seems Poppy was right."

Luke squinted at her in the mirror as he brushed his hair. "How d'you know this?"

"A contact who shall remain nameless," she said with a certain amount of smugness. (Pattie Doyle was a forensic scientist from the technical squad and, unknown to Luke Ryan or indeed Dermot McEvoy, she had helped Grace out with information before. She was a firm believer in *The Sisters sticking together against the common enemy*.)

"And where does this contact get his information"

"No comment." Grace grinned at him.

"And how long does this contact think Carenza O'Connell's been there?"

Grace shrugged. "Don't know yet, I came straight here to pick you up."

"What for?"

She smiled sweetly at him. "Come on, Luke. Give me a break. You know I'm working for Poppy, and she did tell us that Carenza was dead days ago."

"Look Grace. You know you can't come with me. It's more than my job's worth."

"Ahhh Luke . . ."

On the drive to the scene of the crime he told her of his conversation with Free Dalglish-Stuart.

"The poor girl sounds like a T-shirt slogan," commented Grace, uncomfortable with the slight tinge of jealousy she felt when Luke described the younger woman in glowing terms.

"Dermot won't have a minute's peace from Poppy when she finds out about Carenza."

"Free's as convinced as her mother that O'Connell's a murderer," Luke said. "And she's a very normal straight lady. I must say her opinion lends a lot of credibility to Poppy's ranting."

"Really," commented a tight-lipped Grace. The Ballycoyle Woods were cold, grey and leafless in the winter morning. The gate leading to the wood was open but taped off by the uniformed gardai already on the scene. Dermot's car pulled up just as she and Luke got out of her car. They stood in the lane and waited for him.

"All right Ryan, I can do without I-told-you-so!"

Luke pointed to his chest with an exaggerated flourish, "Moi?" he said as Dermot caught sight of Grace.

"And don't even *think* of passing that barrier, Grace," Dermot said.

It was Grace's turn to say, "Moi?"

The technical team had already erected a canopy over the body. Carenza O'Connell was lying on her back fully clothed with her eyes open and a startled look on her face. Her features were swollen and there was a gaping wound at the side of her skull. The pink silk camisole top revealed ugly livid purple patches covering the side of her right arm. In death she looked small and pathetic. She was extremely thin.

Sean Gill, the duty surgeon, was closing up his bag.

"Don't look at me for the cause of death, I'm just here to pronounce her dead," he said, pre-empting Luke's question as he walked off towards the lane.

"Well thanks," said Luke to his retreating back. "Who rattled his cage this morning?"

"I don't know," said Pattie Doyle. "I think he had a round of golf booked or something. We're finished here if you want to have a look. Hello, Grace. What brings you here?"

Grace cringed. Pattie's acting ability left a lot to be desired. She hoped that Dermot hadn't heard her pathetic attempt at sounding surprised.

"Hi Pattie, I just came along for the ride," she said feebly.

Luke gave the two women a knowing look and asked Pattie, "Have you found a weapon?"

Pattie shook her head. "No, but the search team are just starting now. Maybe they'll come up with something." She started to pack her bag. "Oh, by the way, Dr Gill said that she was killed somewhere else and dumped here because of the hypostasis. And because of the rate of decomposition he reckons that she's probably been dead at least six days." She packed the last of the plastic evidence bags into her case.

"That'd make it Saturday or Sunday," commented Luke as he leaned over Carenza O'Connell's inert body. There was a purple bruise around her neck, but apart from that, the hypostasis (lividity of the skin caused by the blood flowing after death by gravity to the lowest parts of the body) and the wound in the side of her head, she appeared to be unmarked.

"Look here, Dermot. It looks as if she may have been strangled," Luke said. He was talking to Dermot but looking over at Grace, who was within earshot at the other side of the cordon.

"The murderer didn't make much effort to hide the body, did he?" remarked Grace. "You'd think he'd have dropped her a little further away from the path. It's almost as if he wanted her to be found."

Dermot nodded thoughtfully. "Hmmm . . . that's if it was a he. Maybe the murderer wasn't capable of carrying the victim any further. Perhaps he was a she."

"Maybe," said Grace. "Though perhaps the body was moved *because* it hadn't been found. Perhaps the perp really did want her to be found."

"Maybe," said Dermot. "We'll see what Leo Yentob has to say. Luke, get the search team to check deeper into the wood, see if they can find if the victim was originally dumped further in here or elsewhere. And then go and break the news to the husband."

Luke went off and Grace walked back towards the lane with Dermot.

"Has Carenza O'Connell's car turned up yet?" she asked.

"No, not yet," he replied.

"Are you going to pick up O'Connell?"

"I'll talk to him, but I think it a bit premature to pick him up," he said. Then it dawned on him. "Oh shit! Poppy Dalglish-Stuart will make a meal of this."

"Does she know yet?"

"No. I'm just going over there now," he said. "I suppose you're tagging along to see Poppy, are you?"

Grace grinned at her old boss. "Got it in one," she said.

They had to wait for Poppy to rise from her bed when they arrived. Compton showed them into her drawing-room at the rear of the house.

"This is more like it," Grace said when they were left alone. The remark was prompted by the disarray that confronted them, which seemed far more in character with her client. Unlike the pristine hall and the dining-room, Poppy's private drawing-room was on the seriously dingy side, definitely influenced by the nineteen-sixties student-bedsit school of interior design. A fat overstuffed couch stood in front of a large marble fireplace, where the makings of a briquette fire was set in the grate. Squashed and deflated cushions were thrown willy-nilly over the couch and spilled onto the floor and threadbare hearth rug. Two enormous hairy dogs lolled asleep, one covering the couch and the other across a mismatched armchair. Grace noticed that the leg of the chair was missing and the corner was supported by a book. The hound on the chair opened one eye, and, unimpressed with the company, went back to sleep. The curtains were open, but the dark day made little impression on the dowdy room. Grace walked over to a small table by the fireplace and switched on a lamp. The bulb lit up and a warm glow reflected off the walls.

Dermot, hands in pockets, wandered over to the sideboard which was covered with dust. It was cluttered and piled high with books. He idly perused the spines, reading the titles. A cigarette end in the ashtray caught his eye and he picked it up and sniffed. He looked over at Grace.

"Old habits die hard," he said.

The door opened and Poppy swept in. "Inspector, to what do I owe the pleasure?" she said. When she saw Grace's expression, she knew.

"You found her," she said.

Dermot nodded. "I'm afraid so, Poppy. I'm very sorry."

"Have you arrested Emmet yet?" she asked matter-of- factly. "Did you charge the swine?"

"No, Poppy. Preliminary findings at the scene suggest she died between Saturday and Sunday and he has an alibi for the whole weekend. We've no evidence to link him to the crime."

Poppy snorted. "You don't think he did it himself, do you?"

"Well forensic might come up with something yet," Dermot said. "I'll let you know how the investigation progresses."

"I hope you do a better job than you did for poor Anabell," Poppy snapped derisively.

"Be fair, Poppy. She was dead and buried before you came to see me."

Poppy stalked over to the fireplace and bent down to light the newspaper and fire-lighters. The flames danced yellow and blue, licking the briquettes. The dogs stirred and the larger of the two rolled over and stretched. Poppy bent over and scratched his grey wiry belly.

"Poor poor silly Carenza," Poppy said to no one in particular. "If I have to do it myself, I'll prove that that swine killed my sister. If it's the last thing I do."

Dermot said, "As you wish. I'll be in touch." He turned to leave.

Grace hung back and, when he turned to see if she was following him, Poppy said, "Grace and I have things to discuss."

After he had gone, Poppy shoved the dog off the chair and sat in front of the by now roaring fire. She patted the seat beside her inviting Grace to sit. The flames of the fire warmed and brightened the room. Compton shambled in with a tray, beautifully set with tea and hot muffins.

"I'm sorry about Carenza," Grace said, meaning it.

Poppy nodded. "Thank you dear, I think you are."

"What did you want to talk to me about?"

Poppy sighed. "What do you think? I want you to gather evidence against my brother-in-law."

Grace was about to direct Poppy towards the gardai but then recalled Phoebe's dire warning about not turning away work. "We'll do what we can," she promised. "You know he has an alibi?"

Poppy frowned. "Are you sure about that?"

"I checked it out myself. He was at a medical conference in Cork. Two hundred witnesses saw him in the afternoon and later he made a speech after the gala dinner. And the receptionist remembers him asking about the underground car park. When I spoke to her on the phone she said that the cars are locked in at night."

"What about the Sunday?"

"He was in the conference hall all day and at another dinner that night. The computer printout shows that his car didn't leave the car park until six am on the Monday morning."

Poppy snorted. "How convenient. What's to have stopped him hiring a car and driving up overnight. His alibi seems a bit pat to me."

"I have to agree with you," Grace said. "Though Mungo thought of that already and he checked out the hire firms round Cork city."

"And?" Poppy boomed.

"No luck I'm afraid. He drew a blank."

Grace suddenly remembered that she had abandoned Luke back at the scene of the crime and that he had no means of transport back to Harcourt Terrace. "Oh my God, I have to go," she said. "I'll phone you soon. And don't worry, if O'Connell's guilty we'll nail him for you."

"I'm in no doubt that you will, my dear," said Poppy. "In fact I'm counting on it."

Luke was not stranded at the Ballycoyle woods, but had hitched a lift with Jack Mulloy to break the news of Carenza's death to her husband.

He was quite astonished by the widower's reaction. He stood staring at Luke for a few moments then gasped, "Oh God, my poor, poor

Carenza." He sat down heavily on the bottom of the stairs with his head in his hands. Luke stood silently for a couple of moments and was about to speak when O'Connell looked up and said, "What happened?"

"I beg your pardon?"

O'Connell frowned. "Did Carenza's lover kill her?"

"We don't know that your wife had a lover or, if that was the case, if the lover killed her."

O'Connell stared at him. "My wife told me in her note that she had a lover, and that she'd gone off with him. What more do you want?"

"Your wife was murdered, doctor. At the moment we have no suspects." He let that sink in. "Her body was discovered about two hours ago in Ballycoyle woods by a jogger."

O'Connell's face was like stone, he leaned on the newel post. "Oh God. But who?"

"We need you to make a formal identification. When could you come down to the mortuary?"

O'Connell didn't appear to be listening. He repeated, "Who did it?"

Luke looked at the floor. "Our investigation's only in its very early stages, Doctor O'Connell. It would help if you could tell us about the last time you saw her, and the circumstances leading up to her disappearance."

"I blame myself. Maybe if I had reported her missing, but I didn't think. Carenza suffered from depression. From time to time she felt she needed to get away. She left a note to say that she had left me for someone else. She had never said anything like that before. That's why I thought this time she had gone for good." He trailed off looking beseechingly at Luke as if waiting for some sort of absolution.

"I doubt it would have made any difference. It would appear that she died very soon after she went missing. What were you doing at the conference in Cork?"

"Doing?" O'Connell enquired.

"Well, were you speaking or just attending?"

"I was delivering a lecture on the Saturday, and I gave a speech at the gala dinner. Then on the Sunday, I delivered another lecture. I left here on Saturday and got home on Monday morning."

"Did you phone your wife between Saturday and Sunday night?"

"I tried, but she'd left the machine on. She sometimes did that if she didn't feel like talking to anyone. But of course she'd probably gone by that time."

"So you don't really know when your wife went missing. She could have disappeared any time between Saturday and Monday, when you returned?"

O'Connell thought for a moment. "Yes, I suppose you're right, I just assumed."

The two stood quietly. Luke broke the silence. "Could you give us a list of your wife's jewellery? There's always the possibility that she was lured away and killed in the course of being robbed."

O'Connell nodded and went to a bureau. After shuffling through some papers he handed Luke a typewritten list.

"It's a list the insurance company had us draw up."

Luke put the list in his pocket. "Thank you. When would you be able to come to the morgue and formally identify your wife's body?" O'Connell didn't answer. "Doctor O'Connell?"

He looked up and gave a shrug. "I'll go after surgery," he said.

"I think under the circumstances, doctor, that your patients wouldn't expect . . ."

O'Connell cut him off brusquely. He appeared to be fully in control of his emotions again. "Nonsense, life must go on. I have patients relying on me, Sergeant."

Luke found that he wasn't at all surprised that O'Connell would calmly go off to work after just learning that his wife had been brutally murdered. He really was a cold fish, or maybe a guilty fish. Though, on reflection, O'Connell's reaction wasn't that of a guilty man, surely a guilty man would feign grief in order to avert suspicion?

"We'll need to search your house and garden, Doctor. As yet we don't know where your wife was killed and there may be some clue here."

O'Connell just nodded and muttered. "Fine, fine. Whatever it takes."

Luke didn't catch up with Grace until he called to see her that evening at Baggot Street.

"Thanks a bunch, Grace," he said frostily when she let him in. "You could have said you weren't going to hang around."

"Where were you?" she said innocently. "I went back for you but you'd gone."

"The best form of defence is attack, eh?" he said. "Go on, admit it. You forgot all about me."

"Well, not exactly forgot," she said. "How did O'Connell react when you told him about Carenza?"

"He seemed to fall apart."

"You're kidding."

He shook his head. "No, he nearly collapsed when I broke the news. He's either a very good actor or he was genuinely shocked."

"Which do you think?" Grace asked.

Luke shrugged. "I'm prejudiced, I don't really like the man. I can't help feeling that it was out of character the way he acted."

"Hmmm," affirmed Grace, "I agree with you."

"Leo Yentob said that the victim was lying on

her side before she was moved, and that the blow to the side of her head alone would have rendered her a vegetable even without the strangulation. A belt and braces job he called it," Luke said.

Grace was relieved that he sounded less peeved with her. She didn't mention that Pattie Doyle had called again to tell her that the forensic examination had revealed fibres consistent with the victim having lain on a carpet, and traces of motor oil. That, and the fact that she had been curled up on her right side with her knees to her chest, suggested that she had been stashed in a car boot until the murderer had dumped her in the woods.

"We searched the house. The lads found traces of blood on the garage floor, so it looks as if she was killed there and then moved."

Grace nodded.

"How did Poppy take it?" Luke asked.

"She was expecting it."

"What are you going to do now? Have you any other cases on the go?"

"Poppy wants us to dig up evidence against O'Connell. Has the missing jewellery shown up yet?"

Luke shook his head. "No, not yet. But we circulated the list to the antique shops. We may get a bite from that. Now. D'you fancy going out for a bite to eat?"

"In a while," Grace said impatiently. "What did the house to house come up with?"

Luke frowned. "I shouldn't be telling you this, but what the hell. A couple of the neighbours pointed towards an odd job man called Paddy Moran. Apparently Carenza took him under her wing."

"Has he an alibi?"

Luke shrugged. "We haven't found him yet, so we don't know."

"I think Poppy's right about O'Connell, even if he has an alibi. She's really convinced he's involved in Carenza's murder," said Grace.

"So is Free. She reckons he needs Carenza's money badly," Luke said. "Though Dermot isn't into that theory."

"I think he's prejudiced against Poppy because of the Anabell business," Grace said.

"That and her tarot card mumbo-jumbo."

"And what do you think?" she asked.

"I've got an open mind. Though Free has a point if O'Connell does need money, especially in view of Poppy's theory about the Anabell thing."

They sat in silence, each mentally turning over the problem.

"Do we know for certain that O'Connell's short of cash?" Grace asked.

"Free thinks so," Luke said. "She reckons he's living way beyond his means."

"So you've no actual evidence other than Free's say so?" Grace said sharply.

Luke didn't seem to notice her tone. "Well, no, but then Free's also convinced he's seeing someone . . ." Luke went on but Grace had stopped listening. She was getting irritated by Luke's constant references to the lovely Free Dalglish-Stuart. Her dented self-esteem wasn't up to it. She felt her jaw tighten. When he had finished what he was saying there was an uncomfortable silence. Luke eventually sensed the atmosphere was not convivial.

"What's the matter?" he asked.

She shook her head. "Nothing."

"Well shall we go and get something to eat then?" he asked.

She shrugged. "If you want," she said stiffly, her face like thunder.

Luke was at a loss. Grace's rapidly changing moods were her least attractive feature as far as he was concerned. And much as he was attracted to her, he was beginning to wonder why he bothered.

"Oh for God's sake," he said, exasperated. "What's the matter with you now . . . Are you coming or what?"

"Why don't you take your precious Free?" she snapped.

Luke shook his head, he was confused. "Take Free?" he said. "Why should I do that?"

Grace remained silent, she was beginning to feel foolish. Finally he turned to the door and throwing up his hands said, "Fine. I'll go on my own."

As the door slammed shut and she listened to his footsteps clattering down the stairs, she cursed herself for being so touchy. She thought about going after him but her insecurity won. She let him go and opted for feeling alone and miserable instead.

Chapter Five

The search team found the murder weapon in Ballycoyle Woods. It was a large claw hammer and the tissue, bone and blood samples from the head matched Carenza O'Connell's. Pattie Doyle also managed to lift a partial palm print and a thumb print from the handle which were, as yet, unidentified.

Dermot was about to go out for a late lunch when a call came into the information room from a Sydney Smith, the owner of an antique shop in the city centre. Dermot called Luke and the two of them went off to follow up the call.

The shop was in a narrow side street just off Capel Street in the city centre where five or six adjacent shops all dealt in antiques, jewellery and bric-a-brac. An old-fashioned bell jangled as they entered and a smart young woman stood behind the counter polishing a silver tray.

Dermot flashed his warrant card. "I'd like to speak to Sydney Smith."

The young woman smiled, "I'm Sydnie Smith."

"Oh!" said Dermot surprised. "You called earlier about the pieces of jewellery."

"Yes," she bobbed below the counter, reappearing moments later holding a Quinnsworth carrier bag which rattled as she placed it on the counter. "A young lad came in with it this morning and I told him to come back after lunch to give me time to value it." She let the sentence hang.

Luke opened the bag and took out a gold bangle.

Sydnie Smith said, "It's eighteen carat and there's an inscription." She turned the bangle while it was still in Luke's hand and he got a whiff of her perfume. The bangle was inscribed *Carenza. Yours forever E*. Luke passed it to Dermot. "Who brought it in?"

"A young lad," said Sydnie. "He said his granny wanted him to sell it for her. If I have any doubts I usually hang onto the stuff until I've checked it out to be kosher. He seemed harmless but maybe a bit, well, slow, if you know what I mean. And most of it's good stuff. Look at the diamond earrings." She picked out a pair of diamond studs set in platinum and held them out in the palm of her hand.

"Could be the odd job man, Paddy Moran," Luke said.

Dermot was nodding. "Perhaps. What time is the man coming back, did you say?"

Sydnie Smith looked at her watch. "In about ten minutes or so."

"Could we wait out of sight somewhere?" asked Luke.

Sydnie ushered them into the back room where they had a view of the shop through a beaded curtain.

About twenty minutes later the bell jangled again and a scruffy lad in denims and an anorak entered the shop and shambled over to the counter.

"Did yeh look at the stuff I left?"

Sydnie looked towards the curtain and nodded. The two gardai re-entered the shop.

"Paddy Moran?" asked Luke.

"Yeh," said the lad, smiling. "What d'you want?"

"Paddy Moran. I'm arresting you for theft and on suspicion of murder. I must caution you that you don't have to say anything at this time, but anything you do say may be used in evidence."

Paddy looked like a haunted rabbit. "Wha!" he wailed "I didn't steal nuthin'."

They picked up the jewellery and hustled him into the car. Paddy shuffled along without making any further fuss.

Back at Harcourt Terrace, Dermot checked

the jewellery against O'Connell's list. It was all there with the exception of a diamond brooch in the shape of a wheat-sheaf.

Before they went in to start the interview, Dermot said to Luke, "We'd better get his social worker down here. He might not be competent and I don't want to take any chances."

Paddy's social worker, Alison Munroe, arrived about twenty minutes later and Dermot took her to one side.

"Thanks for coming down, Miss Munroe. What can you tell me about your client? Has he ever been violent?"

"Paddy? Never. What's this about? What's he supposed to have done?" she asked looking anxious.

"He was trying to sell some pieces of jewellery stolen from a murder victim."

"What has he said to you?"

"Nothing yet. We were waiting for you."

"I appreciate that," said Alison Munroe. "I can't believe he's involved in anything like that, he's harmless, though I should warn you he's very open to suggestion. He might admit to crimes just to curry favour with you. He's done it before."

They walked together to the interview room where Luke and Paddy were waiting. As they entered the room Paddy jumped up. "Alison! I didn't do nuthin'." His eyes were pleading and he was wringing his hands.

"It's OK, Paddy. Sit down there." She led him to the table. "The guards want to ask you some questions. Just answer them, and tell the truth."

"You knows I never tells lies, Alison," he said, looking hurt. He sat down heavily.

Dermot sat down opposite and said to the nervous young man, "Now Paddy, do you want to tell us anything?" Paddy sat looking at his shoes. "Where did you get the jewellery Paddy?" Paddy mumbled something.

"What?"

"I found it."

"Where?"

"I found it at the back of Mrs O'Connell's garden."

"Are you sure you didn't take it from Mrs O'Connell after you killed her, Paddy? And what did you do with the rest of it? A very valuable piece is still missing."

"I never . . . What?" It had just dawned on him what they were saying. "What d'you mean, killed? I never killed no one."

Luke leaned over him, placing the palms of his hands on the table top. "Come on, Paddy, we know accidents can happen. You didn't mean to hit her, but then you panicked. Right?"

Paddy just shrugged. "I never," was all he would say.

Alison Munroe said, "I think we'd better get

you a brief, Paddy." She turned to Dermot. "This should stop until I can get Paddy a brief." She shook her head. "This is stupid, Paddy wouldn't hurt a fly."

There was a tap on the door and Luke went out, returning moments later. "Can I see you a minute, Dermot?"

Dermot got up and the interview was suspended to allow Alison Munroe time to find a solicitor for Paddy.

Outside Luke said, "The thumb print on the hammer matches Paddy's, as near as dammit."

Dermot raised an eyebrow. "Right, don't waste any time. Hustle Alison Munroe to use the duty solicitor. Let's get this interview on the road as quickly as possible."

It took about an hour for Michael Kent, the duty solicitor, to arrive. When they were all seated once again in the interview room Dermot said, "Do you realise that you're still under caution, Paddy?"

Paddy looked at Kent, who nodded, and then said, "Yeh."

Luke placed the hammer in the plastic bag on the table in front of Paddy, saying nothing.

"Paddy, we found Mrs O'Connell."

"You said."

"Where were you between last Saturday lunchtime and Monday morning?" asked Luke. He picked up the hammer and sat on the corner of the table facing their prime suspect. The hammer was level with his line of vision. He looked at it but didn't react.

"Dunno . . . I think I was at the hostel."

"You think? Did anyone see you there?"

"I suppose so. Mister Halloran would'uv seen me."

Alison Munroe said, "That would be Jack Halloran, the warden."

Luke was still sitting on the table holding the hammer in his right hand. He plonked it noisily on the table in front of Paddy. "When did you dump her in the wood, and what did you do with the car?"

Paddy Moran looked at his solicitor for guidance. When Kent nodded he said, "I didn't kill Mrs O'Connell, an' I found the jewellery like I told yeh in the garden."

Dermot looked at Luke who said, "Your fingerprints were on the murder weapon, Paddy. How do you explain that?"

"I dunno . . . I jus' know I didn't kill her. She was good to me. She was kind an' good to me, why would I kill her?" He thumped his fist on the table top to emphasise the point, narrowly missing the handle of the hammer which jumped from the surface with the force of Paddy's blow.

Dermot let him calm down a bit. "Look Paddy, accidents happen. Was it an accident? . . .

that's known as manslaughter, it's not as serious as murder. If you explain what happened the night you went to her house we can judge if it was an accident or not." His voice was coaxing and soft. The good cop, bad cop routine.

Paddy sat with his eyes closed and fists clenched on his knee. "I wasn't at her house when you said. I didn't kill her. I wasn't at the house last week. How many times do I have t'tell yeh?" he said through gritted teeth.

"Then how did your fingerprints get on this hammer?" asked Luke, pushing the hammer towards Paddy. "This hammer whacked and whacked and whacked the side of Mrs O'Connell's head. Then, when she fell to the ground, you put your hands round her throat and squeezed and squeezed and squeezed until she was dead." Luke's face was only inches from Paddy's. Each time he said the word *whacked,* he slapped his hand on the table top in front of Paddy, who sat mesmerised, staring at the hammer, as he flinched back in his chair. "Then you drove her car to Ballycoyle Woods with her in the back and dumped her body."

"I couldn't. I can't drive a car."

Luke looked at Dermot. Dermot picked up the hammer and held it under Paddy Moran's nose. "Have you ever seen this hammer before?"

Paddy shrugged. "It's just a hammer, I dunno."

"Look again, Paddy. It's important."

Paddy reluctantly took the hammer from Dermot and examined it. "It looks a bit like the one Dr O'Connell has in his shed. Yeh, look, it's got tape round the end of the handle."

"Have you ever used it?"

Paddy shrugged. "Suppose so, dunno. Sometimes I had to fix a fence or somethin'. Maybe I did, I dunno."

"This is getting us nowhere," said Luke in exasperation. "Look, Paddy, this hammer killed Mrs O'Connell. Now you say that you didn't kill her. If that's true, how did your fingerprints get on the handle?"

Paddy slumped in his chair again and said nothing.

"I think this would be a good time to take a break now, gentlemen," said Kent. "I would like to talk to my client alone."

Dermot rose from his chair. "I'll send in some tea." He and Luke left the room.

"What do you think?" he asked Luke.

Luke made a face and shrugged. "I don't know. I'll get one of the lads to check his alibi with the warden and if he's ever had a driving licence. I know it doesn't prove he can't drive if he hasn't had one, but it's something the defence will bring up."

"My gut tells me it's not him, I don't exactly know why, but I don't think he's got the wit to dispose of a body and a car. I wonder if Poppy might be right about O'Connell," said Dermot.

Luke, who was taken aback by Dermot's sudden change of attitude, said, "You've changed your tune."

Dermot stopped walking and looked at Luke. "How many times have you been able to pin-point the exact time you left anywhere, and not only pin-point the time but have it on a computer printout to prove it? "

"He calmly went off to work after I broke the news of Carenza's death and said, life has to go on. Do you believe that?" said Luke.

"I know, but unfortunately just because he's a prick, it doesn't prove he's a murderer," said Dermot.

They stood in silence for a moment. "What if he has an accomplice, and between them they set up Paddy?" Luke argued. "It would be easy enough to get his prints on the hammer by getting him to knock a nail in somewhere."

"Perhaps, but who's the accomplice? We have a definite motive with Carenza's money."

"Cherchez la femme?"

"Perhaps . . . Maybe he put Drummond under duress."

"How?" asked Luke. "He'd have to have some pretty serious shit on Drummond to make him commit murder."

"Maybe that's just the point. Poppy suggested that Drummond was implicated in Anabell's death, remember?" said Dermot as they walked down the corridor together towards the CID office. "Organise surveillance on O'Connell. Let's see what floats to the surface. And I think I'll have a word with Drummond."

"What'll we do with Paddy?"

"I think we should charge him, we have enough with his prints on the weapon and it could put O'Connell off his guard."

"Do you really think there's the slightest chance Paddy could have done it?"

"No, not really," Dermot replied.

"Well isn't that a tad harsh, charging him with murder? He'll go out of his mind."

Dermot cast his eyes to heaven in exasperation. "OK, Mr Nice Guy. Charge him with theft of the jewellery. O'Connell only needs to know that we've charged him, he doesn't have to know with what. We'll let him jump to his own conclusions."

Chapter Six

The morning of Carenza O'Connell's funeral dawned grey, stormy and very wintery. Grace and Phoebe had to run through torrential rain from the lane to the little stone church. Carenza was being buried in the Grangetown Church of Ireland cemetery.

They sat at the back of the church and watched the mourners arrive.

"It's a wonder O'Connell's not waiting until after surgery," said Grace acidly.

"Surgery's probably over already," the ex-hooker replied.

The organ played mournfully at the front by the altar, and the pews were filling up with black-clad mourners. Carenza's coffin was at the top of the church covered in wreaths, and a lit candle in a tall brass candlestick stood at each corner. Grace saw Luke come through the door; he had no umbrella and his hair was wet. She hadn't seen him since her fit of pique and she caught his eye but he just looked through her.

"What's the matter with him?" Phoebe asked.

"I think I pissed him off just a little," Grace said feeling a tinge of regret.

"Then you'll have to make the peace," Phoebe said. "He's too cute to blow away that easily, and you're not exactly overwhelmed with offers, are you?"

"Thanks a bunch. I'll just dust off the shelf so you can climb up beside me. Anyway it's too late. I think he's after Free."

"Free what?" Phoebe said, then she grasped her partner's meaning. "Oh. I see."

"I wonder if Poppy and family will come." Grace looked over her shoulder and watched the congregation hurrying in out of the rain, shaking and folding their umbrellas.

"I hope so," Phoebe said. "It'll liven up the proceedings a bit." Phoebe nudged Grace, and in a stage whisper said, "D'you see that man on the third row, second from the end?" Grace peered up the church and her eye picked out the grey-haired man sitting, back ramrod erect, next to a heavyish woman in her late fifties.

"Yes . . . What about him?" she said warily.

"He's an ex-client of mine."

Grace was dumbstruck. The distinguished looking man was all too familiar. Phoebe looked round and seeing her stunned expression said,

"What's the matter? You look as if you've seen a ghost."

"That's my father," she answered in strangled tones.

Phoebe smirked. "Ooops!" she said. "I didn't know he knew Carenza and Emmet O'Connell."

"Well, life's full of surprises isn't it," Grace hissed. "I didn't know my father consorted with prostitutes either." She sat quietly fuming for a few moments "The rotten hypocrite. Mr bloody double-standards. "

"Shhhhh," said Phoebe. "Here's the widower."

Emmet O'Connell arrived accompanied by Brian Drummond and a woman they took to be his wife.

Cassie Drummond was tall, slim and at least fifteen or more years younger than her husband. She had long blonde hair that looked natural and she wore it piled on top of her head, which made her look taller than Drummond. She wore a simple but very expensive looking charcoal grey suit, and walked with the grace of a dancer.

Emmet O'Connell and the Drummonds had taken their seats up at the front and the vicar had started the service but there was still no sign of the Dalglish-Stuarts.

When the vicar was half way through the homily, however, Poppy Dalglish-Stuart and family made a noisy entrance. She swept up the centre of the church like a ship in full sail, clad in a full-length black silk taffeta caftan and turban. She was totally metamorphosised from the bag lady who had called at the offices of Sleuths the previous week. The luxurious fabric swished as she walked past and the heels of her shoes tap-tapped on the stone floor. One end of the turban fanned out at the side, lined with bright cerise and secured with a diamond clip. Grace hardly recognised her. Jack looked altogether more subdued in a conventional dark suit, but his sister, with her ivory skin, high cheek bones and ebony hair, looked stunning in black Armani and three inch stilettos. Her heels tapped in time with her mother's. Following them was a pretty woman whom Grace assumed must be Jack's wife, and two golden haired girls of about six years of age, who looked like twins. The downpour must have ceased because they were all bone dry.

The vicar paused in mid-sentence and waited for the group to take their seats directly behind Emmet O'Connell. He had turned to see what the racket was about and his face turned to thunder when he saw that Poppy and her brood were upstaging him.

The vicar resumed the homily and, when he came to the end and started to extend the sympathy of the congregation to O'Connell for his loss, Poppy's voice boomed through the church.

"Hypocrisy. Save your sympathy. That bastard killed her." She pronounced the word *bah-staahd* and stood with one arm dramatically outstretched towards her late sister's husband, looking for all the world like The Grim Reaper in drag.

O'Connell jumped to his feet. "Have you no shame, woman! At least have some respect for your sister's memory."

"Murderer. Double murderer," she shouted, still standing in the pew. O'Connell took hold of her outstretched arm and tried to drag her to the end of the bench. Jack got to his feet and took O'Connell's hand from his mother's arm. He forced it back so that O'Connell was compelled to sit down or risk having his wrist broken.

"Sit down and shut up and don't even think about touching my mother again," he said, his voice rising. He was a good half head taller than O'Connell who was all of six feet. Grace estimated that Jack must be at least six four.

Poppy turned to her son and smiled. The rest of the family rose to their feet. "We won't be part of this charade," she said. "Come." The family exited with the same panache as they had entered, leaving the vicar and the rest of the congregation open-mouthed and staring.

O'Connell collected himself, straightened his

tie and smoothed his hair. He stood and turned to the rest of the congregation. "I apologise for my sister-in-law's behaviour." He turned back to the vicar. "Perhaps we could continue."

Phoebe and Grace didn't wait for the rest of the service but slipped out and caught up with the Dalglish-Stuarts.

Poppy stopped and waited for the two women.

"What did you think of the service?" she asked.

"Interesting," Phoebe said. "Very dramatic. I have to give you ten out of ten for style."

Poppy introduced Free and Jack and they all shook hands. "When are they going to arrest that despicable man?" Poppy looked back at the church door where the procession, headed by the vicar and chief mourners, was winding its way to the cemetery at the other side of the building. Grace followed her gaze.

"Unfortunately, as you know, O'Connell has an alibi for the time of your sister's murder."

"He'll have got someone else to do his dirty work," cut in Free. "Mother, tell them about the woman."

Poppy nodded. "My sister told me six months ago that she suspected that Emmet was having an affair."

Phoebe looked at Grace. "So it wasn't just the tarot cards or speculation," Grace said, "Were

76

you surprised? Have you any idea who the woman is?"

"Of course I wasn't a bit surprised. I told you, Emmet is incapable of fidelity. My sister was in love with him from the age of fifteen and would hear nothing said against him, even when he dropped her and married Anabell." Poppy laughed a bitter laugh. "Oh yes. Emmet O'Connell always had his eye to the main chance. If he was in conversation with one at a party he was always looking over one's shoulder to see if there was anyone more worthwhile to converse with. He left me in mid-sentence more than once. Anabell had more money than Carenza, hence the elbow for Carenza. Anabell was a silly woman too, God rest her poor tormented soul."

"How did Carenza react to your suspicions about Emmet?" Phoebe asked.

"She was too wrapped up in Emmet's attentions," Free said. "He was acting the poor bereaved widower, letting Carenza bring some light back into his life. Ha Ha."

"And of course he inherited quite a bit from Anabell," Poppy added.

"About two hundred grand," Free said. "But that went on Disney-Medic and his high life. I'd say if you could get a look at his bank accounts you'd see he needs Carenza's money badly,"

"But what I can't understand is, if she was so

in love with him, why not just ask her for it?" asked Grace.

Poppy sighed. "He did. Carenza wouldn't speak to me for nearly five years after they married. Then, about a year ago, she came to see me. I didn't know why at first but I sensed that she was troubled."

"O'Connell said that she had nerve trouble," Grace said. Free snorted.

"I don't doubt it. In the years she'd been married to that worm she became a nervous wreck. Emmet had totally undermined her. She had no self-esteem or confidence and he'd sapped all her strength. If he said jump, she'd just ask, how high?"

It had started to rain again. Poppy said, "Come and sit in the Daimler out of the wet," and they all clambered into the cavernous back of the vintage Daimler, except for Jack and his family who had already climbed into their own car. Grace was fascinated to notice that there was a speaking tube leading through the engraved glass partition to the compartment where a uniformed Compton sat propped up on cushions in the driver's seat. She wouldn't have been surprised if he had blocks tied to his shoes to enable his short legs to reach the pedals.

Poppy continued, "As I was saying, Carenza came to see me six months ago, very distressed. She said that she suspected that Emmet was having an affair. I was stunned, not because I doubted it, but that it had taken her so long to discover the truth."

"You knew for sure that he was seeing someone?" Phoebe persisted.

Poppy cast her eyes up to heaven. "Of course. He was at it all through his marriage to Anabell. How many times do I have to tell you this? Why should the leopard change its spots?"

"O'Connell said that she had gone away alone on other occasions. Did she say anything to you about that?"

Poppy shook her head. "No. But then there was the five year period when we were out of contact."

"I know, but he said she went away four months ago without any warning," Grace said.

"She was with me," Free replied. "We went away to London to see a couple of shows. I thought it would do her good."

"How about his mistress? Did Carenza have any ideas at all about who he was bonking?" Phoebe asked.

"None, but she was beside herself," said Poppy. "She confronted him of course, but he denied it. The silly woman believed what she wanted to believe and she was on cloud nine, convinced that she had imagined it. Anyway, a month ago he told her that he needed more money for the practice. She was going to give it to him, but she overheard him on the phone to his mistress and came running to me first."

"What did you say to her?"

"I advised her to ask for a judicial separation, and told her that he'd been at it for years." Poppy Dalglish-Stuart wiped a rogue tear from her cheek. "I never saw her alive again."

The mourners were drifting towards the lane and Grace caught sight of her mother. "Excuse me, Poppy, there's someone I have to see." She clambered out of the limousine, and hurried off to catch up with her mother who was waiting by the lych gate.

They hugged each other. "Darling, it's lovely to see you," said Alice de Rossa. "But what are you doing here?"

"I could ask you the same," said Grace. "I didn't know you knew Carenza O'Connell."

Alice de Rossa shook her impeccably coifed head. "I don't. Your father knows Emmet O'Connell professionally. But how are you? Kathleen tells me that you all but delivered Andrew and Kiera's baby."

"All but," Grace said sourly. "Have you seen it yet?"

"Her, dear. Her. I went to visit them with Kathleen. She's such a little dote. You know, dear, you really should make the peace. You should do the civilised thing. What's done is done and harbouring a grudge will only make you bitter."

Grace was speechless. She had expected her mother to be on her side, not to be sleeping with the enemy. The traitor read her expression.

"Look, darling, I know you expect me to cut Andrew and Kiera off, but you have to remember Andrew's mother and I have been friends since before you were born. All this animosity is making things very uncomfortable."

"Well I'm sorry about that, Mother. I wouldn't want to upset your social arrangements," Grace snapped.

Alice de Rossa either didn't notice, or chose to ignore the sarcasm in Grace's tone. "Thank you dear. Now about the christening . . ."

Alice de Rossa prattled on but Grace wasn't listening. She could see her father making his way down the path towards them. He stopped suddenly when he saw her, then continued on and stood just behind his wife.

"Hello, Grace. What are you doing here?" he asked.

Alice turned and smiled at him. "I was just telling Grace about . . ."

Paul de Rossa ignored his wife. "I wasn't aware that you knew Carenza O'Connell," he said to his least favourite daughter.

"Well isn't life full of surprises?" she said.

"And coincidences. I was only saying that to my business partner a few minutes ago."

Paul de Rossa frowned. "What are you talking about, Grace?"

She considered confronting him about his relationship with Phoebe Lamplighter, just to cause him the maximum embarrassment but seeing her mother, standing meekly waiting for her adored husband, made Grace stop. "Oh nothing," she said. "How long have you known the O'Connells?"

"A few years. I know him professionally of course. Decent chap. Why do you ask?"

"Just professional interest," Grace said. "His sister-in-law's a client."

"Really?" He sounded surprised "Did she lose her pet cat or something?"

"No. Her sister," said Grace, biting back the urge to tell him not to be such a patronising bastard.

"Poor Carenza. Strange woman. By all accounts she was quite neurotic."

Over his shoulder Grace saw Phoebe getting out of the Daimler. "Oh there's my partner," she said. "You must meet her." She waved and beckoned to Phoebe. Phoebe hesitated, but Grace's parents had both turned round.

"Mummy, Daddy, this is my partner, Miss Phoebe Lamplighter," Grace said, and malevolently watched her father's expression, but, much to her disappointment, he didn't even flinch.

Alice smiled at Phoebe. "I'm so pleased to meet you," she gushed.

Paul de Rossa cleared his throat and formally shook her hand. "How do you do, Miss Lamplighter," he said. "It's a pleasure to meet you. How are you?"

Phoebe, uncharacteristicaly, was reddening from the neck up. "I'm well, thank you," she mumbled. "I'll wait for you in the car," she mumbled and beat a hasty retreat.

"Charming woman," Alice de Rossa smiled up at her husband, inviting his approval of her daughter's business partner.

"Indeed," he said. "Charming. Shall we go, Alice?" He turned to leave and Alice hugged Grace again.

"Don't be a stranger, darling," she said to her. "Call out to see us soon."

Grace gave a hollow promise to do just that and went off to find Phoebe.

"You rotten bitch!" Phoebe raged later as they sat in the car. "You're the one who preached to me about leaving my old life behind. How could you?"

"Well if I'd known you'd be so bloody sensitive I wouldn't have." They sat in silence, waiting for the traffic to clear. "So how long were you seeing him?" Grace asked, trying to keep her face straight.

"Mind your own bloody business," Phoebe snapped.

"Please, please tell me he was into something really, really weird." Grace convulsed with laughter.

"Oh bugger off!"

In the rear view mirror Grace caught sight of Luke making his way down the lane. She decided to try and mend some fences and stepped out of the car. He stopped when he saw her.

"Hello," she said tentativly. "How are you?"

He stood with his hands in his pockets looking down at her. After a moment he said, "Am I in danger of getting my head bitten off?" And, much to her relief, he gave her a lop-sided smile.

She smiled back and shook her head. "No."

"So what was wrong with you the other day?"

Grace shrugged. "Just my galloping insecurity showing," she said. "Is the offer of dinner still on?"

"I suppose I could risk it without a bodyguard," Luke said. "See you later. About eight?"

Back at the office, Grace told Mungo and Xin about the funeral, and of Poppy's assertion that Emmet O'Connell was broke.

"We should get a look at O'Connell's bank statements," Mungo said. "And the Drummond guy should be interrogated."

Grace flinched at the word, interrogated. Coming from Mungo it suggested electric probes invading unspeakable places.

"I agree," Phoebe said. "Grace and I'll do Drummond. You and Xin can take care of the bank statements."

Mungo glowered. "I work alone," he barked.

"Just do it, Mungo," Phoebe snapped. "Xin needs the experience. Anyway she'll watch your back for you."

"Yeh," Xin said full of enthusiasm. Mungo scowled again.

"And what makes you think the good doctor will agree to show you his bank statements?" Grace scoffed.

Three pairs of eyes swung in her direction.

"Oh God," she said. "Here we go again."

Chapter Seven

The Drummonds lived in the same area of Grangetown as the O'Connells, in a similar type of house. The sound of the door bell prompted barking from within and, a couple of minutes later, Cassie Drummond opened the front door holding the collar of a huge grey wolfhound.

"Hello, Mrs Drummond. My name's Grace de Rossa, and this is my partner, Phoebe Lamplighter."

Cassie frowned slightly, then gave Grace a pleasant smile.

"Didn't I see you at the funeral earlier?"

Grace smiled back. "That's right. We're working for Poppy Dalglish-Stuart. I wonder if we could have a word with your husband?"

Cassie frowned again. "What about?"

"We just needed to ask him a few questions about Carenza O'Connell, that's all," Phoebe said casually.

"Oh, I see. Well Brian isn't here at the

moment," Cassie said, smiling again. "But he's due back soon. Why don't you come inside and wait. I'll put the dog away."

Grace and Phoebe watched her walk down to the end of the hall and push the monster dog in through a swing door.

"On your right," she said, pointing at an open door.

The living room was bright and chintzy and full of vases of cut flowers and pot plants. At the far end of the room french doors opened into a conservatory with even more vegetation.

Cassie's open, oval face, now devoid of make-up, had a natural light golden tan. She had changed out of the funeral suit and now wore a coral coloured linen skirt and a white T-shirt. Her feet were bare.

"Sit down. Please. How can I help you?"

"I'm sorry about Carenza O'Connell," said Grace.

Cassie nodded. "Yes, It's awful, truly awful. Poor Carenza, she was such a sweet woman." Grace noted that Cassie Drummond said *poor Carenza* and not *poor Emmet*.

"Did you know her well?"

"Yes, very well. We socialised as two couples a lot."

"And how would you say her health was?" Grace asked.

Cassie Drummond wrinkled her nose. It was

dusted with freckles. "Poor dear, she suffered terribly with her nerves. Sometimes at the last minute she'd cancel an arrangement. Emmet said she had agoraphobia."

"Really? Do you know Paddy Moran, the odd-job man?"

Cassie sat on the arm of the Chesterfield, stretching her long golden legs out on front of her. "I didn't really *know* him. I met him a couple of times, having tea in Carenza's kitchen. Why?"

"You know he was arrested ?"

"Yes I heard. Did he . . . you know?"

"I think he's just been charged with theft," said Phoebe. She got up and walked over to the doors of the conservatory. "Are you the gardener in the family?"

Cassie smiled proudly. "Yes. I'd spend all day at it if I could."

"Did you know Anabell O'Connell?" Grace asked.

Cassie looked taken-aback at the sudden change of subject. "Not as well as I know . . . knew, Carenza. I met her maybe twice when I worked at the surgery."

"Is that where you met your husband?"

"Yes. I was a receptionist there for a couple of years. Brian and I were married just before he and Emmet bought out the practice."

"After Anabell died?" Grace asked.

Cassie furrowed her brow. "What's this got to do with Carenza's murder?"

"Oh, nothing directly," Grace said after a moment. "Anabell was a patient of your husband, I believe?"

"That's right. But what has Anabell to do with anything?" Cassie asked.

Grace turned to her and gave a dazzling smile. "Nothing at all, Mrs Drummond. By the way, was your husband home the night that Carenza O'Connell was murdered?"

"Good grief, you don't beat about the bush, do you?" But Cassie was smiling and not at all aggressive or on the defensive. In fact Grace thought she looked quite vulnerable. "I can't remember if Brian was at home or not. What day of the week was it?"

"It was a Saturday, Saturday the tenth," Phoebe said.

Cassie thought for a moment. "Let's see . . . Saturday the tenth . . . No, he'd have been at a Lions meeting."

"And what time did he get home?"

"About two-ish I think. I was in bed."

"Was that usual?" asked Grace.

"Usual?" She had a puzzled frown on her face.

"Well, what time does he usually get back from Lions meetings?" Phoebe elaborated.

Cassie shrugged. "I don't know, eleven, twelve, no special time. Why?"

Grace disregarded her question. "Do you know if Emmet O'Connell was faithful to Carenza? Does he have a mistress to your knowledge?"

"How the hell would I know? Carenza was a friend of mine, he'd hardly confide in me if he did. Ask Brian."

"Well, did Carenza ever confide in you, did she ever say that she suspected Emmet might be cheating on her?"

"Never," Cassie said firmly.

Phoebe tried a different tack. "Do you like Emmet O'Connell?"

"Yes, as a matter of fact. He's always been kind to me. I know some people don't find him particularly charming, but I can only speak as I find. Would you like some tea?"

Grace was about to refuse when they heard a car pull up outside. Cassie looked towards the window and slid off her perch.

"Here's Brian now," she said, and walked towards the french window. Drummond walked in and Cassie kissed him.

"Miss de Rossa and Miss Lamplighter want to ask you some questions, darling," she said.

Drummond looked concerned for a moment, then gave a strained smile and disentangled Cassie's arms from round his neck.

90

"Fine, would you like to come through to the study?"

The brace of Sleuths followed him through to a small comfortable room off the sitting-room. It smelled of pipe smoke. A dark wood desk in the corner was covered in leather-bound volumes. One was open and Grace noted that they were stamp albums.

"You collect stamps?" she said trying to put Drummond at ease. "I used to as a kid, but nothing on this scale."

Drummond walked over and picked up a thin volume from the bottom of the pile and opened it. "This was my first album," he said proudly. "I started when I was eleven. It's been a life-long passion with me. Do you still dabble?"

Grace shook her head. "No. I haven't the time."

"If we have the motivation, Miss de Rossa, we can find the time for whatever we want to do," he said pompously.

He was a short, dapper, muscular man with a deep tan who looked as if he trained with weights. Close up he was a little taller than he had appeared when she had first seen him at Carenza's funeral.

Grace was still looking at the album. Drummond stood uncomfortably, waiting for her to say something. After a minute he broke the silence.

"Emmet tells me that you're working for Poppy Dalglish-Stuart," he said.

"Yes. She asked us to investigate her sister's murder," said Phoebe.

"Awful thing. Poor Emmet. But how can I help you?"

"How long have you known Emmet O'Connell, Doctor?"

Drummond looked up at the ceiling as if trying to remember. "Since medical school, about thirty odd years, I suppose."

"And how long have you been partners?"

"Fifteen years. Emmet joined the practice the year after I did. When the senior partner retired six years ago, we bought the practice out."

"It's very impressive," said Grace.

Drummond smiled at her." Thank you. We try to keep up with technology. We're computerised and the new surgery was purpose built just after we took over," he went on enthusiastically. "We have ante-natal clinics, a well-woman centre as well as a pediatric clinic."

"That must have cost a bit?"

"Yes, indeed! It's the most modern surgery in the country," bragged Drummond. "We're incorporating a diagnostic programme on our PCs, and mail-merge to call patients in for regular checks."

"It was sad about Anabell O'Connell," Phoebe said out of the blue. "How long were you treating her?" She thought Drummond stiffened slightly as she dropped the bombshell.

"Oh a while," Drummond said non-committally.

"Why didn't her old man treat her? It seems a little silly to call you out when he'd be on the spot?" Phoebe persisted.

"Well he sometimes would treat her, naturally," said the doctor, beginning to look uncomfortable.

"Who diagnosed her last illness?" Grace asked.

Drummond's body language was very agitated. "I don't remember."

"Were you treating her when she died?" Phoebe asked.

"Of course. I signed the death certificate."

Grace could see a film of perspiration glistening on Drummond's upper lip. "She died of heart failure."

"Were you with her when she died?"

"No, but Emmet was. He called me but I didn't make it in time. He tried heart massage, everything." I bet he did, thought Grace. "But it was no good, her heart was enlarged, the muscles weak. Poor Emmet. He was devastated."

Grace couldn't equate the word "devastated", with Emmet O'Connell, whatever Luke Ryan had said.

"Do you know Poppy Dalglish-Stuart well?" she asked.

"Not well. Though well enough to know she's quite mad, totally over the top." He tried to smile as he said it, but the tension caused his face to freeze and the smile turned into a grimace.

"Did you know that she made a complaint at the time of Anabell's death?" Grace asked pointedly.

Drummond swallowed. "Yes, I was aware of that. Pure nonsense. As I said, the woman's quite mad."

"She claimed that Doctor O'Connell cremated his first wife with inordinate haste, and that she didn't hear of her cousin's death until after the funeral."

Drummond was sweating profusely by this time. He cleared his throat. "I wouldn't know about that, Miss de Rossa. But I believe that Poppy Dalglish-Stuart and the O'Connells didn't get on." He mopped his forehead with a large cotton hanky. "I suspect that she's a spiteful menopausal woman just making trouble."

"Perhaps," said Grace smiling. "I believe you're very involved with the Lions club."

Drummond put the album back in its place at the bottom of the pile of books, "I do what I can, but I lead a very busy life. Cassie and I socialise a good deal and the practice is demanding."

"Yes. I'm sure it is. Tell me, did you attend a Lions meeting on Saturday the tenth?"

Brian Drummond still had his back to Grace and was re-stacking the albums. He stiffened again, then turned round slowly.

"Em . . . I'm not sure," he stammered. Grace let the ensuing silence hang and stood staring at Drummond. After a moment Drummond said, "Well, yes. Maybe I did."

"What time did you arrive back home after the meeting?" persisted Grace.

Drummond coughed then cleared his throat. "Eh . . . the meeting finished at about eleven-thirty."

"I didn't ask what time the meeting finished, Dr Drummond. I asked what time you got back here?" Grace said sharply.

Drummond became very agitated. "I don't remember."

Grace sighed and looked meaningfully at Phoebe. Drummond was watching them anxiously. "Do you have a problem with your memory, Doctor?" Grace asked.

"Excuse me?" he stammered.

She leaned back against the desk and folded her arms. "Well . . . You couldn't *remember* who diagnosed Anabell O'Connell's last illness. You can't *remember* what time you got home on a specific night less then two weeks ago."

"What are you implying?" Drummond's face had turned purple.

Grace turned the palms of her hands upwards. "Me? I'm not implying anything." She stressed the word *implying*. "I'm just trying to establish what time you got home on November the tenth, Saturday November the tenth, the night Carenza O'Connell had her head bashed in."

Drummond mopped his forehead again with a white hanky. "I think I . . . I think maybe . . . Maybe you'd better leave. Yes! Leave my house," Drummond spluttered. "How dare you come here making wild accusations . . ."

"Please, Doctor," Grace said. "Please calm down. We're not making any accusations. We're just trying to find out the facts."

"You'll have to excuse my colleague, Doctor," Phoebe said hastily, "She sometimes forgets she's not a cop any more. All we want to do is build up a picture of what happened around the night Carenza O'Connell died. A complete picture. So you'll appreciate we need to know everyone's movements, if only to eliminate them."

That seemed to placate Drummond a little. He mopped his brow again. "Very well. If you put it like that," he said. "He turned back to Grace. "What was your question again?"

"I asked you what time you got home after your Lions meeting on the Saturday night."

Drummond frowned. "It would have been before midnight."

"Are you sure?" Grace asked.

Drummond swallowed, then nodded. "I'm sure."

"That's strange. You see, your wife seems to think you didn't get back until after two."

Drummond gulped, but then recovered. "She's mistaken. I went up to bed around two, but I got home just after midnight."

"Thank you, Doctor," Grace said. "You've been a great help." Drummond mopped his brow again, and appeared to relax a little.

"When was the last time you saw Carenza O'Connell?" Phoebe asked suddenly. Drummond was taken aback; he had assumed when Grace had thanked him that they were finished with him.

"Why do you ask?" he said cautiously.

"I was just wondering if you noticed what frame of mind she was in. D'you know if she had a lover?"

He shook his head violently from side to side, "I don't know if she had a lover or not. Emmet thought she had."

"Yes," persisted Phoebe. "But when was the last time you saw her?"

Drummond was very agitated again. His face was as red as a beetroot.

"I think I saw her on the Saturday evening," he stammered. "I forgot that Emmet had gone to Cork and I called in to ask him something."

"That would be the night she died?" Grace said, shooting a look at Phoebe. "Why didn't you say that before?"

"Why do you think?" Drummond snapped. "I didn't want to be made into a scapegoat. But she was alive and well when I last saw her."

"What time was that?"

"I don't know."

"After your Lions meeting?"

Drummond shook his head. "No. Before. It would have been about seven. I went on my way to the meeting."

"Was she alone?" asked Grace.

"As far as I know," mumbled Drummond. "She was in good form though. She didn't seem upset or afraid about anything."

"Did the gardai talk to you yet?" Grace asked.

Drummond shook his head. "Not yet, but I'm expecting Inspector McEvoy tomorrow. He phoned me at the surgery to say he wanted to interview me."

"Did you murder Carenza O'Connell?" Grace snarled. Drummond to spun round to face her. His face drained of colour and his hands began to shake. He swallowed hard a couple of times then looked her directly in the eyes.

"No I did not," he said emphatically.

* * *

Meanwhile Mungo and Xin were sitting up the road from Emmet O'Connell's gate waiting for him to go out to evening surgery. They hung back a distance when Mungo spotted Jack Molloy and another detective garda in an unmarked Astra.

"It looks as if Harcourt Terrace're watchin' O'Connell," Mungo said. "I hope they stay with him or we won't be able to go in."

Xin rummaged in her pocket and took out a bag of jelly babies. "Want one?" she asked, offering Mungo the bag. He took a fistful and they settled back to wait.

"Wha' time d'you think yer man'll come ou'?" Xin asked. She was rearing to go.

"He should've gone by now. I checked with the centre and he's on duty soon," Mungo said just as the front door opened and O'Connell walked out to his car, carrying a briefcase. The silver BMW swept out of the gate, and Mungo watched it disappear down the road through the rear view mirror. The garda car followed at a discreet distance.

"Come on," he said to Xin, and the mismatched pair made their way swiftly across the road and up the drive. At Mungo's insistence, she had changed out of the lime-green satin dungarees and day-glo orange top into sombre black leggings and sweat-shirt.

Once at the rear of the house, Mungo took

out a set of picks and deftly opened the patio door.

"No alarm," he said to Xin, pointing at the yellow box on the wall above his head. "That's a dummy . . . The mean son of a bitch!"

They started in the study as the obvious place. Mungo opened the drawers of an antique bureau from the bottom up, leafing through the contents and replacing them as he had found them.

"Go to an upstairs window an' keep a look out," he said to Xin. She had just switched on O'Connell's computer and was scanning through the files.

"Wha' abou' this?" she said sounding peeved. "His bank stuff's prob'ly on this yoke."

"Upstairs!" Mungo barked. "We need O'Connell disturbin' us like we need a fuckin' hole in the head."

Chastened, Xin headed for the stairs. As she passed through the hall she saw a bundle of opened letters on the hall window ledge. She picked them up and took them with her up to the front bedroom, and settled herself behind the curtain with a good view of the roadway outside the gate.

Mungo found a folder of bank statements in the top drawer. He copied them with a hand-held copier without reading them, then replaced them carefully.

He had no fondness for computers so he ran up the stairs to get Xin, the expert. Though he was loath to admit it, when it came to computers, he was glad to have her along.

She nearly jumped out of her skin when he stood behind her. The huge man was so light on his feet she hadn't heard him come into the room.

"Jeasus, Mungo! Don't fuckin' do tha'," she screeched, clutching at her chest.

"I thought Ninjas had to be able walk on rice paper without makin' any noise or leavin' a trail," he said in a scathing tone. "And I thought fuckin' Ninjas were supposed to have a sixth sense and hearing like a vampire bat!"

"I was concentratin' on somethin' else," she said stiffly, "Look at this." She handed him a letter. Mungo tilted the letter towards the light from the window. It was from O'Connell's insurance broker, and referred to claim forms he had requested. He copied it also.

"What're the others?" he asked, indicating the small pile of mail on the window ledge. "They look like them condolence cards," she said gathering them up. "Are we done here?"

Mungo nodded and patted his pocket. "Yeh. I copied the bank stuff. Let's get outta here. I want you to take a look at his computer files."

They headed back down the stairs and, as Xin was replacing the letters where she had found them, they heard the sound of a car coming up the drive. The twin beams of headlamps glared through the glass of the front door.

"Shit!" Mungo hissed. "Someone's comin." He grabbed Xin by the arm and hurried her towards the rear of the house. "What the hell's he doin' back so soon?"

Back in the study, Xin switched off the computer and Mungo just managed to silently click the patio door shut as the hall light flooded through the open door of the study. Emmet O'Connell walked through the doorway.

They crept through the shrubbery at the back of the house and climbed over the fence into the garden of the house directly behind the O'Connells'. Mungo was hugely impressed with Xin as they made their way in absolute silence through the bushes, and had a rethink about her abilities with the rice paper.

"Look!" she hissed and pointed to a glass conservatory at the rear of the neighbouring house. It was illuminated by the light of the inner room from which it led. Inside, Cassie Drummond was clearly visible talking to Grace and Phoebe. As they moved out of view, Brian Drummond crossed the open doorway.

"Well I'll be," Mungo muttered.

"Be wha'?" the Ninja asked.

Grace and Phoebe were more than surprised to see Mungo and Xin waiting for them by the car when they had taken their leave of a very jumpy Brian and remarkably cool Cassie Drummond.

"Where's your car?" Phoebe asked.

"We had t' leave it. O'Connell came back and we had to beat it," Mungo explained. "Did yeh know O'Connell's property backs on t'the Drummonds?"

"You're kidding!" Grace said.

Mungo shook his head. "So what did Drummond have t'say?"

"He was very upset," Grace said." He's obviously not telling the whole truth. Though he did admit to seeing Carenza the night she died."

"No kiddin'?" Mungo said.

"He claims it was early in the evening," Phoebe added. "By the way, Grace. What do you make of Cassie?

"Not a lot between the ears," she said. "What d'you think?"

"A bit of an airhead all right, but I think she's genuine . . . Quite sweet really."

"D'you think Drummond could've been bonkin' Carenza?" Xin volunteered. "I mean he on'y needed t'hop over the back fence."

"I doubt it," Phoebe scoffed. "I'd say Cassie has him worn out. Why would he take a mistress?"

"Well, he struck me as a very unhappy man," offered Grace. "Did you believe him when he said he didn't murder Carenza?"

"Did you?"

Grace shrugged. "What would his motive be?"

"What about O'Connell? If Poppy's right about the way Anabell died, he'd be able to blackmail Drummond into killin' Carenza," Mungo said.

"How? Drummond could call his bluff easily enough. I mean, O'Connell would have to incriminate himself in order to point a finger at Drummond," Grace protested.

"I dunno . . . From what you've said about O'Connell so far, I'd say Drummond's in awe of him. I think he'd be too afraid of him to refuse," Mungo said.

Grace snorted. "Come on! We're talking murder here. I don't think Drummond's that stupid. I wonder how much O'Connell had Carenza insured for?"

"I don't know. But I think Mungo's got a point about Drummond," Phoebe said. "I mean if O'Connell persuaded Drummond that Carenza's money was imperative to save the practice, and pointed out that he was up to his neck in Anabell's murder already, it wouldn't be that hard to lean on him."

"But do we know for sure if the practice is short of money?" asked Grace.

Mungo retrieved the roll of photocopies from his pocket and read them by torch light. Eventually he shook his head. "Zilch. This is only his private account, and he's in credit for two grand."

"Is that the only one that was there?" Phoebe demanded.

"Yeh. We'll have to take a look at the medical centre."

"Oh shit!" the ex-cop said. "Not again."

Mungo started to laugh. "Chill out, Gracie. And trust me, I'm a professional."

As they drove back towards Mungo's parked car, Phoebe suddenly said, "D'you think we should start surveillance on Emmet O'Connell?"

"No need," said Xin. "Harcourt Terrace're already on the case."

"That's handy," Grace said. "At least it saves us a few sleepless nights."

"And Poppy a few bob," Phoebe finished wryly.

They stopped at Smyth's for a drink as they were passing the door. Grace saw Dermot sitting on his own up at the bar reading the evening paper, so she left the others and joined him.

"Hello stranger," she said climbing up on the stool beside him. "On your own?"

"Not any more," he said looking up from his paper. "Would you like a drink?"

"No thanks, I've got one over there," she said, indicating the others. "I was wondering if you'd had any breaks in the Carenza O'Connell case."

"Not what you'd call breaks," he said. "How about you?"

"What do you think about Drummond?"

"I'm interviewing him tomorrow. Why?"

"No real reason I can put my finger on," she said. "Are you going to charge the odd-job man?"

"Not with murder. He's got an alibi. We charged him with theft of the jewellery though." He stared into his pint.

"Do you think O'Connell's involved?" Grace asked.

Dermot sighed. "I don't know. I keep going hot and cold on that. I mean, he has a cast-iron alibi and all that. But he's the husband and you know the statistics for the involvement of a family member but . . . well, you know yourself." Grace nodded, she knew very well what he meant. Lack of evidence against the gut-feeling-prime-suspect was a curse.

"Luke Ryan's convinced O'Connell's part of a conspiracy," Dermot said suddenly. "But so far we haven't got a co-conspirator."

"How about Drummond?" she ventured.

"How *about* Drummond? . . . Why are you gong on about him?" Dermot asked. "How's he implicated?"

"Poppy . . ." Grace started, but he cut her off at the pass.

"Come on, Grace. I'm looking for real evidence, not the ravings of Poppy Dalglish-Stuart."

"I wasn't going to say anything about Poppy in relation to Drummond, smart arse!" she snapped. "I was just going to say that Poppy agrees with the idea of a conspiracy, that's all. I think Drummond may be involved. But talk to him yourself and see what you think."

"When did you talk to him?"

"An hour ago," she said. "He's very jumpy about something. And he told me he'd seen Carenza the night she died."

Dermot raised his eyebrows. "Really?"

"Yes. But he said she was OK when he left her."

"Well, he would, wouldn't he?" Dermot said.

"Couldn't you get a look at O'Connell's bank account for the medical centre? Poppy reckons that he's short of money. If she's right, at least you have a motive." Grace harboured the feeble hope that if Dermot got to see the practice bank records, Mungo and Xin wouldn't need to risk another break-in.

"I suppose we could take a peek," Dermot said. "I'll talk to O'Malley about it tomorrow. But if Poppy's right, that still only gives us a probable motive, it doesn't give us any evidence." He drained his pint. "Are you sure you wouldn't like a drink?" he said lifting up his glass and wiggling it at the barman.

"No thanks," she said. "Though I'd love to be a fly on the wall when they read Carenza's will tomorrow. Wouldn't you?" And Dermot nodded. Then she felt a tap on the shoulder. It was Phoebe. She handed Grace her glass.

"Don't you want your drink?" she asked. "We're going to dinner now."

"Oh God, dinner!" Grace said, looking at her watch. "I was supposed to meet Luke an hour ago."

Luke Ryan was not waiting for Grace at the flat on Baggot Street, but then she didn't really expect that he'd hang around for an hour. She was angry with herself for forgetting the time, and wondered how he would feel about being stood up for the second time in as many weeks. She tried his number but only got the machine and so, much as she hated talking to robots, she left a conciliatory message.

Then hunger pangs started to gnaw at her stomach and she rooted in the fridge for something to eat. But all she could come up with was an out of date low-fat yoghurt and an open packet of rashers gone curly and green at the edges. There was nothing for it. Pizza again. She phoned in her order and settled down in front of the TV to wait for it to arrive.

When the door bell rang twenty minutes later she grabbed her purse and ran downstairs to the front door.

Andrew, and not the pizza delivery man, was standing on the step, holding the pizza box. She was gobsmacked.

"I paid the man," he said. Grace continued to stand there dumbfounded. "Can I come in?"

He walked past her, heading for the stairs. "I hope you don't mind me coming round?" he continued. "But I really wanted to see you. To thank you for the other day. I'm very grateful."

"The other day?"

"The baby . . ."

"Oh. The baby. It's OK," she mumbled. "What else could I do?"

As they reached the flat he stood in the doorway to let her past and she caught the familiar whiff of his after-shave. He followed her into the sitting-room.

"Could you get a couple of glasses?" he said, holding up a bottle of red wine that she hadn't noticed before. "We could wet the baby's head."

"Eh . . . I suppose so," she said without enthusiasm, and wandered into the kitchen still slightly stunned. Andrew was the last person she had expected, or indeed wanted, to see. He stood leaning against the wall, hands in pockets.

"Nice place you have here," he said as she rummaged in the kitchen drawer for a corkscrew. She felt uncomfortable, more so when he came up behind her and slipped one hand round her waist whilst he found the corkscrew in the back of the drawer with the other. He kissed her on the nape of the neck. Grace spun round, but his arms were now encircling her.

"What are you doing?" she demanded, but he just smiled and kissed the tip of his finger touching it to her lips. There was an awkward silence. Grace didn't know where to look. She put her hands against his chest to push him away. He tightened his grip, pressing his body against her.

"I've missed you, Grace," he said in a low voice, and bent his head and kissed her on the mouth.

She twisted her head to one side, "Stop it, Andrew. What d'you think you're doing?"

She could feel his breath hot on her face.

"Please, Grace . . . You know how I feel about you. You know you still want me."

"No I don't," she said, shaking her head and pushing her hands harder against his chest, trying to break his grip. "Please stop."

He bent his head again and buried his face in her neck, trying to nibble her ear.

"I still love you, Gracie," he said in the little-boy-lost voice that had always grated on her nerves. "I know you still want me."

Grace was very angry. "What about Kiera? You shouldn't be doing this. She's just had your child, for God's sake."

He dropped his arms, letting her go. "I know," he said, looking down at the floor. "But Kiera was a mistake. Tonight, sitting on my own downstairs while she was feeding it . . ."

"*It?*" Grace cut in "Hasn't *it* got a name yet?"

Andrew looked puzzled and a little irritated by her interruption. "Well, eh, actually we decided to call her Caitlin, after my mother. Anyway," he said, "I suddenly realised how much I missed you."

Grace knew Andrew too well, and as usual he had totally missed the point. "Oh, I see," she said smiling. "You're feeling neglected."

"What do you mean?"

"You know very well what I mean. Kiera has a baby to look after now."

"Yes, yes," he said impatiently. "I know that, and I'll stand by her but . . ."

"Well that's good of you, Andrew," she snapped. "Very fucking good of you." He opened his mouth to speak but she thrashed on. "Don't you think it just a micro-tad late to start missing me?"

"Oh, come on, Grace. Kiera's not the first woman to give birth for God's sake. She doesn't have to make a meal of it."

Grace shook her head. "You hate it when you're not the centre of the universe. Don't you? I thought it was wildly out of character when Kiera went wittering on about you wanting to be present at the birth. I can't see you as the New Man somehow. Changing nappies. Up to your elbows in baby-poo. So what happened to the *You know I've always wanted children* bullshit?"

He was staring at her. His expression said that he still had no idea what she was talking about. "You're pathetic. You can't even remember to use your own child's name." Having gained momentum, Grace careered on, unable to stop. "If there were any mistakes made, it was Kiera, poor sucker, who made them by getting mixed up with you. If you ask me, you resent the fact that she's too taken up with your baby now to spoil you the way you've been spoilt all of your bloody useless life."

He made a grab for her again but she ducked to one side. "Please, Grace. How can you say that? You know that's not true. I've always wanted you. It was Kiera who seduced *me*. I didn't realise what I was throwing away. I didn't appreciate what we had together."

"Oh p-leeease!" she scoffed. "Our marriage was never any great shakes. Your mother and mine were more enthusiastic about it than either of us ever was."

"How can you say that?" he said sadly,

shaking his head. Then he gave a wan smile. "I know you'll come to your senses and see that we were made to be together."

"Jesus . . . You're beginning to sound like your bloody mother." She had to make an effort not to laugh. Not because she thought the situation particularly funny, but because she thought it so surreal. "Get a grip, Andrew," was all she managed to say.

He reached for her again but she stepped back. He was giving her the creeps.

"Just go Andrew . . . Watch my lips. *I don't fucking want you.* Get it through your head. Go home and lie on the bed you made for yourself."

"You certainly know how to hit a man where it hurts, Grace," he said sourly and, gathering up what was left of his dignity, he stormed out.

After she heard the front door bang, she opened the wine and settled back with her pizza. She grinned to herself. Suddenly her self-esteem didn't seem quite so dented.

Chapter Eight

"The red one an' the green, or the blue one an' the red ?" Xin hissed.

"Cut the red and the green," Mungo said. "And take your foot outta my friggin' ear."

"Aw shut up whingin'," the Ninja snapped, as she clipped the red and green wires inside the cover of the burglar alarm. "Wha' now?"

"That's it," he said and helped her down off his shoulders. They made their way round to the rear of the medical centre and stopped by a half glass door. Mungo examined it and attached a suction cup to the centre of the glass.

"Hold on to that," he said handing Xin the flashlight. He then cut round the edge of the sheet of glass avoiding the silver alarm contact strip that was next to the frame. When he was done, he tapped it gently and lifted the glass out in one piece with the suction cup.

"Right," he said as he climbed through the

opening. "Jump over the mat, there's probably a pressure pad under it."

"How d'you know all this stuff?" she asked when they were inside. Mungo tapped the side of his nose.

"You were a spy weren't yeh?" she persisted, but he didn't answer. The lock of the accounts department didn't pose any problems and soon Xin was looking through the computer files. "There isn't even a password on this bleedin' yoke," she said with disgust. "Any eejit could get into it."

After about ten minutes rummaging she said, "I think this is it."

Mungo looked over her shoulder and read the screen. "They're pretty close to the wire," he remarked.

"Closer than you'd think," she answered. "That's just the first page. Look at this." She scrolled the image on the screen and Mungo gave a low whistle.

"I think eighty-five grand overdrawn counts as short of money," he said. "Can you print this out?"

"Is the Pope Italian?"

"No, he's Polish."

"Well yeh know wha' I mean," she said, rattled. She found the print option and hit the right key. It clattered into action. They both cringed at the racket.

"Jeasus! the noise outta tha'!"

Just as the print was reaching the bottom of the page Mungo saw a flashing blue light through the blinds.

"Shit! It looks like the cops," he said, going over to the window and peeping through the blind to investigate. A garda car had stopped by the gate. Two gardai were sitting in the front.

"I don't think we tripped the alarm. It could just be a routine stop. Is that thing nearly done?" he asked urgently. The racket stopped abruptly and she switched off the computer and grabbed the printout. Mungo was still by the window.

"They're gettin' out," he said. "Uh Oh, they're comin' in."

"What do we do now?" Xin said, ducking to one side of the window. The garda flash-lights bobbed up and down as the two Gardai strolled into the car park. They heard the front door being rattled and footsteps along the side of the building.

"The shit'll really hit the fan when they see the back door," Xin observed dryly.

"Then let's not wait around, moron," he answered and opened the window.

"Won't tha' set off the alarm?" she said grabbing his arm.

"Only at the cop shop. We cut the wires to the box," he said as he helped her through.

They ran, cautiously but quickly, down the front of the Centre towards the gate. Then, just as they reached the car, raised voices signalled that the break-in had been discovered. Mungo reversed down the road to avoid driving past the garda car and turned into the first side road that they came to.

"I'd like you to know that I strongly object t' bein' called a bleedin' moron," Xin suddenly announced, and sat grim-faced with her arms folded across her lap.

He reached over and patted her on the leg.

"Just a figure of speech, Killer. You did good tonight," he said and she beamed in the darkness.

Grace heard them coming in just after one and met them in the hall. "How did you get on?" she asked apprehensively.

"No swea'," Xin said casually "We found the bank stuff. They're in over their heads for eighty odd grand," She handed Grace the statements. Grace scanned down the rows of figures. "No one saw you, did they?"

Xin threw her arm around Grace's shoulder and winked conspiratorially at Mungo. "Course not. We're professionals."

Grace gave the pair a weary look. "So you keep saying. But why doesn't that claim fill me with confidence?"

Chapter Nine

Emmet O'Connell sat impatiently waiting for Walter Arrowsmith to begin the reading of Carenza's will. It was three-thirty and Arrowsmith had asked him to attend at three. He couldn't abide tardiness and felt that Poppy was late intentionally, just out of rudeness. He shifted in his seat. Free Dalglish-Stuart and Jack and his brood were already seated, as were Brian and Cassie Drummond, whom Arrowsmith had also asked to attend.

"Walter, I really feel we should get started. If my late wife's sister hasn't the courtesy to be on time I don't see why we should all be inconvenienced."

Arrowsmith took out his gold pocket watch and looked at the time. He couldn't stand O'Connell. Arrowsmith, Wattle, Wattle and Dawber had looked after the Dalglish-Stuarts' affairs for generations and he regarded O'Connell as an upstart.

"We'll give Poppy another few minutes," he

said. He actually had no intention of starting without her, but he was a courteous man and couldn't bring himself to be overtly rude to O'Connell, much as he disliked him.

Emmet wondered why Poppy and her family had been asked to attend. Carenza hadn't spoken to them for years, to his knowledge. She's probably left them some pittance, he thought, smiling to himself.

A few minutes later the door opened and Poppy came in. Walter walked from behind his desk and kissed her on the cheek.

"Walter! how lovely to see you. What a pity it should be in such awful circumstances."

"Indeed, my dear, indeed," he said. "Shall we get started?" He led Poppy to a chair next to his desk and she sat down.

"You look well, my dear . . ." he started to say.

Emmet abruptly stood up.

"For God's sake, Walter, get on with it."

Walter looked coldly at Emmet and deliberately sorted out the papers on his desk.

"We are here to read the last will and testament of Carenza Dalglish-Stuart-O'Connell. The bequests are fairly straightforward." He read from the document before him.

"To my sister, Poppy, I leave our mother's three-strand pearl necklace on the understanding that she passes it on to Free, in her will, also my diamond wheat-sheaf brooch."

Emmet looked over at Poppy and smirked. The hag looks like a tramp, he thought, dressed like that in her bag-lady gear.

Walter added gravely, "The wheat-sheaf brooch has unfortunately still not been recovered by the gardai. However, as soon as it is, I am assured by them that it will be returned. The remainder of the jewellery is being held by the gardai as evidence in a forthcoming proceeding so I shall continue to read the bequests as if that were not the case." Again he paused and looked around the assembled company, then, after clearing his throat he continued, "To my nephew, Jack's, twin daughters, Artemis and Atalanta, the sum of ten thousand pounds each, to be invested by Jack on their account and held in trust until they reach the age of fifteen." There was a ripple of whispering in Jack's corner of the room. Walter continued, "To my niece, Free, I leave all of my jewellery with the exception of any items bequeathed to other parties, and four hundred thousand pounds. In the . . ."

Emmet gasped.

Walter looked up over the top of his half-glasses, paused for a moment then continued, ". . . In the event of her death it will revert to my husband, Emmet, and his partner, Brian Drummond."

Drummond shot a look at Emmet

O'Connell, who looked slightly better pleased, until Walter finished the sentence. ". . . to distribute to the cancer charities of their choice."

Both Emmet and Free looked dumbfounded. Drummond's mouth was gaping open in surprise.

Walter read on. "The residue of my investments, in total, of five thousand pounds and all the remainder of my possessions I leave to my dear husband, Emmet."

So Carenza did have the last laugh on Emmet after all, thought Poppy.

Emmet stood up abruptly. "Five thousand pounds. Let me look at that." He pulled the will from Walter's hands, then Jack's huge hand landed on his shoulder.

"Sit, Uncle. Mr Arrowsmith hasn't finished."

Emmet, who looked slightly abashed, sat down, his face strained and growing puce. Walter pulled the will back across the desk and continued to read.

"To Cassie Drummond, the pearl-drop earrings she always admired, as a memento." Walter Arrowsmith had finished. He sat with his hands folded for a moment before saying. "That is the last will and testament of Carenza Dalglish-Stuart-O'Connell."

Jack said, "Well, I think it would be a nice gesture to go the pub and have a drink to Aunt

Carenza's memory. Will you join us, Walter?" He backed towards the door followed by his wife and the twins.

"Thank you, but no, I think this is a family time," Walter said.

Poppy smiled at her brother-in-law. "I'm sure you're thrilled for Free, Emmet. After all, you married my sister for love, didn't you? Are you joining us?"

He glared at her, then pulled himself together and gave her a frozen smile. He rose to his feet. "Of course. I'd be delighted . . ." He turned and kissed Free on the cheek. She cringed away. ". . . but I'm afraid Brian and I have to get back for afternoon surgery, don't we, Brian?"

Drummond looked distinctly uncomfortable. "Oh. Yes. Yes of course." Then to Cassie, "You take the car, sweetheart, I'll go with Emmet."

Cassie smiled sweetly at her husband and put out her hand for the car keys. "Fine, I have some shopping to do anyway."

The room emptied. Only Free, Walter and Poppy remained.

"Emmet didn't look too happy, did he?" said Free.

"When did Carenza make this will, Walter?" Poppy asked. Walter walked over to the door and closed it.

"Your sister came here three months ago."

He sat down behind his desk. "She was quite distressed. She confided in me that she thought that Emmet was having an affair and she wanted to change her will. In her previous will she'd left him everything. Anyway, she was riddled with doubts until I advised her that, if Emmet was being unfaithful, he didn't deserve to be a beneficiary. If not, then he wouldn't be concerned one way or the other about her wealth."

"Good grief, Walter! How did she react to that?" Poppy exclaimed. "I can't, in the wildest stretches of my imagination, imagine Emmet not being concerned about losing out to that degree."

Walter cocked his head to one side. "She seemed comfortable with my assessment of the situation," he said. After a moment's thought he looked over his glasses at Poppy and added, "I do hope that I acted in an ethical manner."

Chapter Ten

Dermot was called up to Superintendent O'Malley's office the following day.

"What's the progress on the O'Connell murder, Dermot?"

"I'm pretty sure the husband's involved, Frank, but so far we've no evidence."

"I can only give you one more day's surveillance, it's too short on results to justify the expense. Unless, of course, you're expecting something to come of it soon?"

There was a question at the end of the sentence. Dermot had been expecting this.

"I'm going to rattle his cage a bit and search his house again and the car too, this time."

"Are you sure that you haven't just got it in for him? What about the odd-job man? He could be acting dumb, you know. And you have his prints on the murder weapon?"

Dermot shifted in his chair. He suspected that Frank O'Malley had been told to warn him off O'Connell. I wonder if they're the same political colour, he thought bitterly, or perhaps word came from higher up.

"One of the hostel residents puts Moran in the hostel at the time of the murder and so does the warden. And he can't drive, so he couldn't have dumped her in Ballycoyle Woods, or got back. And there's no forensic whatsoever on any of his clothes. I think someone tried to set him up."

O'Malley pursed his lips and swung around on his swivel chair. He looked at Dermot.

"What's O'Connell's motive? He didn't inherit much."

"I think that came as a surprise to him. He was expecting the lot."

"What about the Dalglish-Stuart woman? Her accusation against O'Connell could just be an elaborate smoke-screen. Her daughter did do very well out of it."

"Come on, Frank. According to the solicitor, no one knew the contents of Carenza O'Connell's will, or indeed that it had been changed. Where's the motive there?"

O'Malley sighed heavily. "All right, Dermot, but you'll have to scale things down a bit if you can't get a result soon."

"How about the surveillance?"

"Just another twenty-four hours."

Back in his office Dermot called in Jack Molloy.

"O'Malley only gives us another twenty-four hours surveillance on O'Connell, so I want to put the wind up him a bit. Get a search warrant for his house and car, and go through them like a dose of salts. Take stuff away even if it's irrelevant, anything just to wind him up."

"OK. Will I tell him we're looking for forensic on Paddy Moran?"

"Good idea, but don't sound too convincing and wait for him to ask. Where's Luke Ryan?"

"He's in the District Court," said Jack. "It's the armed robbery at the Ballycoyle Credit Union we got Barry Gibbons for. Gibbons is up on remand again but the book of evidence is ready so he'll be for arraignment to the Circuit Court. It should be over by lunch-time."

"OK," said Dermot. "You and O'Boyle do the search. I've borrowed three uniformed lads to help you. Just frighten the shit out of him."

* * *

Luke was bored to distraction hanging round court all morning but, much to his relief, he was finally called just before lunch. He didn't fancy spending the afternoon in the depressing surroundings of the Bridewell.

Gibbons was arraigned to the Circuit Court, as Luke knew he would be, considering he had been arrested wearing a Charlie Haughey mask, carrying a sawn-off shotgun and a sports bag containing fifteen thousand pounds he couldn't account for. Just as he was leaving he saw Free Dalglish-Stuart trotting down the steps ahead of him. He hurried to catch up with her.

"Hello. I believe congratulations are in order," he said.

Free stopped and looked round. She smiled when she recognised him. "Luke! hello." It was a freezing cold day but she looked warm and comfortable in a dark green cashmere coat that came nearly to her ankles, black leather boots and gloves. Her hair glistened in the watery sunlight. "What are you doing here, or is that a silly question? I expect you have to come here a lot."

"You could say that," he said. "I'm just going to get something to eat, would you like to join me?"

Free looked at her watch. "OK. Posh or greasy-spoon?"

"How about the pub over there?" Luke said pointing to The Pig and Kettle. "I know it looks as if it's swarming with bacteria, but the food's quite good."

"I'll risk it if you will," she said. She flashed him a smile that would microwave a frozen cod steak at fifty paces.

When they were seated and waiting for the food to arrive, Luke said, "How did Emmet O'Connell react to your good fortune?"

"I'm not sure it was good fortune exactly," she said frowning. "The man gives me the creeps, I keep feeling as if I'm next on his hit list!"

Luke raised his eyebrows. "Has he made any threats?"

"No, no. Not as such. It's just the way he looks at me. Did you know that he's going to contest the will?"

That was news to Luke. "No, but I'm not surprised, I'd say Carenza's little bombshell knocked him for six."

"He wasn't the only one! Mother was cackling about it all night." They ate in silence for a while. All of a sudden Free looked up and said, "I know he did it. I just know he did. Anabell as well. Please don't let him get away with it."

"Between you and me, I think he did it too, or at least had it done for him. But if he is carrying on with a woman, he hasn't been near her since the funeral. Have you any ideas about who it could be?"

Free looked surprised, She shook her head. "None," she said.

"How close is he to Drummond? If he was covering for O'Connell when Anabell died, what's to stop him being involved in this?"

"Does he have an alibi?" she asked.

"A very iffy one. He admits to seeing Carenza at about seven the night she died. He was at a meeting that finished about half-eleven and Cassie Drummond verifies that he was home by twelve. But then she would, wouldn't she?"

Free shrugged. "I wouldn't have thought he was the type to bash someone's head in. If he covered for Emmet over Anabell, I'd say he didn't realise there was reason for a post mortem and took Emmet's word for the cause of death. I think he's only realising the implications of that now."

"Perhaps," said Luke. He looked into his glass.

Free liked this tall, laid-back, floppy-haired cop. There was a certain niceness about him. She wondered if he was involved with anyone. *I'd take you home any night!* she thought to herself. "Did you know that there was a break-in at the medical centre the other night?" she asked suddenly.

"Yes. Nothing was taken though, I think the garda patrol disturbed whoever it was. It was probably kids after drugs. I doubt that it's connected with the Carenza business."

Free remembered that she had a one-thirty meeting with a client. She checked the time. It was one-thirty-five.

"Oh bother. I should have been out of here ten minutes since," she said gulping her drink. "Thanks for lunch."

"My pleasure," said Luke, standing up, "I'll be in touch."

I do hope so, she thought.

After he had watched her walk off up towards the Ha'penny Bridge, Luke phoned Dermot at Harcourt Terrace and told him that he was going to talk to Drummond again.

"Good," said Dermot. "Keep the pressure up, O'Malley will only sanction another twenty-four hours surveillance on O'Connell. Jack Molloy's over there at the moment ripping his house apart. Was Gibbons arraigned?"

"Yes," said Luke. "Even Andrew Dillon couldn't get him off when Giles Wheelan produced the Charlie Haughey mask!"

"Good. I'm sending over a search warrant for Drummond's car with Pattie Doyle. Call in as soon as she's finished."

Pattie Doyle took Brian Drummond's car apart but found nothing, and Brian Drummond stuck to his story about being at home at twelve on the night of Carenza O'Connell's murder. Cassie continued to back him up.

As Luke was leaving he said, "Thank you for your help, Dr Drummond. We'll be in touch."

"In touch?" asked Drummond looking even more anxious.

"To let you know how the case develops. Don't get up, I'll see myself out."

As Luke drove down the drive he looked in the rear-view mirror and saw Drummond watching him from the window.

When he got home Grace was sitting on his

doorstep waiting for him. "Hello stranger," he said grinning.

"Sorry about the other night," she said. "Did you get my message?"

He nodded "Yes, but I'm afraid I've a confession to make."

"Oh?"

Luke put his arm round her shoulder and led her up the steps. As he was unlocking the door, he said, "I didn't make it either!"

"What?"

"I was delayed."

She punched him on the arm. "That's a very *all purpose* excuse," she said trying to look annoyed as she grinned back at him.

"I really *was* delayed," he said. He put his hand on his heart and said gravely, "But I'll make it up to you, Grace. I promise."

"Damn right, you will."

Later in her favourite bistro, while they were sharing a dozen oysters he said, "What d'you make of Drummond?"

"I think he's definitely involved in some way," she said. "Then there's the missing two hours."

Luke stopped eating. "What two hours?" he asked.

"His alibi," Grace said. "He says he was home by twelve but Cassie told me that he came in at two. When I asked him about it, he said he got to bed at two, but was home by twelve. Why d'you ask . . . didn't you know?"

"No, we didn't," he said. "She corroborated the husband's alibi. Said he was in by twelve."

"And did you know that the medical centre's in hock for eighty-five grand?" she asked.

Luke's eyebrows shot up to his hairline.

"Yes . . . But how d'*you* know that?" he said.

"Don't ask."

The waiter came and removed their plates, returning minutes later with the entree. Grace looked over at Luke's plate and instantly regretted her own choice of poached brill in lemon sauce. His fetta cheese tortellini in tomato, basil and cream looked far more appetising. She reached over with her fork and pinched a bit.

"The brill looks brill," he said with mock weariness. "Would you like to swop?"

"Well . . . If you're sure . . ."

They exchanged plates. Feeling guilty after the pasta and cream, Grace skipped dessert and, conscience assuaged, helped herself to a couple of spoonfuls of Luke's kiwi fruit and kumquat cheesecake.

"Why don't we go over and tackle Drummond about the lost two hours?" she said suddenly.

"We?"

"Well I'm going anyway," Grace said.

"Now?"

Grace popped that last spoonfull of calorie-laden cheesecake into her mouth. "No. It's early yet. After coffee."

Chapter Eleven

Light flooded from all of the windows of the Drummond residence as they pulled up opposite the front door. There was no answer to the bell. Luke banged the heavy brass knocker several times, but there was still no reply.

"D'you think they're all right?" Grace asked, suddenly apprehensive. She tried the knob and the heavy front door swung open.

"Dr Drummond?" she called. Silence. Luke looked at her and they cautiously walked towards the sitting-room. Everything looked normal. She hurried over to the study door which was ajar and pushed it open with the toe of her shoe. Brian Drummond was sitting in his desk chair looking at the ceiling. The only unusual aspect of the scene was that the chair had tipped backwards. The first view they had of Drummond were the soles of his shoes. Later, Grace remembered that her first thought had been surprise at how small his feet were. She found this quite disturbing considering that the contents of his skull were splattered in a ghoulish pattern over the ceiling and rear wall of the small room. A sawn-off shot-gun was grasped tightly in both of his hands against his belly, between his knees. The force of the blast from both barrels through the roof of his mouth had completely blown away the back, and most of the top of his head.

Grace gave an involuntary gasp and stopped dead in her tracks.

Luke, who was following her into the room, bumped into her back. "What's . . . ?" he started to say, then he too caught sight of the doctor. "Jesus!" he said. "What a mess." He pushed past her. "Not much point in checking for signs of life with half his brains on the wall."

Grace pulled herself together and followed him over to the body. Her mouth filled with saliva and she could feel her stomach rebelling. She swallowed hard and averted her eyes, looking at the desk. She noticed that the stamp albums were now neatly stacked on a table in the corner well away from the desk and, in their place, was a single piece of writing paper.

"There's the suicide note," she said. The handwriting was uncharacteristically legible for a medical man. It read,

I can't go on now that Carenza is dead. It's my fault and there is no way out of it. Lloyd's has finished me. I have nothing left to live for.

"Is that an admission of guilt, d'you think?"

Luke leaned over her shoulder. "It could be," he said.

Grace frowned. "It's a bit on the ungrammatical side isn't it? Shouldn't it read Lloyd's (whoever they may be) *have* finished me?"

"Not if he's referring to Lloyd's of London, in which case it's perfect grammar."

"Oh yes," she said, feeling a little stupid. "But look at that." She pointed at Drummond's hands which, even in death, were still gripping tightly to the sawn-off.

"What about it?"

"Cadaveric spasm."

"What spasm?" Grace gave him a *don't you know* look.

"It's very rare. I saw it once with a suicide in Ranalagh. Leo Yentob pointed it out. It's actually premature rigour mortis, happening at the moment of death."

"Really," Luke said. "Aren't you the smart one." Then at the same instant they both remembered Drummond's wife, now widow.

"Cassie Drummond," Luke said.

"Suicide pact?" Grace said. "If you'll call in and search down here, I'll check upstairs." She turned and hurried from the room as Luke picked up the phone.

The house was eerily silent. Her heart was

thumping in her chest. All the upstairs doors were wide open except for one. She took a deep breath and pushed down on the handle, closing her eyes, as if any horrors that might be within couldn't harm her if her eyes were unable to see them. Gingerly she lifted her eyelids. The bathroom was empty. She realised that she had been holding her breath and exhaled. A little less apprehensively she checked the bedrooms and en-suite bathrooms. Thankfully there was no sign of any further mutilated corpses. One was enough for any evening, especially on a full stomach.

She heard Luke on the stairs. "Nothing up here," she called.

"Didn't he have a dog?" Luke asked as he entered the room. Grace nodded.

The sound of a car engine and the beam of headlamps swept up to the drive. Grace looked out of the window.

"It's O'Connell," she said. "We'd better cut him off before he walks in on Drummond."

They made for the stairs and reached the hall just as they heard a key in the lock.

Cassie Drummond preceded O'Connell through the door. She was laughing at something O'Connell had said but she stopped abruptly when she saw Luke and the expression on his face.

"I'm afraid I have some bad news, Mrs

Drummond," he said. Cassie Drummond started to scream.

The garda team arrived and Grace melted into the background to avoid being asked to leave. The dog was found locked in the garage along with the length of barrel belonging to the double-barrelled shot gun which Drummond must have altered before ending his life in such a dramatic manner. Much later, after the body had been carted off to the morgue in a body bag, Grace saw Luke go into the kitchen with Emmet O'Connell. She wandered in after them.

O'Connell filled the kettle and plugged it in, then sat down at the long pine table. Luke leaned against the wall.

"Why do you think Brian Drummond killed himself?" Grace asked O'Connell. He hadn't noticed her coming into the room behind Luke, and looked sharply in her direction as if the sound of her voice had startled him.

"He was very troubled. He had been, ever since Carenza was found."

"What do you think he means in his note when he talks of it being his fault?" Luke watched his reaction closely. O'Connell sighed and looked down at the floor. He took a while to answer.

"Guilt . . . I think, much as I don't want to, that he may have killed my wife." He was still staring at the floor.

Grace looked over at Luke and raised her eyebrows. *He's good,* her expression said, *he's very good.*

"That's very serious talk, doctor. Why do you say that?" Luke asked.

O'Connell looked up at him. He actually had a tear in his eye. "I don't know. I think they might have been lovers."

That possibility hadn't occurred to either of them, and the implausibility of the suggestion made Grace struggle not to laugh out loud.

"What! Even if that was the case, why on earth would he kill her?"

O'Connell glared at her. "Because I know he was short of money. He was a Lloyd's Name, you know."

"Yes. He said something about that in the note he left," Grace said. "But what's that got to do with his being Carenza's lover?"

"I object to your tone, young lady," O'Connell barked. "In fact I don't know what you're doing here at all. You're not a member of the gardai."

Luke rescued the situation. "I'm sorry, doctor. Miss de Rossa is upset. She found your partner's body." Then to Grace, "Why don't you go and see if you can calm Mrs Drummond down a bit."

Grace was about to protest, but Luke's expression made her realise she was skating on

138

thin ice. She mumbled in reluctant agreement and stalked from the room. O'Connell placated, Luke asked the same question that had caused him so much annoyance moments earlier.

"I've no evidence that they were lovers, just suspicions, impressions. Tell-tale signs I can't put my finger on."

Luke let it go. "OK. But if that's true, why would he kill her?"

"You may not be aware," O'Connell said in a very patronising tone, "but Lloyd's Names have total liability for the losses incurred in insurance cover they underwrite. It's been a very bad few years for the insurance markets; I know his losses were considerable."

"It'd be hard not to know about the Lloyd's Names, doctor," Luke replied stiffly. "It's been all over the papers and TV news. Are you sure he actually lost money? Did he confide in you about his losses, or are you just speculating?"

O'Connell sighed and looked over at Luke again. "Oh, I'm not speculating, Sergeant. I think he said his liability was for over one hundred thousand pounds."

"And was he good for that kind of money?"

Emmet O'Connell sat back on his chair and crossed his ankles. "Not in cash. His assets would cover it, they would have to in order to be accepted into Lloyd's in the first place. I think the reason he may have killed Carenza is that he asked her for money and she must have refused."

"That all seems very speculative."

O'Connell shrugged. "Can you think of any other reason why he would kill her?"

"Well. We don't know that he did, do we?" said Luke. "Tell me, are you a Name?"

O'Connell gave a mirthless laugh. "I was never a gambler, sergeant and, to me, insurance companies are just semi-respectable bookmakers."

"Did Brian Drummond ask you for help?"

"Not as such."

"Excuse me?"

O'Connell walked over to the window. He had his back to Luke and was leaning with his hands on the edge of the sink. "Not in so many words. He hinted but I ignored the hints. Maybe if I'd loaned him some money my dear, dear, Carenza would still be alive." His head dropped and his shoulders shook as if he was weeping. Luke wasn't convinced, but then he couldn't see his face.

After a moment O'Connell took a handkerchief from his pocket and blew his nose loudly. "I'm sorry, sergeant." He cleared his throat. "What a mess, what a mess."

"You were out with Mrs Drummond tonight?"

O'Connell nodded. "Yes. We went to The Point to see Riverdance. Brian detests . . .

detested, Irish music or any sort of dance, as did Carenza. Cassie and I often go to those sort of things together. I suppose Brian knew he'd be safely alone until we came back."

"I see," said Luke. "Where can we contact you if we need to speak to you again?"

O'Connell frowned. "Speak to me again . . . What about?" For the first time he looked uncomfortable.

"Nothing specific, Doctor, but you may be able to help us in our enquiries. After all, you knew Brian Drummond better than anyone."

O'Connell nodded. "I'll be at home or at the medical centre. I'll just say my goodbyes to Cassie before I go." The two men walked across the hall to the dining-room where Cassie and Grace and a uniformed female garda were sitting talking.

Cassie was curled up in the corner of the settee, her legs pulled up under her and her arms wrapped round her body. Her eyes were swollen from crying and her cheeks flushed. She gave O'Connell a weak smile as he entered the room.

"I'll be off, Cassie, I'll see you later. Call me if you need anything," he said. She nodded in reply.

When he had gone Grace said to Luke, "Cassie was just telling us that Brian had been acting very strangely lately. Would you like to tell Sergeant Ryan what you just told us, Cassie?"

Cassie Drummond sniffed and nodded. She uncurled herself and sat up on the settee, looking straight into Luke's eyes.

"Brian lied to you when he said that he was at home by midnight the night that Carenza died. He tried to make me believe that he was in and that I only woke up when he came to bed. But I couldn't sleep. I went down at one-thirty to get a glass of water and he wasn't in then." She started to cry again. "Do you think he killed Carenza? Do you really think he *would* do that?"

Luke side-stepped the question. "I understand from Emmet O'Connell that your husband was in some financial trouble. Do you know anything about that?" he asked.

"He was a bit old-fashioned, Sergeant, he never talked about money with me, he thought that I wouldn't understand."

"So you had no idea that he had money worries?"

"I knew he was worried about something." Tears slid down her cheeks and she wiped them away with the back of her hand. "But he wouldn't confide in me. It was very hurtful. Now I can see why. Poor, poor Brian, he must have been so desperate."

"It seems so, Mrs Drummond," said Luke.

142

"I'm afraid that I'll have to ask your permission to search the house."

She didn't seem to grasp what he was telling her. "Search . . . but why?"

"Emmet O'Connell seems to think that your husband and Carenza were lovers, and that he may have killed her."

"Yes. He told me. I can't believe it, but it makes a lot of things fit into place."

"Such as?" Luke asked.

Cassie wrapped her arms round her knees again and shivered. "Oh . . . he was jumpy and restless. A wife can sense these things. Sometimes he smelled of soap when he came in late, as if he had just showered." She looked up at Luke, her eyes filling with tears. "I tried to pretend it wasn't happening. But what chance did I stand against Carenza, she was so rich." She looked down at the carpet. "Of course I didn't know it was her, I never suspected. I thought she was my friend."

"If your husband did murder Carenza, there may be evidence here." When she didn't answer Luke said, "We could get a warrant."

Cassie sighed. "No no . . . go ahead. Search where you like."

She got up and went over to a sideboard and poured herself a large drink which she swallowed in one gulp. It made her cough.

A commotion in the hall signalled Dermot's

arrival on the scene. He stuck his head round the door and gestured to Luke.

"Is there anyone who could come over to stay with you?" Grace asked the widow. The alcohol had put a bit of colour back in Cassie Drummond's cheeks.

"Emmet phoned my mother. She's on her way over. Thank you," she said in a shaky voice. Then out of the blue she asked, "Are you married, Grace?"

Grace said, "Yes . . . Eh . . . Well I'm separated, actually."

"Aren't you lucky," Cassie said.

"What d'you mean?"

Cassie sniffed and then started weeping again. "At least you can still see your husband. I'll never see mine again."

Aren't you lucky, Grace thought.

Chapter Twelve

It was after two when Luke dropped Grace off at Baggot Street. The search of the Drummond house had uncovered correspondence from Lloyd's of London requesting that Brian Drummond honour his liability for the sum of one hundred and thirty-four thousand pounds. Also there was a handwritten document in the form of a contract between Drummond and Carenza O'Connell. It was an agreement for Carenza to lend Drummond one-hundred and fifty thousand pounds, interest free over ten years. The agreement was unsigned but dated one week before Carenza's death. There was no sign of the diamond brooch in the shape of a wheat-sheaf.

Phoebe's light was on so Grace went up to acquaint her with the latest news.

"Where the hell have you been?" Phoebe asked.

"Brian Drummond blew his brains out tonight. Why d'you ask?" answered Grace.

Phoebe looked stunned. "What do you mean, blew his brains out?"

"I mean literally. Luke and I found him with his brains dripping from the ceiling of his study. The suicide note implies that he killed Carenza, but I'm not so sure."

"Christ!"

Grace slumped down on Phoebe's Italian leather couch. "That's not all. O'Connell tried to tell us that Drummond was having an affair with Carenza. Can you believe that? I mean he must think we're complete eejits."

"Why? Who's to say Drummond wasn't bonking Carenza? Maybe Xin had it right when she pointed out that he only needed to hop over the fence," Phoebe observed.

"Oh p-leeeease! . . . You were the one who blew that idea away." Grace snorted. "Of course there was the loan agreement."

"What loan agreement?"

Grace told her, and of the Lloyd's of London debt.

"There you are then," Phoebe said. "I rest my case. Why else would she lend him all that money interest free, if he wasn't giving her one?"

"Well, she didn't part with any money, did she, smart arse?" Grace said.

"OK. Maybe he did kill her then. Maybe he tried to get her to lend him the money, drew up the agreement. Then, when she refused to sign, in a fit of desperation he bludgeoned her to death. He'd have had the time to do it after the Lions meeting. And enough time to dispose of the body."

"That's true," Grace conceded. "And his car's clean so he must have used her car and dumped it somewhere afterwards. Poppy won't be too thrilled if her bête noire is off the hook."

"Oh God! Speaking of bête noire," Phoebe suddenly burst out. "Your parents have been in an accident . . . That's why I was trying to find you. Your sister, Faith, phoned about two hours ago."

Grace shot up in her seat. "What kind of accident? What happened? Are they all right?"

"I don't know. Faith just said that your parents were driving back from somewhere and they were involved in an accident. They're in Vincent's Hospital."

"How serious is it? Oh God, I should be there. How badly hurt is my mother?"

Phoebe grabbed her arm. "I don't know but I'll drive you. I don't think you could manage to get there in one piece carrying that huge guilt trip on your back."

By the time they arrived at Vincent's, Paul de Rossa was in theatre having surgery, and Alice de Rossa was in a private room, heavily sedated. Faith, and Grace's older sister, Hope, were sitting in a waiting room. Faith jumped up when she saw Grace.

"Grace. Where were you?" she burst into tears and threw her arms round Grace's neck. Grace hugged her sister and looked over Faith's shaking shoulders at Hope.

"What happened? How's Mummy?"

Hope stood up and joined them. "Mummy's not too bad. Just superficial stuff. But it looks as if Daddy could have broken his back."

"Oh my God," said Grace. "How long has he been in theatre?"

"About an hour. Professor Ambrose is working on him. Charles said he's the best in the field so . . ." She started to cry and couldn't finish the sentence. The door opened. Phoebe came in with a tray of coffee.

"I thought you could all do with this." Phoebe produced a naggin of brandy and laced the coffee with it. Grace introduced her partner to her sisters.

"Who was driving?" Grace asked after a while.

"Mummy was . . . But the accident wasn't her fault. A drunken driver shot out of a side road right into the passenger side. Daddy was trapped. They had to cut him out."

Grace was relieved that her mother hadn't been in the passenger seat, then she felt instant remorse. Her relationship with her father was based on his assumption that she would always disappoint him, and her bloody-minded efforts to make sure that she did.

"A shrink would make a meal of your relationship," Phoebe had said to her not many weeks before. "In my opinion you're really seeking his unconditional love." Grace had scoffed at what she considered to be psychobabble, but Phoebe had persisted, "OK. Why do you do exactly the thing that you know for certain will get right up his nose? I think you're testing him."

"Well then he's failed miserably, hasn't he?" Grace had snapped in reply. Now she felt guilty and unhappy. What if he was paralysed? What if he died? When she thought about it, she had to admit that Phoebe was closer than she knew to the truth. Even as a tiny child she remembered trying to get her father's attention by being unbelievably bold.

He had been away studying in America when she was born, and he hadn't seen her until she was four months old. Consequently he had never been able to relate to her. He had been present at the birth of all his other children. Grace always sensed his awkwardness with her.

Charles Heaslip, Hope's husband, put his head round the door. "Paul's out of surgery," he said. "They're taking him up to intensive care now." The three sisters gave audible sighs of relief. He caught sight of Grace. "Hello, Grace. You can go up and see your mother soon."

"How is she, Charles? Is she going to be all right?"

He nodded his head. "Yes she was lucky. She's mostly suffering from shock. But I'm afraid Phillip Ambrose's prognosis isn't so rosy for your father."

"I thought you said he was out of danger," said Grace.

"I said he's out of surgery," Charles said. "But there's a very strong possibility that he'll be a quadraplegic."

"Oh my God."

Hope groaned, and flung herself into her husband's arms. Grace felt an overwhelming dread and sense of guilt as if somehow it was her fault. God was punishing her. Faith, who had gone very white in the face, swayed slightly. Phoebe grabbed her.

"Here, take a drop of this." She handed Faith the brandy naggin. Faith took a hefty swig and handed the bottle to Grace who followed suit.

"How soon will they know?" Grace asked.

Charles shrugged.

"Difficult to say. Maybe forty-eight hours or so. When the swelling on the spine subsides a bit."

The door flew open and Charity, the

youngest of the four de Rossa girls, burst in. "I got your message," she said to Faith. "What happened? How's Mummy?" Faith led her over to a corner and explained.

"Did anyone get in touch with the boys?" Grace asked, suddenly remembering her brothers.

"I tried to reach Eoin through the aid agency, but you know what communications are like in Bosnia," Hope said. Grace didn't, but she could imagine. Eoin was Paul de Rossa's favourite and eldest son who was working for the UN in Bosnia. "But Michael's on his way. He's jumping a flight from Boston in a couple of hours."

Michael was Grace's favourite and the youngest of her siblings. Like her he was, if not a black sheep, definitely on the grey side in his father's eyes. He had studied medicine on the insistence of his parents, but when he qualified he'd dropped out and was currently waiting tables in Boston, whilst trying to break into his great love, the music business. He wasn't earning megabucks, but he was far happier that he had ever been as a doctor.

"Look. I don't think there's any point in all of you staying here for the night," Charles said. "Paul is stable now and you'll be called if anything happens."

That suited Grace. She hated hospitals at the

best of times, and was the first to make a move to leave. She called in to take a look at her mother. Alice was deeply sedated but didn't look too bad apart for bruising to her face and a crepe bandage on her right arm. Grace crept over to the bed and kissed her on the forehead. She stirred slightly but didn't wake.

The night sister wouldn't let her into intensive care to see her father but she peeked through the window. Paul de Rossa looked wretched, wired up to the monitors and drips. And worst of all, he looked helpless. She had always been accustomed to her father being in control.

Phoebe was waiting for her in the car. "Are you OK?" she asked as Grace got into the passenger seat.

Grace nodded. "He looked awful. What if he's paralysed? How will my mother cope? He'll be impossible to live with."

"I suppose she could always bung him in a home," Phoebe said.

Grace cringed. "Your sensitivity never ceases to amaze me, Phoebe," she said. "Have you ever thought of being a bereavement counsellor?"

"Oh shut up," said Phoebe. "I'm just saying it like it is." They drove in silence. The roads were empty.

"I'll go and see Poppy first thing," Grace said as they pulled up outside Baggot Street. "I suppose there's no sign of any new client on the horizon?"

"Mungo has a security gig lined up," Phoebe said. "Some teeny bopper band at The Point. But that's it."

"We could do with a decent time-consuming, expensive surveillance job with Christmas coming up," Grace commented.

Phoebe agreed. "With a bit of luck Poppy'll still have a bee in her bonnet about O'Connell. We could always steer her in that direction. And don't even think of trying to talk her out of it if I can persuade her," Phoebe warned.

"With penury staring us in the face I'll help you to do the persuading," said the ex-cop.

Chapter Thirteen

Grace dreamed about Drummond and, as she looked down at his body, the face turned into that of her father. She awoke with a start, disorientated, as Xin plonked down a mug of coffee on her bedside table.

"Sorry abou' yer auld fella," she said. "Phoebe told me abou' him and yer ma."

Grace looked at the clock and struggled up into a sitting position. She was feeling groggy for want of sleep.

"Christ. It's after eleven." She groaned. "I have to go and see Poppy, and ring Vincent's. Why didn't you call me?" She grabbed her dressing-gown and swung her feet to the floor.

Xin pulled back the curtains. "I rang Vincent's a while ago. Yer ma's awake, an' she's OK, bu' there's still no change in yer da. He's ou' of intensive care, bu' the neurologist still doesn't know if he'll walk again."

"How come they gave you the information?"

Grace asked, aware of how difficult it was to prise any information other than, *as well as can be expected* from hospital medical staff.

"I said I was you."

"Oh," Grace said, slightly miffed that Xin had got away with it.

"I'll be goin' downstairs now," Xin said. "I'm helpin' Mungo t'interview bouncers for The Point gig."

Grace stood under the shower and let the hot stream of water play on her stiff shoulder muscles. The heat eased the tension and she began to relax a little. After hurriedly throwing on her clothes, she headed downstairs and bumped into Phoebe, halfway down.

"Don't bother going into reception," she said. "It's full of Neanderthals."

"Xin told me," Grace said. "Shall we go straight over to Poppy's to break the news?"

Compton answered the door of the Dalglish-Stuart residence and showed them into Poppy's sitting-room. Phoebe, who hadn't been to the house before, was just as bemused as Grace had been on her first visit.

The hairy dogs looked as if they hadn't moved since Grace's last visit and adorned the settee and armchairs like fur-covered cushions. Poppy rose as they were shown in.

"I assume you've come to tell me about Brian Drummond," she said.

"Yes, we have. When did you hear?" Grace asked.

"Inspector McEvoy rang me this morning at some ungodly hour," Poppy said. "He tried to tell me Drummond blew his own brains out. More like O'Connell did for him as well."

"There's no doubt that it was suicide, Poppy," Grace said. "When Luke Ryan and I found him he still had the gun in his hand. He was in an awful mess."

"I told you so, Mother," Free said. They hadn't heard her come into the room behind them. "The Inspector said he confessed to killing Aunt Carenza. Is that true?"

Grace said, "He left a note. It said Carenza's death was his fault. Personally, I don't think that's an admission of guilt."

"There, you see?" Poppy barked at her daughter. "I told you it wasn't a confession."

"What else could it be? How could he be more plain?" Free said astonished.

"Well. If I was confessing to a murder I'd say I murdered Carenza, or I killed her. Not, it was my fault. Wouldn't you?" asked Grace.

Free shrugged. "Not necessarily."

"I agree with Grace. It all sounds rather third party. Like he did something that was responsible for, or caused someone else to murder Carenza," said Phoebe.

"Oh come on!" Free snorted. "That's a bit far-fetched. You sound like Mother."

"Well I agree with her," Poppy barked. "As sure as night follows day, Emmet O'Connell had Carenza killed in the belief that he would get his hands on her money. If only we could prove it."

"Do you have any ideas yet about who he could be seeing?" Grace asked.

Poppy shook her head.

"That's if he is still seeing anyone," Free cut in. "The gardai were watching him for two weeks and didn't come up with anything. I think we should let sleeping dogs lie."

"That's typical," Poppy sneered at her daughter. "You don't care about justice. You're just happy with your little nest egg."

Free's face went white with rage. Her lower lip began to tremble. "How can you say that, Mother? You know how I loved Aunt Carenza. I just think you're on a fool's errand, that's all." She turned and fled from the room.

"Stupid girl," Poppy said to no one in particular.

Comptom shambled in through the door. "Will you be requiring anything, madam?" he asked.

Poppy shook her head and waved him away. "No, go away Compton. On second thoughts, bring in a jug of hot port. We are about to have a council of war."

Phoebe looked at Grace and gave her a sly

wink. Grace felt awkward. She didn't like the idea of exploiting Poppy, despite her fighting words of the previous night. But she realised that the dwindling finances of Sleuths, Investigation & Security Specialists, called for desperate action, however unethical.

Compton returned with a tray, jug and glasses. Poppy poured out three steaming hot toddies. The three women sat around the fire and Poppy, after draining her glass in one swallow, said, "I think Emmet will be off his guard now, so I want you to mount round-the-clock surveillance."

"That comes expensive, Poppy," warned Phoebe.

Poppy snorted. "I don't care what it costs. Just give me his head on a plate."

Grace felt herself blush, but perhaps it was the hot port. "O'Connell had Carenza insured, you know," she said.

Phoebe jumped in. "That's another thing. We could probably hack into the insurance company's computer and check how much he got paid out. That might just count as motive."

"Could you do that?" Poppy sounded very impressed.

"Of course Poppy. We're professionals." Phoebe replied. Grace's heart sank.

"Wonderful," said Poppy. "Go ahead and do it."

When they got outside Grace hissed, "How the fuck are we going to hack into a computer? Are you out of your mind? You should've quit while we were ahead. And I wish you'd stop using the line, *We're professionals,* it's getting on my nerves."

"Chill out, Grace," Phoebe said smiling. "We got the surveillance job, didn't we? At least we'll live to fight another day. Now, do you want to go on to Vincent's to see your folks?"

Phoebe dropped Grace and went back to the office to organise the first surveillance shift on O'Connell.

And Grace went to see her mother.

A familiar voice greeted her as she opened the door of Alice's private room. Kathleen Dillon, the mother-in-law from hell, was sitting on the bed holding forth about something. They looked towards the door as it opened. It was too late for retreat.

She hurried towards the bed and embraced her mother.

"How are you feeling?" she asked. Then without much enthusiasm, "Hello Kathleen. How nice to see you."

Kathleen waited for her to disentangle herself from her mother, then offered her cheek to Grace, who gave it a peck.

Alice smiled bravely at her daughter. "I'm fine, darling," she said. "But your poor father

159

isn't so lucky, I'm afraid." Her eyes were watering up.

"I'm sure he'll be fine, Mummy," said Grace, trying to sound confident. "Professor Ambrose is the best there is. If anyone can get Daddy on his feet, he will."

Alice squeezed her hand. "Thank you, dear. You're so sensible. I'm just being a silly old woman."

"Why haven't you been to see me for ages and ages?" Kathleen asked Grace.

"Well you know how it is . . . under the circumstances I find it a bit awkward." Grace felt smug in the knowledge that one of the good things to come out her desertion by Andrew was the absence of his mother from her life.

"Nonsense!" Kathleen gushed. "After you practically delivering my grandchild. What's awkward?"

"I believe they're naming the baby after you, Kathleen," Grace said, rapidly diverting the conversation.

"Yes, yes," said the proud grandmother, "Though I think it was a close run thing between Caitlin and Grace."

Grace cringed. "Do you need anything, Mummy?"

Alice de Rossa smiled. "No dear. To see you is enough. You've all been so good, it makes the heartaches of rearing children worthwhile."

"Perhaps you could ask that nice nurse to send in some tea and biscuits," Kathleen said.

"Fine," Grace answered. "Then I'll just pop along and see Daddy. I'll call in again before I go." She retreated. Alice and Kathleen had resumed their conversation before the door had closed.

Paul de Rossa had been moved to a private room from intensive care. He was lying flat on his back with his head and shoulders screwed into a metal cage contraption. He looked like something from a horror movie. The nurse on duty warned her to stay no longer than two minutes and not to tire him out.

"How do you feel, Daddy?" she asked, immediately regretting the stupid question.

"How do I look?" he answered. She was sure he tried to smile.

"Not terrific," she said. "I just saw Mummy. She doesn't look too bad, though Kathleen Dillon was with her so I suppose there's always a danger that she'll be bored to death."

There followed one of the awkward silences that always seemed to happen when father and daughter tried to make small talk. Grace walked over to the window and looked out. Dublin Bay looked beautiful in the crisp winter sunshine. "The view's lovely," she said lamely.

"You know, don't you?" he said.

"Know what?" She assumed he was referring

161

to his injury and didn't know what he had been told of his chances of paralysis.

"About your friend, Miss Lamplighter."

Grace's heart leapt in her chest. "Yes. I know . . . but I haven't said anything to Mummy." He started to speak but she cut him off. "It wasn't to spare you. Not for you. But for her. I know how much it'd hurt her. She adores you, though God knows why. You don't deserve her."

"I know," he said simply. "It won't happen again."

"Even if you can walk?" she snapped and instantly wished she hadn't. "I'm sorry. That was cruel."

"But an honest observation," he said without malice. Another uncomfortable silence followed.

"Michael should be here soon, and Faith's trying to contact Eoin." She felt horribly embarrassed. Her father's sex life was the last thing she wanted to discuss with him. Later she reflected on what a failure she was at communicating with either of her parents about even everyday things, let alone anything of importance.

"How is your business venture progressing?" he asked after a while.

"Very well. Marvellous in fact . . . Well actually not very well . . . There, I've done it again . . . I've succeeded in disappointing you,

162

haven't I?" she asked, feeling a mixture of anger and sadness.

"You don't disappoint me, Grace."

"Only because you don't expect anything anymore." She fought to stop the tears that were welling in her eyes. "I only ever wanted you to be proud of me."

"I am."

"Are what?"

"Proud of you. I'm proud of you all. I'm just not very adept at showing my emotions."

"You're proud of me?" She made no effort to hide the sarcasm in her tone. "Right!"

"Don't be like that, Grace. I *am* proud of you. I'm proud of your courage, and the fact that you've never been one to take the easy ride. And as for disappointment? Well, I think it is I who have disappointed you."

You've got that right, she thought.

He closed his eyes and, as if it were a signal, the door opened and a nurse came in.

"I think you should go now," she said gently.

Grace nodded to the nurse and left without saying goodbye. It was only on the way back to Baggot Street in the taxi that she remembered that she hadn't said goodbye to her mother.

* * *

Meanwhile, back at the ranch, Phoebe was cross-

163

examining Xin, who was wearing her computer-buff hat about her knowledge of hacking.

"I don't hack. I'm not tha' interested in it. Whose files d'you want t'get inta anyway?"

"Well, for instance. What if we wanted to check out how much Emmet O'Connell collected on Carenza's life policy. How would we go about it?"

Xin shrugged her shoulders. "It's quite straightforward. First yed have t'have a Modem."

"What's that?"

Xin gave her a withering, *don't you even know that much* look, and sighed. "A phone link t'other computers. Righ'? I think your Ronan has one."

Phoebe nodded and resisted the urge to make a sarcastic comment.

"Then we'd need t'know the name of the insurance company."

"We have that."

"Fine. Then we have t'find ou' what network they're on."

"How do we do that?" Phoebe asked, disappointed that they had fallen at such an early hurdle.

"Me brudder can find tha' out."

"What then?"

Xin shook her head slowly from side to side and gave a low whistle. The way the washing-machine man does just before he tells you that he can't possibly fix it for under a couple of hundred quid, and you'd probably be better off buying a new one anyway.

"Well, now we come t'the hard bi'." She paused to give that little bombshell time to sink in. "Once we're in the network, we need the righ' password t'get inta the insurance company files."

"How do find out the password?" Phoebe asked. "Would your brudd . . . brother know that too?"

Xin shook her head. "No. The on'y way is t'keep tryin' passwords till yeh strike lucky. There's a problem wit' tha' too."

"Oh God. What now?"

"After yeh enter the wrong password three times, the computer aborts yer call, an' yeh have t'start all over again, an' there are millions of combinations for passwords."

Phoebe was beginning to regret her bravado with Poppy. If hacking was so bloody complicated why did people bother to do it at all?

"There is a way round tha' of course," Xin added after another pause. "There's special software programmed t'stop the computer abortin' the call. An' it enters every possible password. All the hacker has t'do is sit an' wait for the righ' one."

Things were looking up. "So where do we get this software?" Phoebe asked hopefully.

"Dunno," Xin said. "Your Ronan migh' know. Why don't yeh ask him?"

"How would he know? He wouldn't be into that kind of thing."

Ronan was the son Mungo had delivered of Phoebe in the New York taxi cab. He was also a computer wizard, though Phoebe had no idea if he was a hacker.

"Will yeh cop on t'yerself," the Ninja said, unable to believe that Phoebe would be so naive about her own son. "Anyway, if he isn't, he mus' know some other smart-arsed computer-nerd kid who is."

Phoebe thought about that. On balance, Ronan was the only answer. She resolved to phone his headmaster on some pretext and then get Mungo to pick Ronan up from boarding school the next day. She smiled to herself when she thought of her son. It would be an added bonus to have him for the weekend.

Chapter Fourteen

Three days later Luke got caught in a traffic jam on his way back to Harcourt Terrace. As he drove round a bend in the road, he saw the cause of the hold-up. A garda car was parked by the footpath and there was a small group of people standing out in the road. As he drew level, Poppy's protesting voice drifted in through the open window. He pulled in to the kerb and got out after having half a mind to just drive on and leave her to it.

The two uniformed officers were trying to reason with an irate Poppy, who was beating them back with a placard on which was written in bold, albeit artistic lettering, O'CONNELL IS A SERIAL KILLER.

She stopped when she saw Luke. "Have you come to arrest me, Sergeant Ryan?"

"I hope not, Poppy."

The garda looked at Luke. "D'you know this woman, sir?"

Luke took him by the arm and led him to one side.

"What's the story? What's she been doing?"

The garda looked back over his shoulder at Poppy.

"We got a call from the medical centre. Apparently she has some kind of vendetta against one of the doctors."

"Yes, I know about that. But what's she been doing?"

"Just marching up and down outside. There wasn't any offence until the doctor came out to get into his car, then she got abusive and chased him back inside. They had to lock the door to keep her out. That's when we arrived."

The other cop was still talking to Poppy and rapidly losing patience, by the look on his face.

"Look," said Luke. "Give me a minute, will you."

He walked over to where Poppy was standing, still brandishing the placard. "What's the problem?"

The cop said, "This woman's in danger of being done for a breach of the peace, that's the problem."

"Give me a minute, Sean, will you," he said to the cop. "I might be able to sort this out." Then out of the side of his mouth, he added, "Without the paper work." The cop stood back and threw up his hands. "She's all yours."

He turned back to Poppy, who had the placard ominously raised above her head. "OK Poppy. What's all this about?"

She stopped the placard in mid-swipe. "Is that a serious question?"

"OK, I have an idea what the problem is," he conceded. "But d'you think that this is the right way to go about it?" He was standing in front of her now. She lowered the placard to the ground and pouted.

"You above all people should know that I have no other way open to me to air my grievance," she said in a weary voice. He took her elbow and led her to the footpath.

"Look, Poppy, being done for threatening behaviour and a breach of the peace isn't going to further your cause one bit. People will just think you're a nutter."

Poppy burst out laughing. "So what's new, young man?"

Luke looked at her imploringly. "Please, Poppy, just let me take you home before O'Connell decides to make an official complaint."

It had started to drizzle. She looked up at the sky, then over at the medical centre, where the staff and patients could be seen peering out of the windows. After a moment's thought she said, "All right. But only because it's started to rain and I don't want to catch my death of cold."

Luke settled her into the passenger seat and put the placard in the boot.

The garda driver came over to him. "We've just had a shout to a disturbance at Killigrews. What do you want to do with this one?"

"Did Doctor O'Connell make an official complaint?"

"No he didn't."

"Then leave it with me. I'll take her home."

Emmet O'Connell watched from his office as Luke's car drove away carrying Poppy. The crowd, sensing that there was going to be no further violence, dispersed.

"Will that woman never stop haunting me?" he asked himself.

Free was just about to put her key in the lock when she heard the sound of car tyres crunching on the gravel. She turned and a look of amazement crossed her face when she saw Luke Ryan pulling up with her mother perched in the front seat of his car.

"What . . . ?" she started to say, then, seeing the legend on Poppy's placard as Luke took it out of the boot, shut her mouth abruptly and gave Luke a despondent look. He shrugged in reply.

"Mother, you have to stop this," she said.

Far from repentant, Poppy snapped, "Stop patronising me dear. Now, shall we have tea?" and sailed past both of them into the house.

Free stared after the retreating figure. "What happened?"she asked Luke.

"I came across her outside O'Connell's surgery trying to do damage to a couple of cops with the placard. Apparently she tried to attack your esteemed uncle-in-law with it too, but he fled."

"Is he going to press charges?" she asked.

"Your guess is as good as mine," he said. "But I doubt it. He won't want the publicity."

"Are you coming in?"

Luke shook his head. "I think I'll give it a miss, thanks." She looked disappointed so he added by way of explanation, "I'm still on duty."

She smiled at him. "Thanks for rescuing Mother, though it would have served her right if you'd let them arrest her."

"Perhaps," he said laughing. "But do you think the Irish judicial system could cope with you mother?"

* * *

Poppy was laying down the law at the dinner table later that evening to Free, who was trying desperately to stay calm.

". . . and I said to Luke Ryan. The only reason I'm leaving is because I don't want to catch my death of cold. But mark my words, Free, I'll be back there tomorrow and every day for as long as it takes."

"Mother, you have to stop this. You could end up in prison if Emmet prosecutes."

Poppy burst out laughing. "Better women than I have spent time in prison for their beliefs, my dear. That's the trouble with the young today, no staying power. First sign of discomfort and they run home crying."

Free was about to remind her mother that she had done just that, but thought better of it in case Poppy took it as a challenge. Instead she stayed silent and went back to her vegetarian shepherd's pie in the hope that her mother would forget about the whole thing.

"And another thing," went on Poppy, "he'll be after Cassie Drummond soon if he runs true to form, and then she'll be the next victim. And, when she is, my conscience will be clear. Your Sergeant Luke Ryan won't be so bloody patronising then, will he?"

I think he was being condescending, not patronising thought Free, smiling to herself. "No Mother, I don't expect he will."

Poppy droned on for the rest of the meal. Free switched to automatic pilot, refusing to rise to her, deep in her own thoughts. Her mother drove her up the wall ninety percent of the time but she didn't want to see her carted off to prison. She resolved to go and see Emmet the following day to try to dissuade him from bringing charges, or at any rate to find out what his intentions were.

"You're not listening to me!" Poppy's shrill voice intruded, snapping her back to the present.

"I am, Mother, honestly I am. I was just thinking that maybe you should try and think of some other way of getting at Emmet. I mean, I don't see what you can do from prison."

"Who says I'll go to prison anyway, girl. Emmet will probably take out an injunction or something."

"Yes I know, but then if you ignore it, you'll be in contempt of court and they can throw away the key, so you'll be playing right into his hands."

This seemed to catch Poppy's attention. Her bravado evaporated a little at the thought of having to do prison time. Despite what she'd said to Free earlier, she didn't fancy being locked up . She'd always suffered a little from claustrophobia. But her natural arrogance took over. "No, my dear, you're wrong, he wouldn't dare take me to court."

Free gave her a wry look. "I wouldn't count on it, Mother. I wouldn't count on it."

* * *

Grace had always been of the opinion that surveillance was the next most boring pursuit after watching paint dry. It left her listless and grumpy. And didn't do her skin or bladder any good either due to the diet of crisps and canned fizzy drinks she consumed whilst sitting for eight hours at a stretch trying to be invisible.

Watching Emmet O'Connell was particularly tedious, and for the last three days she had drawn the late shift. She reached into the glove compartment and rummaged for something to eat, but all she could find was the heel end of a packet of extra strong mints. She dusted the fluff off the top one and popped it into her mouth. *What am I doing here?* she asked herself, *Poppy won't be any the wiser if I just go home.* He wasn't the Boston strangler, whatever Poppy might think. And Drummond, however improbable, was firmly in the frame for Carenza's murder.

The mobile phone chirped. It was Phoebe.

"How are you getting on?" she asked.

"Same old routine," Grace said. "He got in from evening surgery an hour ago. But check up on me in a couple of hours in case I've atrophied. Hang on, he's coming out. I'll get back to you." She hung up the phone and started the engine, grateful for a bit of action.

Much later, back at Baggot Street she sat with Phoebe in her kitchen drinking hot whiskeys.

"O'Connell drove round to pick up Cassie Drummond and they went to the Cafe en Seine on Dawson Street. They definitely looked as if

174

they were on a date. They were really relaxed together."

"History repeats itself," Phoebe remarked. "He's not wasting any time moving in on the widow, is he?"

Grace towelled her hair, she was only just beginning to get warm after the drenching she had got waiting outside the restaurant where Emmet O'Connell had brought Cassie Drummond. "No, he isn't," she said. "And her husband's not even buried yet. Neither of them seemed particularly heartbroken either. I wonder if he's been seeing Cassie Drummond all along."

"It's possible. It really would open up a whole new can of worms if they were. But she doesn't strike me as the type to cheat on her husband. What do you think?"

"I don't know," Grace said. "What's the type? I didn't think Kiera was the type to cheat on her best friend, and look where it got me!"

The sound of footsteps on the stairs made Phoebe jump up from her seat and rush to the door. Mungo came in moments later followed by Ronan. She hugged her son.

"Hello Ronan," Grace said, genuinely pleased to see the youth. "Did you have a good journey?"

The boy beamed at her. He was still as slight as ever and, if anything, looked even younger than his twelve years. His complexion, usually pallid and on the adolescent spotty side, was rosy and flushed from the ride on the pillion of Mungo's Harley-Davidson. He squinted at her through his round wire-framed spectacles.

"Hello, Grace. Isn't this exciting? Do we have to break into somewhere again?" he asked. He was referring to an incident that had occurred earlier in the year whilst Grace had still been in a member of the gardai. She and Phoebe had found it necessary to do a spot of breaking and entering into a snooker hall to find evidence against a couple of gangsters who were trying to kill Phoebe and frame Grace.

"Not into a building this time, Ronan. Just into someone's computer," she said. "We knew you were our only man as far as hacking was concerned."

"Well I'm hittin' the hay," said Mungo. He looked exhausted after the long ride to collect the boy. "I'm on the early shift in the mornin', and I've got to contend with six thousand screamin' ten-year-olds at The Point gig tomorrow night. How long d'you guys think this friggin' surveillance is goin' on for?"

"Either as long as Poppy will pay," said Grace, "or until O'Connell incriminates himself. Anyway, don't knock it, Mungo. It's paying the rent at the moment." She felt a little hypocritical considering how close she had come to playing truant herself earlier in the evening.

Phoebe, who had been fussing round the cooker, plonked a cup of Ovaltine on the table in front of Ronan.

"I really should start hacking in now," he said, "it could take a very long time."

"How long is *long*?" Grace asked.

Ronan shrugged his bony little shoulders. "Hard to say. How long is a piece of string? It could take a couple of days at worst. It depends how soon we get lucky."

"A bit like us and the surveillance, hey kid?" Mungo said from the doorway, and they heard him chuckling as he made his way downstairs.

"Oh wow! Can I go on surveillance with Mungo?" Ronan asked excitedly. "Please can I? Can I?"

"We'll see," his mother said, suddenly feeling very middleaged. She caught Grace smirking and glared at her.

Xin's brother, David, who was, much to Grace's surprise, a computer engineer with the Department of Defence, had come up with the network that the Clerical & Widows Insurance Company subscribed to. Subsequently Ronan linked up by means of his Modem telephone link to the network and took out a small three-and-a-half inch computer disk from the inside pocket of his blazer.

"Is that it?" Phoebe asked. "Will that find the password?"

"Eventually," Ronan said. And, crossing his fingers, loaded it into the disk drive. The screen lit up and Ronan dialled up the network and then typed in a command on the keyboard. His computer beeped a couple of times and columns of data started to scroll slowly up the screen.

"Do we have to wait up until this thing does the business?" Grace asked, fearful that Ronan would say that they did.

"No. I'll set up an alarm to wake me. I'll call you as soon as we get in."

"Fine," said Grace, "I'm for bed then."

After Grace had gone, Phoebe watched her son tinkering on the computer keyboard. Then she asked tentativly, "Do you do this hacking thing much?

"Not any more," he said, "I grew out of it."

Phoebe nodded. "I see. Where did you get the disk from then?"

"My friend Osbourne and I wrote it last year. It was our first year, sort of unofficial, project. We did it just to see if we could, really."

Phoebe said, "Oh," again. She was becoming accustomed to her son amazing her with his cleverness.

"I think I'd like to go to bed now." He got up from his desk.

"Of course, darling." Phoebe rose from where she was sitting on his bed.

She kissed him goodnight and, as she got to the door he called after her, "you won't forget about Mungo and me going on surveillance together, will you?"

"We'll see."

She quietly closed the door after her.

Unlike every one else in the house, she didn't feel tired so she wandered back into the kitchen and made herself another hot whiskey. She sat at the table inhaling the comforting fumes. Her mind wandered back to the time when Ronan was a baby.

Things had been very different then. She ran a successful up-market escort agency in Manhattan called Executive Recreational Services. She lived in a penthouse above the shop on Central Park West, and money had been no object. She hated being short of money now and her spending seemed to go into overdrive whenever that situation arose. Her credit card had turned into a flexible fiend and was teetering on the brink. At times she wondered about the wisdom of a straight business venture as opposed to her years of hustling. Those years had been far more profitable, and only for a vicious Big Apple cop whose palm she hadn't greased sufficiently, she'd still be on the pig's back.

These days she hurtled from one financial crisis to the next.

She had been born in Galway of middle-class parents with whom she didn't get on and, at the age of eighteen after a secretarial course, she had emigrated to America. Dissatisfied with the meagre lifestyle clerical jobs afforded, she took an evening job with an escort agency. After a few weeks she made the discovery that the other girls were making far more money than she by offering extra services. Gritting her teeth she finally plucked up the courage to do the same. After the first time it wasn't quite so bad. She was always careful about the men she chose to proposition. Phoebe was beautiful, and also very resourceful. She made sure to keep up-to-date files, both written and photographic, on all of her clients, including their preferences and peccadilloes so that if any should turn nasty, she had the means to bring them to heel. After working for two years, one of her regulars offered to give her the backing to open her own agency. Phoebe vowed that hers would be the most prestigious, high-class, discreet agency in the city. And her files, instead of being an insurance measure, were a ready-made client list. All new clients had to be vouched for by those existing. She gained the reputation of employing only the most beautiful of girls who had to be both cultured and charming. By this time she was working in an administrative capacity, having decided that that was where her true talents lay.

Ronan's father had been charming and shiftless. She bumped into him (literally) in the mid-seventies in a bar in Greenwich Village. He and Mungo had just returned from Vietnam and she was immediately attracted to him. They both moved into her apartment the following week. Those were the days of her flirtation with drugs, both organic and mind-bending, and there was every danger of the casual caller being whisked off on an unexpected psychedelic trip by merely walking into the drug-laden atmosphere. Travis was as slight and sinewy as Mungo was large and muscular. He was not particularly good-looking in the conventional sense, but very sexy in a hang-dog sort of way. Basically Travis was a card-carrying sadistic bastard, but he was like no one Phoebe had ever met before and she was blind to his failings. After a couple of months, the two men went on the road. As Phoebe said years later when explaining her relationship with Travis to Grace, "They thought they were Jack Kerouac or Dennis fucking Hopper in some road movie, and just took off on my new Harley."

They turned up out of the blue five years later, minus the Hog, and that night Phoebe became pregnant with Ronan. Travis was the love of her life, flawed though he was. As soon as he heard she was pregnant, he disappeared, and she never saw or heard of him again. Mungo, who had a serious drug problem by that time, for some reason decided to stay. The war had messed up his head, and she often heard him crying out in the night with unspeakable nightmares. Four months before Ronan was born, she got up in the night to ease her terminal heartburn and found him unconscious and close to death. She rushed him to hospital where they pumped him out and then she paid for his drug rehab in Betty Ford. He came home two months later, leaner and rather fragile. Phoebe nursed him back to health.

In the early hours of a February morning, in the middle of a snowstorm, Phoebe went into labour. She fell into a blind panic.

"Chill out, Phoebe. I'll get a cab. No problem," Mungo said calmly. He got her coat. "Where's your purse?"

"In the bedroom," she wailed. "But look outside, Mungo. It's a fucking blizzard out there."

He walked past her and returned with her bag. "Stop moanin'", he barked, and took her by the arm. The doorman panicked when he saw them emerge from the elevator.

"Ain't no cabs runnin', sir," he said helplessly. "Not in this. Did you call an ambulance?"

"No, George. No time," Mungo said patiently. "Look after Miss Lamplighter. I'll be back in a minute." Mungo, assisted by the agitated doorman, helped Phoebe over to a low sofa by the wall. She awkwardly eased herself down.

"Don't leave me!" she wailed as he headed for the door.

He stopped and bent down in front of her. "I have to find a cab, Honey." He gently stroked the side of her face. He'd never seen Phoebe this afraid before. "Hang on in there. George here'll look after you. I'll be as quick as I can." George stood and looked helpless.

"Sure I will," he said without conviction.

Mungo hurried out into the night. The freezing air took his breath away as he opened the glass entrance door. He bent into the howling gale and the blizzard, and disappeared from Phoebe's view. Another contraction doubled her in pain. George stood by, still looking helpless.

Twenty yards along the street, Mungo turned right into Central Park West. Through the swirling snow he saw a set of red rear lamps, about twenty yards ahead, making slow progress away from him towards Columbus Circle. He broke into a run. The ground was slippery under his feet and he slithered a few times, nearly losing his balance.

He caught up with the lights. They belonged

to a Yellow Cab. The driver stalled when he caught sight of Mungo's huge bulk overtaking him. Mungo pulled open the door.

"You fer hire?" he asked sliding into the front passenger seat.

The cab driver, a small, red-haired Irish American, thrust a fist full of green bills at him.

"Here" Take it. Have it all. Just don't hurt me." He cowered against the driver's door.

"I just want to rent your cab, Moron. I ain't fuckin' muggin' you." The driver stared at him blankly.

Mungo jumped out of the cab and ran round to the driver's side. He wrenched the door open and dragged the whimpering driver out, frog-marching him round the cab and stuffing him into the front passenger seat. Then he leapt back in to the cab and gunned the engine.

"I gotta pregnant woman in labour back there." he said.

The cab driver relaxed. "Why didn't you fuckin' say so," he said. "Let's get movin'."

Mungo glided to a halt outside the apartment building and leapt out, closely followed by the driver. Phoebe was puffing and panting, trying to control the pain.

"You got a cab. I don't friggin' believe it!" George said.

Mungo and the cab driver helped Phoebe

across the slippery pavement to the back of the cab.

"You drive," Mungo said, getting into the back with Phoebe. The cab driver headed towards Columbus Avenue.

"Roosevelt Memorial's about the nearest hospital," he said. "I'll head for Columbus and 59th."

"Whatever," Mungo said. The cab crawled along slowly past the Dakota building.

"Can't you go any faster?" Phoebe sounded as desperate as she felt. "Oh God!"

"I'm doin' my best, lady."

Progress was slow. After ten minutes they were only four blocks further on.

"How far is it now?" Mungo asked.

"We're only on 67th," the driver replied. "The hospital's still seven blocks away." He turned round in the seat. "How's she doin'?"

Phoebe let out a scream.

"Not well," Mungo said. "You'd better pull in. Things are happenin' fast here."

The cab driver slewed into the curb and cut the engine.

"What's he doing?" Phoebe moaned. "You've got to get me to hospital. Now!"

"No time, Honey. Just relax," Mungo said, sounding slightly tense. "Can't you send out a Mayday or somethin' over the radio?"

"Radio's dead," The cab driver said. "It's the snow."

Phoebe groaned. "Oh God. I want to push. What should I do?" She grabbed Mungo's arm.

"I think I see a cop car," the driver said. He jumped out of the cab and stood in the middle of the road waving his arms.

Mungo delivered Phoebe's baby and the cops arrived just as Ronan gave his first mighty yell.

* * *

Grace had been curious about their relationship and had on one occasion asked her if Mungo was gay.

"No, Grace. Mungo isn't gay," Phoebe replied, rather huffily. "If you must know, his balls were half shot-off in an ambush in Vietnam."

"Good grief!" Grace said. "Does that mean he can't . . . you know?"

"What do you think?" Phoebe snapped.

"OK, OK. I was only asking," Grace said. "So what is your relationship?"

Phoebe shrugged and gave a heavy sigh. "I suppose we love each other in our own way. But then it'd be impossible for us not to. With what we've been through together and all."

"And what about Ronan? Doesn't he ever ask about his father?"

"He did once, ages ago, when he was about seven or eight," Phoebe said.

"So what did you tell him?" Grace asked.

Phoebe said, "I told him the truth."

"Poor Ronan."

"He's better off without Travis around," Phoebe said. "Anyway, Mungo's a better father than Travis could ever be. And Ronan loves him to death."

After the incident with the rotten cop Phoebe was deported. Her funds were confiscated and she was left penniless. She returned to Dublin and started to pick up the pieces. It took time but, with the experience she had gained in America, after three years she was earning well and entertained a very upmarket, highly recommended clientele.

Ronan was sent off to boarding school and had no inkling of how his mother earned her living. The recession followed in the late-eighties and things were once again not so lucrative. Her downfall came about when she fell foul of two Dublin criminals who had a strong desire to emulate the Kray twins. They made a serious attempt to barbecue her by torching her house while she was still inside. Around this time she was also coming to realise that she was getting very close to her sell-by date. Reluctantly she and Grace found themselves in business together.

The sound of running water woke her with a start. Ronan was at the sink getting a glass of water.

"What's the time?" she asked, stretching her stiff neck and rubbing her eyes.

"It's just after four," said the boy. "You should go to bed."

Phoebe smiled at him, she loved him madly, more than life itself. It always amused her when she found herself in the position of the child, and he in that of the adult.

"Any luck yet?" she asked.

"Not yet," he said. "Now go and get some sleep or you'll never get up in the morning."

Chapter Fifteen

"Well there you are then. That proves it!" Poppy said. "I told you he was carrying on with someone all along."

Grace had just reported Emmet O'Connell and Cassie Drummond's assignation of the previous night. Compton had shown her into a rickety glass conservatory at the rear of the house. It looked out on an overgrown lawn where two goats were grazing knee deep in grass. Even on the dreary December day, the south-facing room was awash with light. Grace shivered with cold because the elderly ramshackle glass structure did little to keep in the heat radiating from a pot-bellied iron stove in the corner. Poppy had solved the problem, clad as she was in layers of woollens and scarfs, and a stout pair of Doc Martens peeked out from under her skirt. She wore fingerless gloves and was working on a large abstract canvas.

"Proves what?" Grace asked as Poppy turned

back to look at the work in progress. "Who's to say he isn't moving in on the widow like he did with Carenza after Anabell was killed?"

That hadn't occurred to Poppy. "I suppose so," she conceded. "There would be a certain symmetry to events if he were, wouldn't you think?"

"You could say that," Grace replied. "Cassie didn't seem particularly upset about her husband, mind you. What do you want us to do now? D'you want us to carry on with the surveillance?"

"For the time being. Emmet isn't as clever as he thinks he is. Besides, it might just save that poor girl's life."

"It could take a long time before he attempts anything with Cassie, you know," Grace ventured.

"I don't care about the cost," Poppy said imperiously. "Money means nothing to me. It's not important." She paused for a moment, then added, "I'd prefer it if you didn't mention my plans to Free. She doesn't approve of the way I spend my money. Not that it's any of her business."

"What's none of my business?" Free asked. She had just walked into Poppy's studio and had missed the start of the conversation.

"I was telling Grace that you're peeved with me for picketing the medical centre."

Free looked annoyed. "I think it's very much my business if you're carted off to Mountjoy. You shouldn't let Emmet O'Connell become an obsession, Mother. It'll only make you more bitter."

"What do you mean *more* bitter," Poppy snapped at her only daughter. "I am not in the least bit bitter. I am merely on a quest for justice. Anyway, why are you defending Emmet? You know as well as I do that he instigated the whole thing."

"I'm not defending him. I think you're wasting your time and money, Mother, that's all. And remember, he wouldn't budge when I tried to talk him out of pressing charges against you for attacking him the other day. You'll have to be more careful. Anyway, the gardai have closed the case. They've accepted Brian Drummond's confession. Why can't you?"

Grace heard a phone ringing somewhere in the house and a couple of moments later Compton shuffled in and informed her that the call was for her. She left Poppy and Free squabbling and followed him out to the hall.

"Ronan got inta the Widdas an' Clerics data base. An' O'Connell picked up a hundred grand on Carenza . . ." Xin babbled then, before Grace could get a word in she went on, ". . . We were just goin' t'do a print ou' when I saw he had a policy on Doctor Drummond."

"How much for?" Grace enquired.

"Two-hundred-an-fifty-thousand fuckin' smackers. Can yeh beat tha'. An' he's pu' in a claim already, with yer man not even cold."

Grace was shocked. She wondered for just an instant if O'Connell *had* murdered Drummond, then she remembered the cadaveric spasm, and the shotgun clenched in Drummond's hands. "It's been a profitable few weeks for the good doctor, whichever way you look at it then, hasn't it?"she said, almost to herself.

"Yeh . . . An' that's not all. Ronan suggested we see if Drummond was insured with the Widdas as well, seein' as we were inta their data base anyway."

"And?" Grace said.

"An' he was. Bu' there was a note on the file sayin' tha' it was null an' void, cos he topped himself."

"So that leaves Cassie Drummond in big trouble. I wonder if he had a mortgage on the house."

"Dunno," Xin answered. "There's no mortgage protection policy on the data base. That means she'll have to cough up for the Lloyd's debt now, won't she, poor cow? An' she migh' even lose her house."

A thought suddenly struck Grace. "She still owns half the medical centre. Drummond's share. I wonder if that's what O'Connell's after."

"How much would tha' be worth?" Xin said, thinking aloud.

"Haven't a clue," said Grace. "But he's already picked up three-hundred-and-fifty grand. Even after he pays off the overdraft, he'll have a decent amount of change left. He could offer Cassie peanuts for her share at the moment and I'd say she'd sell. I wonder if she knows about his insurance windfall from her late husband? I may just pay her a visit on the way back to the office. Where's Phoebe?"

"She's ou' trying to drum up some business, I think," said Xin. "She got a call from some Polish fella ou' in Blackrock."

"What kind of business?"

"Dunno exactly. She said he was an ol' friend. I think it was somethin' to do with the fella's business."

I sincerely hope so, Grace thought, anxious in case the sudden downturn in their cash flow had tempted her partner back into hustling.

Oh, before yeh go," Xin said, "yer brudder came inta the office. Yeh didn't tell me he was such a babe."

Grace smiled to herself "My baby brother? . . . Yes I suppose he is. Where is he now?"

"He went over t'Vincent's. Said he'd catch yeh later."

Grace went back into Poppy's studio and told her about O'Connell's recent financial good fortune.

"How do you know this?" Free asked astonished.

"They chopped into the insurance company's computer," Poppy said smugly.

Free looked even more dumbfounded. "Chopped?" she said.

"Your mother means hacked," Grace said. "We hacked into Widows and Clerics data base."

"You can't possibly think it's just serendipity now, child. Emmet made this happen. He engineered it. He pressured Brian Drummond into killing Carenza, then drove him to suicide."

"How?" Free demanded. "How would he drive Drummond to suicide?"

"Despair child, despair. He probably suggested that Drummond try to get the money for Lloyd's from Carenza in the knowledge that her certain refusal and then the resulting murder would drive him over the edge, leaving the way clear for him to get his hands on the whole of the practice, and the lovely Cassie to boot. I suspect that even his exclusion from the will was just a minor set-back. Ask Grace. She and Sergeant Ryan found Brian Drummond with his brains blown out. What else but despair would drive a man to do that to himself?"

"Luke Ryan? How come you were with him when you found the body?" Free asked.

"We were having dinner and just decided to

go over to ask Drummond about something," Grace said. "Why do you ask?"

Free flushed. "Oh no reason," she said, stammering slightly. "I didn't know you knew him that well."

A gust of wind slammed a branch against the glass of the conservatory, making Grace jump.

"It's getting wild outside," Poppy said. "I think I'll put the goats in."

Grace took the opportunity to leave. "I'll be in touch," she told Poppy. "I'll pop in to see Cassie Drummond on my way and drop a few hints about Emmet. I'll bet she doesn't know he picked up the two-hundred-and-fifty grand either. That little morsel should stir things up a bit."

Poppy eyes glinted malevolently.

"Do that, dear. Go and make some mischief."

* * *

Mungo's car was parked, unobtrusively, near to Cassie Drummond's house. Grace parked further down the road and walked back to join him. "Is O'Connell in there?" she asked.

"Yep," he answered. "Went in about half an hour ago. Did Xin call you?"

"About the insurance pay-out?" Mungo nodded. "Yes she did. I'm going to stir things up a bit when O'Connell leaves. See if she knows how much he's in profit up to now."

They sat in silence watching Cassie Drummond's front gate. The weather had worsened and rain was now lashing down, battering off the roof of the car. Mungo switched on the windscreen wipers and de-mister. "This is a waste of time," he said after a while. "My butt's gone dead sittin' here for no good reason. What does the old broad think he's goin' to do?"

"I don't know. But I agree with Poppy that he's involved, and I'd hate to see him getting away with it." The rain eased and Emmet O'Connell's silver BMW swept out of the gate. Grace hopped out of the car and Mungo set off in cool pursuit.

Cassie Drummond looked surprised when she opened the door to find Grace on the doorstep.

"Hello, Grace," she said. "What do you want?"

"I was just passing so I thought I'd see how you are," Grace said. "May I come in?"

Cassie stood back. "Eh . . . I suppose so." She led Grace through to the kitchen. Two empty coffee cups stood on the kitchen table along with a half-empty bottle of brandy.

"We're burying him tomorrow," she said. "I hate funerals."

"How are you coping?" Grace asked. "With the debts I mean. Was Brian insured?"

Cassie poured herself a glass of brandy and picked up a typed letter from the dresser.

"Would you like one?" she asked, lifting the bottle. Grace shook her head. "How am I coping with his debts? Well the stupid bastard went and blew his brains out so they won't pay out on his life policy, will they? Basically I'm buggered." She threw the letter down on the table in front of Grace who recognised the logo of Widows and Clerics on the letterhead.

"What are you going to do?"

Cassie sat down at the table opposite her and took a sip of her drink. "Well, Emmet's been very good to me. I don't know what I'd have done without him."

I'm sure, Grace thought.

"He's going to buy out my share of the medical centre, thank God, otherwise I'd lose the house."

"Do you know how much your share's worth? Have you had an independent valuation by an accountant?" Grace asked.

Cassie frowned. "Why would I do that? Emmet wouldn't cheat me."

"Don't be so sure."

Cassie's face turned to thunder but her voice was even and unemotional. "Emmet's always treated me with respect. He'd never cheat me. You're as bad as his bloody sister-in-law, but there's some excuse for her, she's barking mad."

"Look at the facts, Cassie. First Anabell, then Carenza. And did you know Emmet had your husband insured for two-hundred-and-fifty

197

thousand pounds? I bet Emmet bloody O'Connell didn't tell you that."

Cassie's face said that she hadn't known that, but she recovered quickly.

"What has that to do with anything? Brian killed himself, or are you trying to say that was Emmet's fault too?"

Grace stood up from the table. "All I'm saying, Cassie, is, if Emmet O'Connell put his arm round my shoulder I'd check to make sure he wasn't sticking a knife between my shoulder blades."

"How dare you! . . . Get out of my house," Cassie screamed. Grace, surprised at her sudden ferocity, ducked as Cassie picked up the brandy bottle again, afraid that she was about to throw it. "Get out of my house and keep your filthy accusations to yourself."

Grace stood her ground. "What are you getting upset about, Cassie? Why are you so sensitive about Emmet? I was only saying it wouldn't do any harm to check out the value of your only asset. That's all."

"No you weren't. You think Emmet killed Carenza and Anabell. Well he didn't." Tears of anger were running down her cheeks. "He wouldn't cheat me. He loves me."

Grace was stunned by Cassie's admission. "Are you lovers?" she asked.

Cassie sat back down at the table and put her head in her hands. "Mind your own business."

"I take it that's a yes?"

Cassie looked up at her. "Just because we're in love it doesn't mean that Emmet killed Carenza, for God's sake. He was going to ask her for a judicial separation."

"What about Brian? Did he know about you, or was he keeping it in the family and bonking Carenza?"

Cassie sniffed. Her bottom lip was quivering. "I didn't know he was having an affair with Carenza until Emmet told me. I don't think he knew about Emmet and me."

"Do you know what I think, Cassie?" Grace said. "I think your late husband and Carenza *weren't* having an affair at all. I think Emmet just threw that into the pot to complicate matters. And if your husband *did* kill Carenza, I think it was because your precious Emmet put pressure on him to do it. He couldn't afford to leave Carenza. He needed her money to save the practice."

"That's bullshit, and you know it!," Cassie screamed. "She didn't leave him her money, did she?"

"He didn't know that though, did he? He thought he was in for the lot."

Cassie sat looking down at the table top. Eventually in a weary voice she said, "Just get out of here and mind your own business."

Grace walked to the door. "Think about it, Cassie. At least get an accountant's assessment of the value of the practice." The widow didn't reply. Grace left her sitting at the kitchen table.

Chapter Sixteen

Grace stood waiting for the lift to take her up to her mother's room in the private wing of St Vincent's hospital. She fervently hoped that Kathleen Dillon wasn't around. The bell pinged as the lift doors opened. Michael stood in front of her.

"Fancy seeing you here," he said, sweeping her off her feet in a huge hug. He hadn't changed in the two years since they had met, except that he had a healthy tan and his hair, now sun-streaked, touched his shoulders.

She was thrilled to see him. "When did you get in?" she asked.

"I was on standby so I couldn't get out until yesterday," he said. "Then they had to dump us at Shannon because of the storm, and they bussed us up in the early hours of this morning."

"Poor you. You must be knackered. Have you seen Daddy yet?"

The grin left Michael's face. "He looks grim. I haven't seen his consultant yet, what's the score?"

"He may be a quadriplegic."

"Christ! Is that for sure? How will Ma cope?"

Grace took his arm and they wandered over to a waiting-area and sat down. "Not quite for sure," she said.

"Professor Ambrose said he might improve, but they'll have more idea when the swelling round his spine goes down."

"How's he taking it? He was asleep when I looked in."

"Hard to say," Grace said. "But you know Daddy. He'll make Mummy's life hell if he's paralysed. I don't know how she'll cope."

"She'll just have to get a nurse to come in, I suppose," he said. "Anyway it might not come to that."

"Did you see her?" she asked.

"Yes. She seems fine, bruised and battered, but fine. I had the usual *I'm only a silly old woman* routine, and *just seeing you makes the pain of childbirth worthwhile.*"

Grace laughed. "I had that too."

"Kathleen Dillon was holding forth when I called in. She said something about being a grandma. Is there something you're not telling me? Do I have a nephew or niece I don't know about?"

"No, you have not," she said. "My esteemed husband dumped me for Kiera Lyons nearly a year ago. She had the baby, not me."

Michael looked more than surprised. "Jesus! Did you know they were carrying on?"

"Eventually," she answered. "But that's not the half of it. She chose to go into labour and give birth in my office."

He burst out laughing. "You're not serious?"

"Believe me . . . I'm deadly serious," she said.

"Faith told me about your new business venture. How are you enjoying private enterprise?"

"It has its ups and downs. But it's OK so far. But how are you doing? Are you nearly rich and nearly famous yet?"

Michael grinned at her. "I should be so lucky," he said. "By the way, can I stay at your place? I love Hope dearly, but I don't think I can cope with Charles's disapproval and his pontificating about me not fulfilling my potential and all that crap."

"No problem," Grace said. "In fact, if the mother-in-law from hell's upstairs I'd sooner go over to Baggot Street now and get you settled in, if that suits you?"

"It suits me fine." He picked up his travel bag.

"Let's go."

Xin went all coy when Grace introduced her

to Michael. "We met already," she said and even the white pancake make-up couldn't mask the fact that she was blushing madly. "Are yeh stayin' here with Grace?"

"Yes he is. Is Phoebe in?" Grace tried not to smile. She had never seen the super-cool Ninja embarrassed before.

"No she's still off talkin' to yer man in Blackrock. Shouldn't you be relievin' Mungo? He called in on the mobile a while ago an' he was not a happy camper."

"Shit!" Grace looked at her watch. "I forgot the time. Can you help my kid brother settle in?"

Xin's face lit up. "No problem," she said, grinning up at Michael. "It'd be my pleasure."

* * *

Luke was on a rest day, but he decided to go along to Brian Drummond's funeral anyway. His presence increased the attendance by one third; only the widow and the deceased's mother-in-law had bothered to turn up apart from the priest. He was surprised that O'Connell wasn't there until he remembered that it was now generally accepted that Drummond had murdered Carenza O'Connell.

The service was indecently short. Just the minimum prayers and ritual. Just enough to assure that the dear departed was now winging his way to the hereafter. Cassie Drummond remained dry-eyed throughout but, since she must have been cheating on her husband for however long, that didn't surprise him at all.

He called in to Harcourt Terrace on the way past and was more than a little surprised to find that Free Dalglish-Stuart had left a message for him. It read *Please meet me at Lorenzo's Bistro at one.*

He wasn't able to reach her by phone so he decided he had better go. It was not often he was invited out by a beautiful rich and intriguing woman, and he felt it rude to leave her just sitting there, not knowing if he was going to show up or not. On the way he dropped his car into the garage for a long overdue service.

She was already seated when he arrived and waved to attract his attention. "I'm glad you could come," she said. "I was anxious to repay you for rescuing Mother the other day."

"There's no need . . ." he started to say but she waved him into silence.

"Really. I insist," she said firmly. The waiter came over and they ordered.

"Your mother's a very unusual lady," he said after a while. Free burst out laughing.

"That's a very diplomatic way of putting it. I used to be embarrassed by her when I was a child."

"No kidding?" he said in mock disbelief. "I can't think why."

"You know what it's like," she said, appearing to miss the irony, "you want your parents to look like your friends' parents and she certainly didn't fit any stereotype. Not having a father was a bit inconvenient too. I used to spin stories about him being a racing driver who was tragically killed in a race. Can you believe that!"

"What was she like then?"

"Not a lot different from now really. Though she was away a lot in Nepal during her spiritual phase. And then she lived in a tee pee in West Wales for a couple of summers. Great Aunt Dorcas, that's Anabell's mother, wouldn't let her take us after the first time, but I don't think Mother minded. She was never very maternal, or practical."

"You seem to get on quite well now."

She shrugged again. "I suppose so, but only since I've been an adult. She can't relate very well to children. In a way I suppose we really just tolerate each other."

"For someone you just tolerate, you seem to get very prickly if anyone says a word against her." He grinned to take the harm out of the remark.

"Blood's thicker than water at the end of the day," she replied. "She's very moody, of course. I think it's a hangover from the large amount of dope she used to do in her hippy days. They say LSD stays in the system for years, you know."

Their pasta arrived and Luke poured the wine. "How does Jack get on with her?" he asked.

"Fine, as long as he doesn't have to spend any time with her. I think she's quite fond of the twins, particularly since she hardly ever sees them."

"Did you miss her, I mean, with her not being around when you were a kid?"

She raised her eyebrows and rocked her head from one side to the other, in a sort of, *did I? didn't I?* gesture. "Sometimes," she said finally. "Though a summer in the tee pee in Llanabythyr cured me."

"How do you mean?" he asked.

"Have you ever spent two months living in a tee pee during a wet Welsh summer?" she said. He shook his head. "Believe me, you'd hate it as much as I did. And the mud . . . You wouldn't believe the mud. It was horrendous. Jack didn't mind it that much. He ran wild. But I'm not that intrepid, I couldn't bear the primitive conditions, and the brown rice and lentils."

Luke looked across the table at her. She waved her exquisitely manicured hands as she spoke, punctuating the sentences. He certainly couldn't imagine her up to her knees in mud and five miles from the nearest shower.

"Has she still got a bee in her bonnet about Emmet O'Connell?" he asked.

"As much as ever." She sighed. "By the way, did you know Emmet and Cassie Drummond are lovers?"

"Yes. Grace de Rossa told me," he said. Free's heart sank slightly. He and Grace seemed to be very close. She wondered just *how* close.

Grace meanwhile was following Emmet O'Connell without much enthusiasm. He headed for the city and parked in the Drury Street car park. Grace pulled into a parking bay a few slots away and then followed him on foot. He briskly made his way towards Grafton Street and she had to break into a trot to keep up. The Christmas lights brightened the dull day and lunch-time shoppers hurried in and out of the shops, mentally ticking gifts off their Christmas lists.

O'Connell crossed Grafton Street and walked down South Anne Street towards Dawson Street. *I bet he going to Lorenzo's again,* she thought to herself.

"Oh my God, Emmet's coming in," Free suddenly said, shrinking down in her seat. Luke looked over his shoulder and saw Emmet O'Connell walk over to an empty table in the corner.

"What's the matter?" Luke said. "What are you afraid of?"

"Can we just leave?" she asked stiffly. "I don't want to talk to him. I don't want another scene. It's too embarrassing."

Luke shrugged his shoulders. "As you wish," he said and signed to the waiter for the bill.

"Oh God, he's seen me . . . he's coming over." She was going scarlet from the neck up.

"Hello, Free. How are you?" O'Connell said.

Free recovered well and switched on a dazzling smile.

"Nice to see you, Emmet." She even sounded as if she meant it."

"Hello. Sergeant Ryan, isn't it?"

Luke stood. "Doctor O'Connell," he said and gave a nod. O'Connell pulled out a chair.

"Do you mind?" he asked and, when neither of them objected, sat down at the table.

"I'm sorry to intrude." He looked directly at Free.

"But I wanted to apologise for my attitude the other day. I was angry and upset. But my rudeness was unforgivable."

Free opened her mouth to speak but he cut across her.

"Please, let me finish. I want you to know that I've decided not to press charges against your mother, and I also don't intend to contest Carenza's will."

"But why?" Free blurted out. "You were so angry about it. I thought . . ."

"No, no, not angry. Shocked. I was shocked to think that Carenza would cut me off. But, under the circumstances, I feel the dignified thing to do now is to accept Carenza's wishes. And I also think there's no point in wasting the court's time with your mother."

Free looked stunned and didn't notice the waiter place the bill on Luke's plate. Despite her invitation, he felt obliged to pick it up.

"Anyway. I just wanted you to know of my plans," he said and rose from the table just as Cassie Drummond hurried in out of the rain.

"I think your lunch date's just arrived," Luke said.

O'Connell smiled stiffly and said, "Oh yes. So she has." He hurried over to Cassie and kissed her on the cheek before they sat down at the corner table.

"Well! The cheek of them," Free hissed. "And she's still in her widow's weeds. She only buried Brian this morning."

"I know," Luke said. "And a pitiful affair it was too. Only Cassie and her mother were there. Emmet didn't even bother to show up."

"Can we go now, please?" Free said.

Grace was sheltering out of the rain in the newsagent's doorway when she saw Luke and

Free coming out of Lorenzo's and hurrying towards Grafton Street. She stared after them in disbelief. Her battered self-esteem and her raging insecurity kicked. *Sod this,* she thought, setting off after them. *O'Connell's not going anywhere for an hour.*

She followed them as far as Stephen's Green and saw Luke getting into the passenger side of Free's car. *Get a grip* she told herself. *You're meeting him tonight. Stop being paranoid. There has to be a perfectly innocent explanation.*

* * *

"Calm down, Free. You're doing sixty and we're on Leeson Street," Luke said, gripping the dashboard, knuckles white.

"Sorry." She slowed down. "I'm just wound up. It's Emmet. He gives me the creeps." She drove on over Leeson Street bridge.

"You can drop me anywhere here," he said.

"Won't you come for a drive?" Free asked suddenly.

"A drive?"

"Oh God . . . It's this whole business." She sounded close to tears. "Between mother ranting on about Emmet. And the will. And then meeting him in the restaurant like that. I suppose I just need some friendly company."

He felt sorry for her, and a little awkward.

"OK," he said. "Why don't we drive out to Enniskerry or somewhere for a walk. That'll clear your head. It never fails with me."

* * *

Grace was in a foul humour by the time she got back to Baggot Street. The rain and Luke Ryan had depressed her, so she had given up on O'Connell and gone to Neary's for a drink. One drink led to another and she was the worse for wear by the time she made her way unsteadily up to the Green for a taxi back to the office at around five.

"Where've yeh been?" Xin demanded. "I've been trying t' get yeh on the mobile fer ages."

"Oh . . . em . . . I left it in the car in Drury Street car park."

"Well, what are yeh like!" Xin said in disgust.

"Oh shut up!" Grace flopped down on the sofa and closed her eyes. "Where's Michael?"

"He an' Phoebe went off somewhere." Xin said. She sounded disgruntled.

"Where?"

Xin shrugged "Dunno."

"Well that's just wonderful. She's supposed to be doing the evening shift," Grace snapped. The drink and the events of the afternoon were making her decidedly grumpy.

Mungo put his head round the door. "We're off," he said.

"Off where?" Grace snarled.

He looked over at Xin. "Who rattled her cage?"

Xin sniffed. "She's been like that since she came in." She switched off the computer and reached for her coat. "I'm goin' home. She might be in better humour when she sleeps it off."

Mungo shrugged, then draped a mohair rug over Grace. She was already snoring softly as he closed the office door quietly after him.

* * *

Meanwhile Luke and Free were driving back towards the city. She was in better spirits. They had spent a pleasant afternoon walking in the fresh air, and had warmed up afterwards sitting by a roaring fire in The Wayside Inn.

"Thanks for humouring me," she said. "I hope you don't think I make a habit of hijacking men for the afternoon."

"No problem," he said. "Any time."

"Look, Why don't we make a night of it? Stop somewhere for dinner or something?" she said hopefully.

"Sorry, I can't," Luke said, "I'm afraid I've something on already."

"OK." She blushed in the darkness and tried not to sound disappointed. "It was just a thought."

Luke felt very awkward. It was obvious to him that she would like to see him again and he wondered how he could let her down gently.

"Em . . ." he started, "I really enjoyed your company this afternoon, Free, but it's only fair to tell you that I'm sort of involved with Grace de Rossa."

"How involved?"

Luke cleared his throat. "Quite involved. We've been seeing each other for a while."

Free chuckled and playfully thumped him on the shoulder. "Oh, don't be such a boring stick-in-the-mud! What harm would an innocent little dinner do? She needn't ever find out."

"Look, no offence, Free. But I'd rather not."

Free was glad of the darkness as she felt the heat rise to her face. A feeling of utter humiliation overcame her.

"Don't give it another thought," she said lightly. The car suddenly swerved to the right.

"Oh hell. I think I've got a puncture." She pulled into the grass verge and switched off the engine. Could things possibly get any worse?

"I'll take a look," Luke said.

He came back a moment later. "Yes, it's a flat. Give me the keys and I'll get the spare and the jack out."

Free handed him the keys and he walked round the back of the car. She followed with a torch. He opened the boot and she held the beam steady while he rooted for the jack.

"Where's the tyre iron?" he asked.

"It's in there somewhere," she said. He searched around until he found it and then lifted out the spare and bounced it down onto the road, rolling it to the verge. She held the flash-light as he changed the tyre.

"I can do this, you know," she said.

"I don't doubt it." Luke grinned. "But I'd seem a bit of a wimp if I left you to it. Anyway I wouldn't want you to chip your nail varnish."

When he had finished, he let down the jack and dumped it back in the boot and then dropped the flat into the tyre-well. It wouldn't sit in properly so he said, "Give me the flash-light, will you? There's something stopping the tyre from fitting in here properly."

Luke shone the torch into the recess. Something shiny caught his eye. He reached down and picked it up.

Chapter Seventeen

Grace woke up with a start. For a moment she didn't know where she was. Her mouth felt like the bottom of a budgie cage. The clock above the desk said seven-thirty. Someone had thrown a rug over her where she lay on the sofa, and had left the desk lamp on.

She stretched, rubbed her eyes and swung her legs to the floor. The whole house was silent. When she got her head together she went upstairs to shower and change for her date with Luke. She felt stupid and juvenile, remembering her irrational reaction when she saw him leave the restaurant with Free Dalglish-Stuart.

She fervently hoped that O'Connell hadn't gone berserk and bludgeoned Cassie Drummond to death on the one occasion in the last week when he hadn't been under surveillance.

She felt much better after a long hot shower

and took time applying her make-up and deciding what to wear. She ruefully reflected that she hadn't taken that much care with her appearance until Free Dalglish-Stuart had appeared on the scene.

By nine, she was getting edgy. By ten, she was annoyed. And by the time she heard Mungo and Ronan coming in after The Point gig at around eleven, she was livid.

Michael and Phoebe breezed in just after midnight, by which time she strongly resembled an anti-Christ.

"Well, I hope you had a good time," she snarled at them as they came through the door. "You were supposed to be doing the late shift."

"Get a grip, Grace . . . Poppy won't know the difference," Phoebe said. "What's your problem?"

"Are you OK, Gracie?" Michael asked. "You seem a bit tense." The concern in his voice brought her back down to planet earth.

"I'm sorry," she said. "I've just had a pig of a day. I shouldn't take it out on you. Especially when I abandoned the surveillance myself this afternoon."

Phoebe raised her perfectly arched eyebrows in surprise. Saint Grace deserting her post. That was a turn-up for the book.

"How did you get on with your Polish friend?" Grace asked. "Did he put any work our way?"

"No, it didn't work out," Phoebe said, not elaborating.

Grace persisted. "Why not? What did he want?"

"Let's just say he was a Pole I wouldn't touch again with a barge." Phoebe glared at her and quickly changed the subject. "I thought you had a date with Luke Ryan."

"I was stood up, wasn't I?" Grace admitted miserably. "And I saw him having lunch with Free Dalglish-Stuart this afternoon, so I suppose that's that. Where were you two anyway?"

"We went out for a bite to eat," Michael said. "By the way, Hope called and said the old man's got some feeling back in his arms and chest."

"Really?" Grace was slightly cheered. "That's promising, isn't it?"

"Yes. Quite promising. The feeling returns from the neck downwards, so it remains to be seen how much will come back but, as you said, It's looking hopeful."

"Is Ronan back yet?" Phoebe asked.

"Yes," said Grace. "About an hour ago." Then, after a pause, "Phoebe . . . What's the matter with me?"

"Where do you want me to start?"

Grace felt miserable. "Thanks a bunch. But what is it about me and men? Or is it just men in general? Why can't they have the decency to be up-front? Why do they always have to sneak off and see someone else on the quiet?"

"Always, is rather a sweeping statement. I'd say your main problem is that you jump to conclusions," Phoebe commented dryly. "You don't know he's *making free* with Free. I assume it's Free we're talking about. And anyway, how many times have you stood the poor sucker up in the last few weeks?"

"That's not the point. Anyway if he's not with her, where is he?" she moaned. "It can't be work. Today's his rest day."

"Just tell me where he lives and I'll go round and break his legs, Grace." Michael put a comforting arm round her shoulders. "The rat doesn't deserve you."

"Take no notice of her, Michael," Phoebe said. "She wasn't that interested in him until she thought he was after someone else."

"What do you know?" Grace snapped. "Who said I was that interested now? I'm just a tad pissed-off that he's messing me around, that's all."

"Me thinks that the lady doth protest too much," said Phoebe, unable to resist the temptation to wind her up.

"Me? I don't care if I never see the bastard again," Grace huffed.

The phone rang and Phoebe picked it up.

"No it's Phoebe. Really! . . . when?" they heard her say. "And where is he? . . . I don't know . . . OK. I'll tell her." She replaced the receiver.

"That was Dermot McEvoy," she said to Grace. "You know that man you never want to see again?"

"Yes. What about him?" Grace said, irritated.

"Well he didn't take you out tonight because he's in hospital. He was the victim of a hit-and-run."

Grace felt as if she had been thumped in the solar plexus. "What hospital? How is he?" she asked, shocked to the core.

"He's in Vincent's Accident and Emergency."

Grace sat down heavily. "Oh God. I feel awful. I should go over there."

"I'll drive you," Michael said. "Where's your car?"

"Shit! I left it in Drury Street car park."

Phoebe took her car keys from her bag and handed them to Michael. "Here. Take mine."

Dermot met them in the corridor and Grace introduced her brother.

"What exactly happened?" she asked him.

"It's hard to know," Dermot said. "He was found on the side of the road not far from Enniskerry at around eleven. He'd obviously been run over by a car, and he'd been there quite some time."

"Oh my God. Did he see who did it or anything?"

"He hasn't regained consciousness," Dermot said. "But his car's in for service, so how he got all the way out there is anyone's guess. Mine is that he was dumped on the road, then run over. And more than once by the look of his injuries."

"But who'd do that? Why?"

"Oh come on, Grace, he's a cop. There are plenty of people with a grudge who'd be capable." .

"How badly is he hurt?"

"Both legs and pelvis broken, plus the right arm, left wrist, collar bone, fractured skull, possible brain trauma, loss of blood . . . do you want me to go on?"

Grace winced. "When was the last time anyone saw him?" she asked.

"It was his rest day. He called into Harcourt Terrace after Drummond's funeral, picked up a message and that was it. No one saw him after that."

"I did," Grace said. "I saw him coming out of Lorenzo's in Dawson Street at around two with Free Dalglish-Stuart."

"I'll talk to her in the morning," Dermot said. "She might be able to tell us where he went after she left him."

"He was supposed to pick me up at half-eight," Grace said. "I was bad-mouthing him to Phoebe because I thought he'd stood me up. I feel terrible. I wonder when we can see him?"

"He's still in surgery."

"God! I hope he'll be all right."

The three of them sat down by the wall. For someone who hated hospitals with such a passion, she was spending an inordinate amount of time sitting round this particular one. She wasn't even sure why she was waiting. From the sound of things, Luke wouldn't be out of surgery for some time, let alone be able to say what had happened to him. "What was Luke working on?" she asked. "Who'd want to kill him?"

Dermot lit a cigarette, then he remembered that he was trying to quit and looked round for an ashtray. There was none, only a flower pot below the No Smoking sign so he used that instead. "I can't think of anyone off-hand who'd make such a serious attempt to kill him," he said. "Though I suppose Poppy Dalglish-Stuart would blame Emmet O'Connell for it, along with the Holocaust, the Bosnian war and break-down of the cease-fire."

"That's not funny, Dermot."

"No. I suppose not," he said getting up. "Let's go home and come back tomorrow."

Chapter Eighteen

Grace went along to Vincent's very early. She couldn't sleep anyway, and her visiting list was growing longer by the day. She called in to see her mother first. Thankfully, eight-thirty was far too early for Kathleen Dillon.

Alice de Rossa was propped up against a mountain of pillows watching breakfast television and nibbling on a croissant piled high with butter and strawberry jam. The bruising on her face was turning yellow and the swelling had subsided a good deal.

"You look a lot better today," Grace said. "How d'you feel?"

"Very sore, darling," Alice replied. "In fact I'm in considerable pain, but I'm afraid with all my allergies they can't really risk too many pain killers. Have you seen your father?"

"Not yet," Grace replied. "I'm going up after I leave you. Though it's promising that some feeling's coming back in his arms, isn't it?"

Alice gave a weak smile. "Yes dear, but Faith

says Eoin isn't coming. Don't you think that's just too bad?"

"I'm sure it's not his fault, Mummy. He can't just jump on a plane, you know. He is in the middle of a war zone."

Alice sniffed. "Where there's a will . . ." She pushed away her tray. "Just move that, will you, dear. It's the first bite to have passed my lips in days but I can't manage a morsel more." Grace wheeled the table down to the end of the bed. The pile of crumbs and scrapings of butter and jam left in the dishes told her it had been a pretty large bite.

The door swung open and Charity breezed in laden with flowers and fruit. She had always been able to manage their mother better than anyone. Grace knew that she would cajole Alice out of her self-pity.

"You look better today, Mummy," she said. "Hi, Grace. How are you?"

"Fine thanks, Charity," replied Grace, backing towards the door.

Charity plumped her mother's pillows. "Did you see Michael today, Mummy?"

"Not yet, dear. And did you know Eoin's not coming? It's too bad, isn't it. Still, I suppose you all have your own lives to lead. You're all too busy to visit your sick old mother."

"Hush, Mummy. You know that's not true. And I'm sure Eoin'll do his best."

"Well I'll just pop up and see Daddy," Grace said, seizing her opportunity. "I expect Michael will pop in later. I'll call in again before I go." She hurriedly closed the door behind her.

Paul de Rossa was still flat on his back. Michael was sitting by the bed. They appeared to be deep in conversation so she decided to call in later and headed up to intensive care.

Luke was lying in the same bed that her father had occupied only hours before. The stress of the previous few days had wound her up to the degree that when she saw him almost totally encased in plaster from head to foot, limbs suspended in traction, she had to fight to stop a fit of hysterical laughter. He looked like something from a Monty Python sketch. The hysteria subsided and she felt hot tears welling in her eyes. Dermot walked up the corridor and stood beside her. They both looked at Luke through the window of the off-limits ward. "Is he going to be all right?" she asked. Her voice was shaky.

"The quacks don't know yet. He's still in the coma. Between you and me, I think they're worried about that." That wasn't the news she wanted to hear. Dermot, sensing her distress, put his arm round her. She gave a couple of sobs, then pulled herself together and rummaged in her pocket for a tissue.

"How are your parents?" Dermot asked.

"Mother's on the mend, but it's too early to say with my father." She felt tears welling up in her eyes again. She coughed and blew her nose, trying to hide her embarrassment. "Did you see Free Dalglish-Stuart?" she asked in a shaky voice.

Dermot shook his head.

"No. Not yet. I'm on my way there now. I suppose you'd like to tag along?"

"Yes please."

Compton answered the door to them. In the harsh morning light he looked even more cadaverous.

"I'd like to speak to Free Dalglish-Stuart."

"Miss Free is not at home, sir," he replied.

"I see," said Dermot. "When will she be back?"

"I'm afraid I have no idea, sir. Miss Free didn't come home last night."

"Is that usual?" asked Grace.

"As you ask, madam. No, it isn't."

"Oh my God!" Grace hissed, dragging Dermot by the arm. "Do you think O'Connell could have done her in?"

Dermot laughed. "Now that's bordering on paranoia, Grace."

Grace was agitated. "No, Dermot. You see, I was supposed to be watching him. Poppy was determined. Anyway, I got pissed off when I saw

225

Luke coming out of Lorenzo's with Free, so I buggered off and got smashed in Neary's instead of watching O'Connell."

"Just because you weren't watching O'Connell, it doesn't mean to say he clobbered Free. I suppose you're going to tell me he tried to kill Luke too. For God's sake, Grace, you're beginning to sound like Poppy."

Compton coughed. "Excuse me, sir."

Dermot had forgotten that Compton was still there.

"Miss Free did say she would be out for dinner last night."

"There. You see!" Grace was devastated. "He did stand me up. He *did* spend the evening with *her.*"

"You're not listening, Grace. The man said she was eating out last night. Not that she's having an affair with your boyfriend. You don't know she was having dinner with Luke."

"What's the commotion?" Poppy, swathed in a threadbare crimson silk kimono, pushed past Compton.

"It looks as if your daughter's missing," Dermot said.

"Missing?"

"She didn't come home last night, madam," Compton muttered.

Poppy smiled smugly. "She's probably with

226

that nice Sergeant Ryan. She spent the day with him yesterday."

"Sergeant Ryan was the victim of a hit-and-run last night," Dermot said gravely. "He's in intensive care."

Poppy's hand flew up to her throat. "Oh my God! So where's Free?"

"Are you sure she was with him all of yesterday? Are you certain she was having dinner with him?" Dermot asked.

Poppy nodded. "Yes. She phoned me from some pub out in the wilds of Wicklow."

"That's where Luke was found." Grace gave Dermot a there, *you see,* look.

"You'd better come in," said Poppy.

"Can I use your phone?"

While Dermot was calling the office, Poppy and Grace went into her sitting-room. Poppy paced furiously. Grace felt sick. It was bad enough that Luke was seriously ill, without knowing that he'd two-timed her, and with Free of all people. What did *she* have that was so wonderful? Apart from beauty, brains, wonderful dress-sense and being filthy stinking rich. Grace sank down into Poppy's squashy sofa and felt sorry for herself. The larger of the two hairy dogs licked her hand. *God! even the dog's sorry for me,* she thought. *What a loser.*

"If it wasn't for the fact that you were

watching Emmet, I'd say he's at the bottom of this," Poppy said.

Grace cringed. "Well, eh, the thing is, Poppy, I don't know where O'Connell was after about two, yesterday afternoon."

"What d'you mean, gel. Of course you know. You were following him."

"Not exactly."

"What do you mean, *not exactly*?"

Grace swallowed hard. "I mean, I lost him. He gave me the slip."

Dermot bustled into the room. "I'll be off, Poppy. I'm heading out to join the house-to-house team in Enniskerry. I'll let you know as soon as we have any news."

"What about Emmet O'Connell? Why aren't you talking to him?" Poppy snapped. "You should be talking to my brother-in-law."

"All in good time, Poppy," said Dermot wearily.

"But the trail will be going cold. You're giving him time to cover his tracks! He might have killed my daughter. For God's sake, man!"

"Look, Poppy," Dermot said, trying hard to hold on to his temper, "there's nothing so far to implicate Emmet O'Connell."

"Hrmmph," snorted Poppy. "You said that about Carenza and Anabell."

"And, if you remember, Brian Drummond confessed to killing Carenza, Poppy. So please, don't waste my time with your stupid theories. Anyway, Free may not even be missing. Does she have any particular friend she could be with?"

"I'm telling you, she was with Sergeant Ryan. She phoned me and told me so. And, if you weren't such a stupid individual, you'd be out looking for her now. You'd have arrested that dreadful man."

Dermot glared at Poppy. Abruptly, he turned and stormed out of the room, banging the door behind him.

"Well!" Poppy exclaimed. "What a rude man."

"I think he's upset about Luke Ryan," Grace said.

"All the same, that's no excuse for such crass stupidity. Is the man blind?"

Compton came in bearing a tea tray. He placed it on the sideboard and left the room. Poppy continued to pace.

Grace got up and made for the door. "I think I'll go over and talk to O'Connell," she said.

"Always assuming you can find him," Poppy snarled at her retreating back.

Grace called in at the office en route to O'Connell's. She felt in need of some moral support.

Mungo was out, but Phoebe and Xin were in reception. She told them how Luke was and about her visit to Poppy's.

"So what makes her think O'Connell's responsible?" Phoebe said. "He's certainly no axe to grind with Luke Ryan."

"I don't think she's open to reasonable analysis," Grace said, glumly. "I feel such a prat. If only I'd stuck with O'Connell, at least we'd know if he was involved or not."

"How did she take it when you told her you weren't watching him?" Phoebe asked, half-smiling.

"I had to be a bit creative. I told her he'd given me the slip."

"Well there's no use cryin' over spilt milk," Xin observed wisely. "And, speakin' of which. Are yeh sure Luke was seein' yer wan?"

"It's beginning to look that way," Grace said. "But where is she? And if someone had it in for Luke, why not wait till he was alone? Why grab Free?"

"That's always assuming that Luke was the actual target. Maybe Poppy's not so far off the truth," Phoebe said.

"What d'you mean?"

"What if O'Connell *has* done for Free, and Luke just got in the way?"

"OK. So where is she then?" Xin asked. "Why didn't he zap her on the spot. An', from what Grace says, whoever attacked Luke seemed pretty determined to make sure he was dead."

"I suppose he'd have to," said Grace. "I

mean, Luke'd be able to identify him, wouldn't he?"

"Yes. But where's Free? Why wasn't she lying at the side of the road too?" Phoebe asked.

"Your guess is as good as mine." Grace was now harbouring strong feelings of guilt. "God! If only I'd stuck with O'Connell, maybe Luke wouldn't be lying in Vincent's now."

"Get a grip, Grace! "Phoebe snapped. Guilt-trips really irritated her. "Mungo's watching O'Connell now. O'Connell's over at the health centre doing morning surgery. Why don't we go to the restaurant and check out what time he left there yesterday. Then we'll go over and talk to him. You never know. The poor sod might even have an alibi."

"Oh. I do hope so," said Grace with real conviction.

Chapter Nineteen

Dermot found Jack Molloy in the front bar of The Wayside Inn, enjoying a pint of the black stuff. Molloy looked embarrassed at being caught in the act.

"I missed breakfast," he half-heartedly explained. Dermot gave him a wry look. "What's the story?"

"Ryan and Free Dalglish-Stuart were here round five yesterday. They sat over there by the fire." He indicated the huge, now ash-filled, open fireplace with his glass. "The barman said she used the phone and they left about twenty minutes later."

"Was anyone else in at the time?"

Molloy shook his head. "No. But he saw them arrive, and he said the woman was driving."

"What car?"

"He thinks it was a big Volvo, but he's not sure." Dermot scratched his chin. "They could have been followed. It'd have been dark outside. If Luke was being targeted, whoever was doing the hit could've been parked a couple of yards down the road, out of sight."

A young barman bustled in, clattering a crate of mixers on to the counter.

"This is Brian Bourke, Dermot. He was on yesterday evening."

Dermot nodded at the young man. "And you're sure you saw nothing unusual round the time Sergeant Ryan and his friend were in?"

Brian shrugged. "Like what?"

"Anything," Dermot said.

Brian thought about it. Eventually, he shook his head.

"No. Not really."

Dermot thanked him, and he and Jack Molloy went outside.

"You know, Dermot. If it was a hit, I'd have expected a two-men-on-a-motorbike job, wouldn't you?" Molloy speculated.

"Perhaps. Why? . . . D'you think maybe it was Free Dalglish-Stuart they were after?"

"It's a thought," Molloy said.

Dermot snorted. "So that brings us back to O'Connell."

"Maybe. He's next in line for the money."

"You subscribe to Poppy's theory?"

"Why not?" Molloy said. "She got the loot in the will. I can't think of a better motive. Don't be put off the idea just because Poppy Dalglish-Stuart suggested it."

"Point taken," said Dermot. He slammed the car door and wound down the window. "Finish up here and I'll head over to see O'Connell."

"What're you going to say to him?"

Dermot put the car into gear. "Haven't a clue," he said. Jack Molloy stood back to avoid being showered with chippings as Dermot accelerated away.

* * *

Lorenzo's was closed. Phoebe peered through the glass door, then tapped it with her car keys to attract the attention of a waiter, who was setting up tables for lunch. He sauntered over and opened the door. He was a tall, slightly chubby, young man. Good-looking, but slightly camp. He wore a badge stating that his name was Eugene.

Phoebe flashed her best smile and said, "Hi, Eugene. I'm Phoebe Lamplighter, and this is my colleague, Grace de Rossa. I wonder, were you working yesterday at lunch-time?"

The waiter nodded, furrowing his brow. "Yes. Why?"

"May we come in?" Grace asked, sidling past him into the dining area. "We need some information."

"What about?"

Grace explained. "We're making enquires

about a couple of customers you had yesterday at lunch-time."

"D'you work for the papers, or something?" he asked warily.

"No, no," Phoebe said, flashing her pearly white teeth again. "We're private detectives."

"Wow! Really?" he said, intrigued. "What d'you want to know?"

"Shall we sit down," Phoebe suggested, pulling out a chair.

"OK," he said. "I'll get us some coffee."

Grace and Phoebe sat down. "Well, isn't this all-girls-together," Grace remarked under her breath as Eugene rattled coffee cups behind the bar. Phoebe kicked her under the table.

Phoebe set the ball rolling. "Do you know Dr Emmet O'Connell?"

"Sure. He's a regular."

"And he had lunch here yesterday."

"Yes. How did you know that?" Eugene placed three cups of coffee on the table and sat down.

"It's our job," Grace said, dead-pan. "Do you know the woman he had lunch with?"

"Yes. Mrs Drummond. His partner's wife. I told you, they're regulars."

"Can you remember what time they left?" Phoebe asked.

Eugene nodded. "Sure. They had a steaming row and she stormed out before she'd even started her entree."

"Really? What was the row about?" asked Grace.

Eugene shrugged. "How the fuck would I know? She just started yelling and waving her arms about."

"And what did *he* do?" Grace looked over at Phoebe.

"Nothing. He just sat there, taking it all," Eugene said. "Though he looked livid."

"So have you *any* idea what started it?" asked Phoebe.

"Not really. Though she kept looking over at a couple who were sitting over in that corner." He pointed at a small table at the back of the room. "The doctor was talking to a woman and her fella when Mrs Drummond came in. Maybe it was that."

"What did the woman look like?" Grace asked.

"Tall, short black hair, well dressed in a beautiful green cashmere coat. It looked like a Louise Kennedy, though I could be wrong. Anyway, where was I? Oh yes, she was good-looking in a snotty sort of way. I've seen her in here before."

"Have you seen her with the man before?" Phoebe could hear the tension in Grace's voice. She squeezed her arm.

Eugene shook his head. Grace visibly relaxed.

"So Dr O'Connell was speaking to the couple in the corner when Mrs Drummond came in. Then she and Dr O'Connell started this ding-dong?" Phoebe asked.

"Well, not until after the couple in the corner left," Eugene said. "And I don't know for sure that's what they were arguing about. It was lunch-time. I was busy." He looked apologetic. "Is he carrying on with the one in the corner, or something?"

"Why d'you ask that?" Phoebe said.

Eugene grinned. "I've been at this a long time. You get used to spotting those who shouldn't be together, if you know what I mean? Nudge, nudge, wink wink. Nuff said."

"What about Mrs Drummond? D'you think the doctor's having it away with her?" Grace asked, conspiratorialy.

Eugene leaned forward towards Grace. "For months," he said, pursing his lips.

"How many months?" Phoebe asked.

Eugene said, "Six or seven, give or take."

"And what makes you think he could be having it off with the woman in the corner?" Grace was bemused. Free and O'Connell hated each other.

"Well I don't *know* if they were. I was putting two and two together when Mrs Drummond reacted the way she did, that's all."

"Right," Grace nodded. "And how long after Mrs Drummond did Dr O'Connell leave?"

"About five minutes. He called for the bill, paid and, I suppose, he went after her. I don't know."

Grace patted Eugene's arm. "You've been a great help, Eugene. Thanks."

"Don't mention it," he said, getting up from the table. "Is there anything else?"

"I'll let you know," Grace said.

When they were back outside on Dawson Street, Phoebe said, "At least you know it was Luke's first time in there with Free."

"There are other restaurants in the city, you know," Grace replied tartly.

"For God's sake, Grace. Chill out, will you? You're only looking for sticks to beat yourself with. At least give him the benefit of the doubt till he can give you his side of it."

Grace sighed. "You're right. But I feel so jealous. I know it's stupid, but I can't help it, and I hate it. I've never been jealous of any one before."

They walked back towards the car park.

"I know this is bordering on the surreal, but d'you think that it's just possible that perhaps it was Free and not Luke who was the real target of the attack last night?"

Grace stopped. "You're not thinking about O'Connell again, are you?"

"No."

"So who?"

238

"Look how jealous you are of Free," Phoebe began.

"I'm not!"

"You just admitted that you are, Grace."

"Ok. So what! D'you think I zapped the smug little bitch, or something?"

"No, no," Phoebe said. "But what if it was an ex-boyfriend of Free's? What if he followed her and, in a fit of jealousy, he kills Luke and kidnaps Free?"

"It's a thought, I suppose," Grace conceded.

"Let's put O'Connell on hold. He's not going anywhere," Phoebe suggested. "We'll go over and see what Poppy can tell us about Free's love life."

Meanwhile, Dermot pulled in to the kerb outside Emmet O'Connell's house. He climbed out of his car, crossed the road and walked back fifteen yards to where Mungo was parked. Mungo lowered his newspaper and wound down the window.

"How long have you been on his tail?" Dermot asked.

"Whose tail?"

Dermot gave him the two fingers.

Mungo grinned. "OK. Since six this morning." He scratched the back of his head and yawned.

"So where's he been?"

"Health centre, Cassie Drummond's for half an hour, then back here about twenty minutes ago."

"Does he know you're following him?"

Mungo grinned again. "Course not. I'm a professional."

"Sure," Dermot said, sarcastically. He turned and headed back towards O'Connell's house.

"Have a nice day," Mungo said, going back to his paper.

O'Connell wasn't best pleased to see Dermot.

"What do you want now, Inspector?" he snapped.

Dermot ignored his ill temper. "I need to ask you a few more questions, Doctor."

"What about this time? Does that blessed woman never give up?"

"I'm looking into a hit and run incident, Doctor. One of my officers was run down last night."

O'Connell nearly blew a fuse. "Oh, for pity sake! Do you feel it necessary to accuse me of every crime that's committed in the city, Inspector?"

Dermot put up the palms of his hands. "No, Doctor. I'm not accusing you, but I need to ask you a few questions to eliminate you from our enquiry, that's all."

"I suppose the hag's behind this," he commented, still seething.

Dermot ignored the comment. "Sergeant Luke Ryan was run down last night and left for dead. It seems that Free Dalglish-Stuart was with

240

him at the time, as far as we know, and now she's missing."

"Missing? What do you mean, missing?"

"I mean, Doctor, that no one's seen or heard from her since yesterday. And, taking into account the circumstances, it looks as if she could've come to some harm."

"Good God!" O'Connell seemed genuinely shocked. "When did this happen?"

"Early yesterday evening, out in Enniskerry." Dermot paused. "Where were you between, say, four and eleven last night?"

O'Connell shook his head. "This is ridiculous," he muttered. "Between four and eleven, you say?" Dermot nodded. "Let's see," O'Connell said. "At four I would have been at home. I went to see Mrs Drummond at about five. Then I went back home again."

"What time was that, Doctor?"

"I suppose it would have been about five-thirty."

"What then?"

O'Connell lost his rag. "I decided to drive aimlessly around Co Wicklow, where I bumped into your sergeant and Free, whom I proceeded to run over." He was spitting venom. "And then I came home again, but not before dismembering Free's body and stuffing it into bin-liners which I just happened to have in the boot of my car. What the hell do you think? I came home, for God's sake. End of story, you moron."

Dermot disliked being called a moron, particularly by the likes of O'Connell. "There's no need for that attitude, Doctor. I'm just following procedure," he said stiffly. "Believe it or not, you're not the only person we're interviewing."

O'Connell looked embarrassed. "I'm sorry," he said with ill-grace. "It's the strain of the past couple of weeks. Forgive me."

Dermot nodded. "When was the last time you saw Free Dalglish-Stuart?"

Without hesitation O'Connell said, "Lunchtime yesterday. I met her by chance in Lorenzo's on Dawson Street."

"And did you speak to her?"

O'Connell nodded. "Yes, as a matter of fact. I told her that I've decided not to contest my late wife's will. It was an amicable meeting. Good grief! Now you come to mention it, she *was* with your Sergeant Ryan."

"Did you speak to anyone after you arrived back here last night? Were you alone?"

"No I didn't speak to anyone. Yes I was alone," O'Connell said flatly. "What now, Inspector? Are you going to arrest me?" He held out his wrists contemptuously.

Dermot snapped his notebook closed. "No, doctor, I'm not going to arrest you. Yet." *Don't tempt me,* he thought. "I'll be in touch." He turned on his heel and marched down the drive. O'Connell stood at the door and watched him walk away.

Chapter Twenty

Poppy was reluctant to accept the possibility that Free's disappearance could be linked to anyone other than Emmet O'Connell. Eventually Grace managed to talk her round.

"Look, Poppy. We have to look at everything. What if it isn't O'Connell? What if something happened to Free simply because we ignored *any* possibility, even a remote one?"

"Did you talk to Emmet yet?" Poppy asked.

"Not yet. But he's not going anywhere. Mungo's got him under surveillance as we speak," Phoebe replied. Poppy stalked up and down the same piece of mat. Grace could have sworn that she'd worn a track since the morning.

After a while Poppy said, "I don't know what I can tell you."

Grace said, "Did Free ever break off a romance with anyone?"

Poppy shrugged. "I suppose so."

"But can you think of anyone specific?" Phoebe asked. "Someone who might bear a grudge?"

Poppy stared down at her feet, then shook her head. "No. The truth is, my daughter doesn't seem to have much luck with men."

Tell me about it, Grace thought.

Poppy went on, "About three years ago, you see, she was jilted."

"Jilted?"

Poppy nodded, still staring at the floor. "Yes. He was a nice young man. I think Free was madly in love with him. Sadly, he didn't feel the same."

"You mean they were engaged?" Grace didn't know why she was so surprised.

"Maybe *jilted* is the wrong word," Poppy said. "Free thought the young man, I think his name was Tim Mc-something, felt the same way about her. She's inclined to be obsessive about things. Anyway, in the end he got fed up with it."

"How d'you mean? Fed up with what?" Grace asked.

"He couldn't handle it. Her constant phone calls. She was very jealous and possessive. If he even looked at another woman, she'd make a scene."

I know how she feels, Grace thought. She blushed.

"So what was the upshot?" Phoebe asked.

"He left. She had a breakdown," Poppy said, matter-of-factly. "She's been very wary of men since then. I was so pleased when she took up with Sergeant Ryan. He's the first man in whom she's shown any interest in a long time. And from what she told me, he feels the same way too."

Grace tried to ignore the stab of pain in her heart.

Poppy looked at her imploringly. "What could have happened to her, Grace? Where is she?"

Grace had never seen Poppy look so vulnerable. She felt sorry for her.

* * *

"Let that be a lesson to you," Phoebe said smugly as they drove out of Poppy's gate.

"Let what be a lesson to me?"

"You'll drive Luke away if you carry on the way you are," Phoebe said.

"I think that's rather shutting the stable door, don't you?" Grace snapped. "Call Mungo and see where O'Connell is now."

Phoebe sniffed and rummaged in her bag for her mobile. She dialled Mungo. "Shit! Either his phone's switched off or his battery's flat," she said.

"Never mind. Let's go over to O'Connell's

anyway. If he's out, we can always pop around the corner and see what Cassie has to say, so it won't be a wasted journey." Grace did a U turn and headed towards Grangetown.

There was no sign of Mungo's car near Emmet O'Connell's house. They rang the doorbell anyway. No reply.

"I wonder where he is?" said Grace.

"Hopefully, not too far from Mungo," her partner replied. "Let's go see the widow-woman."

There was no reply to the widow-woman's doorbell either, but her car was parked in the driveway. Grace banged the heavy brass knocker in case the bell wasn't working. Still no reply.

"Maybe she's in the back garden," Phoebe suggested. They made their way round, through the side gate, to the back of the house. A dog started barking, though there was no sign of it. Cassie wasn't in the garden, but the back door was slightly ajar.

Grace called out, "Cassie."

The barking was coming from the garage. Phoebe looked through the window. The wolfhound threw himself against the glass and Phoebe jumped back alarmed. "Jesus! He's going mad. Why's he locked in?"

Grace felt suddenly anxious. She made for the back door, hoping against hope that Cassie hadn't decided to follow in Brian's footsteps.

She couldn't face brains dripping from the walls a second time.

"Cassie," she called again, pushing the door open with her toe.

The dog, now in a frenzy, threw himself against the garage window. The glass shattered and he jumped through. Phoebe leapt for the open back door, shoving Grace ahead of her. She banged the stout door behind them, shooting the bolt. Grace slithered on the wet quarry tiled floor and landed, winded, in a heap by the fridge. The back door shuddered with the force of hurtling angry canine.

"God! I hate dogs!" Grace said with passion.

"What the hell's happened here?" Phoebe said.

Grace looked around. The kitchen was a mess. Shards of a smashed coffee mug lay in smithereens by the table, the oil-cloth cover was half-dragged to the floor. She rubbed her behind. It was damp from the spilled coffee. Phoebe made for the hall. Sugar from the broken sugar bowl crunched under her feet.

"Cassie!" she called urgently. Silence.

Grace got out her mobile and dialled Harcourt Terrace.

"Dermot McEvoy, please . . . Grace de Rossa."

Phoebe cautiously walked down the hall and

looked through the open door of the sitting-room. Everything looked perfectly normal.

"Cassie?" she called again.

Dermot sounded grumpy. "Hello, Grace, What d'you want?"

"Dermot. We're at Cassie Drummond's. I think something's happened to her. She's not here, and it looks as thought there's been some sort of struggle. The place is a mess."

"I'll be right over," he said, and hung up.

Chapter Twenty-One

A full search of the house revealed no clues to Cassie Drummond's whereabouts. But it was evident that something was seriously wrong. A dog handler had to be called to subdue the wolfhound with a sedative dart. The poor creature was beside himself. Some primeval instinct told him that something had happened to his mistress.

"Well, I hate to admit it, but there's only one common denominator in all of this," Dermot said. "And that's O'Connell."

Grace and Phoebe agreed.

"More than you think," Grace said. "You know they had a ding-dong row in Lorenzo's yesterday?"

"How do you know?"

"We talked to the waiter. Apparently O'Connell was talking to Free Dalglish-Stuart, who was with Luke, if you remember, when

Cassie came in. Anyway, after Luke and Free left, Cassie and O'Connell had a blazing row."

"What about?"

"The waiter didn't know," Grace said. "He said Cassie stormed out of the place, and O'Connell followed her about five minutes later."

Dermot scratched his chin. "Where is he now? Mungo's still on him I suppose?"

"He should be," said Phoebe. "But his mobile's down so we can't get hold of him."

"Great!" Dermot sneered.

"Don't be so fucking high and mighty," Grace snarled. "You were the one who blew away the O'Connell theory, out of hand, remember? If it wasn't for us, you wouldn't know where to start looking for him."

"So where is he then, smartarse?"

"God! You two can be such children," Phoebe said in disgust. "I'll call the office and see if Mungo's been in contact."

Grace and Dermot looked suitably chastened.

"Sloots. How may I help yeh?" sang Xin's voice at the other end of the line.

Phoebe winced. *I should be used to this,* she thought.

"It's me, Xin. Have you heard from Mungo?"

"Yeh," Xin said. "He called from a pay-phone. His battery's dead."

"Where is he?" Phoebe asked.

"Still followin' yer man."

"We've established that, Xin," Phoebe said patiently. "Where was he when he last called in?"

"Some hotel ou' in Kilternan."

"Did Mungo say what he was doing? Was he with anyone?"

"He said yer man looked as if he was waitin' fer someone. Bu' then he had t'hang up quick, 'cos yer man was on the move."

"Call me as soon as you hear from him again," Phoebe said, and hung up. "Mungo's still with him. Last Xin heard, they were at the hotel in Kilternan."

"What the hell's he doing out there?" Dermot asked, almost to himself.

"Search me," said Phoebe. "Mungo said he looked as if he was waiting for someone."

Dermot made for the phone. "I'll put out a call for him."

Grace's mobile chirped. "Grace de Rossa."

It was Xin.

"Hang on, Dermot," Grace called after him. "What's the story, Xin? Where's Mungo?" she asked.

"It's not abou' Mungo. It's your Ma, Grace. She's had a terrible haemorrhage."

"You mean my father?"

"No. I mean yer ma. Faith phoned from Vincent's. Yer ma's in surgery."

"Oh my God! But she was OK. What happened?"

"Dunno, Grace. Bu' I tink yeh should get over there. An' pronto."

"What is it, Grace?" Phoebe looked alarmed.

"It's my mother. I've got to get over to Vincent's."

"Why? What's happened?" asked Dermot.

Grace hurried towards the door. "I'm not sure. But she's in surgery."

"I'll drive," Phoebe said. "I'll call you as soon as I hear from Mungo, Dermot."

The two women ran from the house. The traffic was awful, as it always is when you're in a hurry. Phoebe weaved in and out, hand on the horn, prompting shaken fists and shouted insults.

"What's the matter with your mother?"

"I'm not sure. Xin said she's had a *terrible haemorrhage*. I think she might mean a *cerebral* haemorrhage."

"Oh dear. I hope not," Phoebe said lamely.

Alice de Rossa was still in surgery when they arrived at Vincent's. Faith met them in the corridor, two polystyrene cups of dark liquid in her hands. The three women walked back to the waiting room together to join Charity, Michael and Hope.

"What happened? How is she?" Grace asked.

"She had a seizure," Hope said. "Charles said

it looks like a subdural haemorrhage. He's assisting in surgery now."

"What does that *mean*?" Grace said. "Will she be OK? Is it serious?"

"It's serious." Michael put his arm round her shoulder. "But not necessarily too serious. It's possible she could make a full recovery."

"Yes. But what *is* it?" Grace persisted.

"Ma's bleeding in between the dural mater and the arachoid membrane. That's the cavity between the scull and the brain. But she was diagnosed within minutes of the seizure . . . Charles is assisting David Patterson. He's the best neurosurgeon around, so there's every hope . . ." Michael trailed off. He didn't want to give his sisters false hope, but at the same time he didn't want to upset them unnecessarily. Time enough for that if the unthinkable happened.

Grace sat down. It was so unfair. Her mother had only been bruised. She'd been recovering well. Why did this have to happen? "How's the old man?" she asked. "Does he know what's happing?"

"Professor Ambrose decided against telling him just yet," Hope said. "At least until they see the extent of the damage."

"Damage? You mean brain damage?" Grace was shocked.

"Possibly," Michael said. "We'll have to wait and see."

Phoebe said, "Look Grace, I'm no help here. I think I'll get back to the office."

Grace had forgotten about Phoebe. "OK. I'll let you know what happens here," she said. "And thanks for bringing me down."

Time dragged by. It was growing dark outside. Grace looked at her reflection in the glass of the window. She could see her brother and sisters behind her, talking in subdued voices. *Are they feeling as guilty as I am?* she wondered. *Why are my parents such a constant source of guilt? Is it just me, or is it like that for everyone?* She tried to take her mind off things and picked up an ancient copy of *National Geographic*. She couldn't concentrate. Listlessly she threw it to one side. It skimmed across the glossy cover of *Marie Claire* magazine and fell to the floor. Michael bent down and picked it up.

"Would anyone like coffee?" she asked.

"I'll go," Michael offered.

"No. It's OK. I feel like stretching my legs," she said.

She needed air. The cloying heat of the hospital, along with the stress of the past week, was getting to her. *When all this is over I'll probably die of adrenalin deficiency,* she ruefully reflected.

She passed ICU on the way down the corridor.

Luke.

She hesitated, then walked on. They

wouldn't let her in anyway. Besides, he'd probably prefer to have Free visit him, if she turned up again in one piece, that is. She felt a lump in her throat. Tears stung her eyes. She swiped them away angrily and hurried for the lift.

Outside the air was stinging. She could see her steamy breath. She went over to a low wall and sat down, hugging her arms around herself to ward off the cold. She was utterly miserable. Most of the people in the world whom she really cared about seemed to be tapping on death's door. She let go, and cried.

For her mother, for her father and for the disappointment she felt about Luke. She'd really trusted him. Big shuddering sobs shook her shoulders, and stole her breath. Oblivious to the curious looks of passers-by, she sat there and howled for a good ten minutes until she felt better. Then she dug out a soggy tissue and wiped her eyes and blew her nose.

"Grace! I've just heard. How is your poor, dear, mother?"

A familiar figure bustled towards her and Kathleen Dillon, close to hysteria, flung herself at Grace and wrapped her arms around her neck.

The words, *straw,* and, *camel's back,* crossed Grace's mind and she had to fight hard not to snigger. Somehow Kathleen had broken the tension.

"She's in surgery, Kathleen. But Michael says it's hopeful. Let's go up and see if there's any news." She put an arm around Kathleen and they headed for the lift.

Kathleen looked up into her face. "Are you all right, dear? You look as if you've been crying." She sounded genuinely concerned.

Grace smiled at her, and squeezed her shoulder.

"I'm fine now, thanks, Kathleen. There's nothing like a good howl to clear your head."

"I know, dear, I know." Kathleen said. "All this on top of everything else. But never mind. Every cloud has a silver lining."

Grace stopped. "Like what?" she said. "Where's the silver lining?"

Kathleen smiled at her. "Little Caitlin of course. My beautiful little granddaughter. And to think that you all but delivered her. You must be so proud."

"And so lucky to have such a wonderfully sensitive mother-in-law," Grace said through gritted teeth as she stepped into the crowded elevator.

"Don't mention it, dear," Kathleen replied, oblivious of Grace's sarcasm. "You know how much I care about you."

After a lengthy interval, Charles came in to the waiting room, still in his green scrubs. They all jumped up.

"It's not as bad as we first thought," he said. "We've relieved the pressure on the brain and the bleeding's stopped. So far there's no sign of brain damage." Grace heaved a sigh of relief. Charles continued, "we'll know more in the morning."

"Can we see her?" Hope asked.

"Best not," Charles said. "Why don't you all go home? There's little point in waiting here. I'll phone if there's any change."

Kathleen, forever the drama queen, decided, stoically, to hang around. After all, Alice de Rossa was her oldest friend. *A friend in need,* and all that. Grace was too weary to talk her out of it, even though she knew that Kathleen expected her to.

"Whatever you like, Kathleen," she said.

* * *

Faith gave Grace and Michael a lift back to Baggot Street.

"I think we were supposed to talk Kathleen out of staying," Grace said. "I hate it when she plays those silly mind-games. I never know what the right answer is. Mother's the same." She caught her breath. "Oh God! I'm such a bitch. I shouldn't have said that."

"Relax, Grace," Michael said. "I think mind-games are a thing with their generation."

257

"Anyway," Faith added, "who are we to stop her being a martyr."

They stopped on the way to pick up a take-away. Faith declined the offer of a late-night snack. When she dropped them off outside Baggot Street, Phoebe's light was on, so they called in.

"How's your mother?" Phoebe looked concerned.

"Could be worse," Grace said. "We'll know more in the morning. Any news of Cassie?"

"Not as yet," Phoebe said.

"Shouldn't you have taken over the night-shift, watching O'Connell?" asked Grace. "Mungo's done a double-shift already, covering for me."

Phoebe pinched a slice of Grace's pizza. "No need," she said. "Acting on information received from yours truly," she pointed a beautifully manicured finger at her chest, "Dermot McEvoy picked him up a couple of hours ago. He's getting the third degree as we speak."

Chapter Twenty-Two

"How many times do I have to tell you?" O'Connell said, "I don't know where Free bloody Dalglish-Stuart is." He shifted sideways in his chair and crossed his legs, placing his elbow on the desk. His fists were clenched.

"So where were you the night before last, say, between five and eleven?"

"I've already told you. I was at home."

"So you say," Dermot said. "But there doesn't seem to be anyone to corroborate your alibi."

O'Connell gave a strained laugh. "If I'd realised that I'd need an alibi, Inspector, I'd have gone out to a very public place, or asked friends round to the house. Sorry I can't help you."

I'll wipe that grin off your face, you bloody smug bastard, Dermot thought.

"I'm glad you think that there's something to laugh at here, Doctor. One of my officers was badly beaten and left for dead the other night."

"I know, you told me, and I'm very sorry about your colleague," he said. "But his attack, and Free's disappearance, have absolutely nothing to do with me."

Dermot tried a different tack. "Why were you out in Kilternan tonight, Doctor?" He was sitting across the table from O'Connell. Molloy was standing by the door with his arms folded.

"I had a meeting."

"Who with?"

"Not that it's any of your business, Inspector, but it was Cassie Drummond."

"So why go all the way out there to meet her? You only live round the corner?"

"I don't know. You'll have to ask her. I had a fax. She was supposed to meet me in Kilternan, but she didn't turn up. I was on my way to her house when you stopped me."

"Do you normally communicate by fax?" Dermot's voice was incredulous.

"Sometimes it's more convenient." O'Connell said. He looked a bit strained. "If I'm with a patient, it saves me being disturbed . . . Look, what's this about?"

"Cassie Drummond's disappeared," Dermot said, without emotion.

O'Connell took a sharp intake of breath. "Disappeared? When?"

"When was the last time you saw her?" Molloy asked.

"The day before yesterday, around five in the evening. I told you this already."

Dermot tapped his pen on the table top. After a pause he said, "I have reason to believe you saw her yesterday. "

O'Connell shook his head. "No. That's not correct. And what do you mean by *reason to believe?*"

Dermot dropped the bombshell. "Did you know that Poppy Dalglish-Stuart has had you followed?"

O'Connell snorted. "That wouldn't surprise me in the slightest."

"Dr O'Connell. I don't think you're paying attention," Dermot said. "I said, Poppy had you followed, so you'll realise that we know you stopped off at Cassie Drummond's yesterday in the morning. You were followed, man."

O'Connell sat staring at Dermot. He slowly and deliberately took out a cigarette and lit it. "Correct me if I'm wrong, Inspector. But you asked me when I last saw Mrs Drummond," he said. "When I called on her yesterday, she was out. So you see, I'm telling you the truth."

"Then why were you in her house for over half an hour?"

"I wasn't *in* her house, Inspector. I was *outside* her house. Her car was in the drive so I assumed, wherever she was, she wouldn't be long. Eventually I gave up. But I expect my esteemed sister-in-law's told you this already."

Dermot shifted uncomfortably in his chair. What was it about this man that he found so offensive? It was a toss-up between everything he said and everything he did. *Obnoxious prat.*

"How long do you intend to keep me here?" O'Connell asked.

"Until you've told us what we want to know," replied Molloy, as he sat down next to Dermot.

"This is preposterous," O'Connell hissed under his breath. "Are you suggesting that I somehow got into Cassie's house. Knocked her senseless, then spirited her away in the boot of my car, or something. All in the space of thirty minutes?"

"Well, did you?" Dermot asked.

O'Connell pushed his chair back noisily and stood up.

"This is ludicrous!"

"Sit down!" Dermot snapped.

O'Connell hesitated for an instant, then sat down.

"That's better."

O'Connell stared at the wall. Dermot could sense he was rattled.

"Were you annoyed when your wife cut you out of her will in favour of Free Dalglish-Stuart?"

"What are you suggesting?"

"What d'you think?" Dermot said.

O'Connell stayed silent. He tapped his heel on the floor in annoyance. The colour was rising up his neck.

"What did you argue with Cassie Drummond about in Lorenzo's?"

"None of your bloody business," O'Connell snapped.

"Maybe you lost your temper with her when you visited her yesterday," Dermot said. "Maybe you killed her in a fit of rage."

"No I didn't," O'Connell said.

"I thought you said you didn't see her yesterday?" Molloy said.

"I didn't see her yesterday, you moron! I told you, she was out. And I never lose my temper!"

O'Connell lost it. His voice shook and his face was red. He was half-standing, half-sitting with his hands flat on the table. Flecks of saliva foamed at the sides of his mouth.

Dermot looked round at Jack Molloy. "I rest my case," he said. The two men sat staring at O'Connell.

Emmet O'Connell stared back, then abruptly sat down.

"D'you know what I think, Doctor?" Dermot said after a while. "I think you were livid with her for making a scene in the restaurant. I think you went round to see her. To have it out with her, and you lost your temper, just as you did now."

O'Connell took out a white cotton hankie and mopped his brow. "I've had enough of this," he said. "I want to see my solicitor."

"I thought you said you didn't need a solicitor." Dermot tried unsuccessfully to keep the sneer from his tone.

O'Connell glared at him. "Are you refusing my request for legal representation?"

Dermot pushed his chair back from the table and heaved himself to his feet. It had been a long day. Jack Molloy pointedly looked at his watch. Dermot shrugged his eyebrows in reply.

"Jack. Take Doctor O'Connell to the public office and let him use the phone," he said wearily. "I'll be in my office."

Mindful of the fact that Emmet O'Connell couldn't be held for longer than six hours, Damien Egan didn't hurry himself. He arrived ninety minutes after O'Connell's call, then spent a further half-hour in conference with his client.

"He's taking his bloody time," Molloy commented. He and Dermot were standing in the corridor outside the interview room.

"You said it yourself, Jack. The clock's ticking. Egan knows we've nothing concrete on O'Connell by now."

"On the other hand . . ." Jack Molloy said hopefully. Pattie Doyle hurried down the corridor towards them. She had a thin red file in her hands. Dermot's face brightened up.

"Thank's for bringing this over so soon," he said as he took the file from her hand.

"Don't count your chickens, Dermot," she said, half apologetically. "The car came up clean."

"Shit!"

The door opened and Damien Egan came out.

"When you're ready," he said.

Dermot looked at Jack, and they followed him back into the room. O'Connell was still sitting in the same seat. Egan sat down beside him.

"My client has nothing further to say to you, Inspector."

"This is your advice?"

"No," O'Connell said. "It's my decision. I'll not dignify these proceedings further by answering your ridiculous questions."

Dermot shrugged. "What's so ridiculous? Don't try and tell me you were overjoyed when Free Dalglish-Stuart got your wife's estate. You've plenty of reason to want her out of the way."

"I won't pretend I wasn't angry," O'Connell said. "But why would I do her harm? Under the terms of the will, I wouldn't benefit even if she were dead. Where's your motive now? And what about Cassie Drummond? Why in God's name would I want to harm her?"

"I'm not saying you *intended* to harm Cassie Drummond. And, as far as your late wife's estate is concerned, with Free out of the picture, you're responsible for distributing the funds," Dermot said.

"To a cancer charity of my choice," said O'Connell.

"Right," sneered Molloy.

O'Connell leapt from his seat and grabbed Molloy by the lapels.

Egan jumped up and grabbed his arm. "Calm down, Emmet!" Then to Dermot. "I really must protest, Inspector. These insinuations are inexcusable. Unless you've hard evidence against my client, I demand you let him go."

Dermot checked the clock. O'Connell had been in custody for just under six hours.

"If you go through to the office, Detective Garda Molloy will see that your property's returned to you," Dermot said wearily.

"Where's my car?"

"It's parked round the corner in Adelaide Road," said Molloy.

"No doubt I'll be seeing you again, Doctor," said Dermot.

O'Connell glared at him, then pushed past through the doorway.

"I hope you're not thinking of harassing my client, Inspector," Egan said.

Dermot grinned malevolently at him. "Would I?" he said innocently.

* * *

Techno music wasn't really Xin's thing but she'd enjoyed herself, bopping the night away. It was two-thirty am and ZOMBIES was emptying. Xin was there with Lorna and a gang of her workmates. Lorna Mountjoy was tall, blonde and thin as a bean pole, and bore no resemblance whatsoever to her younger sister, Alice, aka Xin. Lorna was a civil servant. She and the rest of the girls worked at the Department of Foreign Affairs. Majella was totally wasted and Lorna was supporting her sagging body.

"What's she like!" Xin commented.

"Ah, give the girl a break. It's her bleedin' hen nigh'," Lorna said.

"Huh . . . I'd never've guessed," Xin said smirking. "Some people just can't hold their drink. Fifteen Bacardi and black an' she's anyone's!"

"That's easy for you t'say," Lorna sniggered. "You've been on bleedin' Seven-Up all nigh'."

"My body is a temple," Xin said. They both burst out laughing.

Majella was Lorna's best friend and it was her last night out with the girls, in theory anyway. Lorna eased the almost comatose girl onto a chair. The set of huge plastic boobs were slightly askew over her Addidas crop top and her blonde streaked hair was covered by a blue hairnet. A miniature plastic penis dangled from her nose by a thin piece of elastic.

"Give us a hand t' get her t' the car," Lorna said.

"Where're the others?"

"They went on ahead t'Leeson Street." Xin said. "Are yeh game?"

"Too right, I'm bleedin' game,"

The two sisters hoisted the bride-to-be to her feet and made their way outside.

"Jeasus! she's heavy," Lorna said.

Fortunately, Xin's car wasn't parked too far away so they half dragged, half carried Majella. They had to stop a couple of times to let her vomit. This seemed to perk her up a bit and she made it the rest of the way to the car under her own steam.

"Where to now, girls?" she asked, before passing out again on the back seat.

"D'you think we should give Leeson Street a miss?" Lorna asked half-heartedly, looking over the back of the seat at Majella.

"She'll be grand," Xin said. "She'll kill us if we take her home too early."

As Xin turned into Adelaide Road, she caught a glimpse of a familiar figure. She jammed on the brakes.

Lorna screeched as her head bounced off the dashboard.

"What the fuck are you doin'?"

Xin ignored her. She was too busy peering through the rear-view mirror.

Yes. She was right. Emmet O'Connell, large as life, was standing beside his silver Beemer talking to another man.

"Why've we stopped?" Majella stirred into life in the back seat.

Xin watched as O'Connell got into his car and started the engine. She let him drive past her and then followed at a discreet distance. When she turned right over Eustace Bridge, instead of left into Lower Leeson Street, Lorna said, "Where're we goin'?"

"Sorry girls, this is work," Xin said. "I have t'folla yer man."

"Wha'?"

"Yer man there," Xin said. "In the Beemer."

"Are we there yet?" Majella had stirred again.

"Who is he?" Lorna was getting interested.

"Emmet O'Connell. He murdered both his wives."

269

"Jeasus!"

O'Connell drove straight home to Grangetown. Xin kept on his tail and parked ten yards down the road from his house.

"This is great," Lorna said. "What d'we do now?"

"Just sit here," Xin said. "It's known in the business by us professionals as surveillance."

Majella snored loudly on the back seat.

Chapter Twenty-Three

Free Dalglish-Stuart swerved to a halt on the gravel driveway. She stumbled blindly from the car and ran up the steps. She was wet and dishevelled. Her hair was plastered to her head, her tights torn and she was shoeless. She hammered the knocker and leaned on the bell. Tears streamed down her face.

"Mother, Mother! Help me! Help me!" she screamed, then collapsed onto the step.

Chapter Twenty-Four

"Yeh have t'get me me own personal mobile phone," Xin said. "We nearly lost yer man. If there hadn't been a phone box at the end of the road, we'd've been knackered."

Xin was holding forth to Grace. She looked even more bizarre than normal. The tight-cropped top and cycle shorts were a sight to behold.

"It's me club gear," she'd said defensively, tugging the legs of her shorts down over her mauve mottled thighs as Grace eyed her up and down. "I didn't go home, wha' with watchin' yer man all night."

"OK. Point taken, Xin," Grace said. "Fair play to you, picking up O'Connell like that."

"How come they let 'im go?"

Grace shrugged. "His time was up. They can only hold him for six hours. I suppose Dermot couldn't drag together enough evidence to charge him."

Xin yawned.

"You better go home and get some sleep, Xin," she said. "You must be dead on your feet."

"Ninjas don't need no sleep."

"Even so," Grace said, trying to hide a smile.

The phone rang. "Sloots. How can I help yeh?"

Xin handed the receiver to Grace. "It's Mungo."

"Hi Mungo. What's happening?"

"All hell's broke loose down here, Grace."

"Down where?"

"I'm at O'Connell's house. The cops've just carted him off in a cop car. Lights flashin', sirens goin', the works."

Grace couldn't take it in. "But they only let him go a few hours ago."

"I had a word with McEvoy. Free Dalglish-Stuart turned up this morning."

"Dead or alive?"

"Alive," Mungo said. That's all I know. McEvoy wouldn't say no more."

"I'll phone Poppy. See what she can tell us," Grace said and hung up the phone.

Phoebe strolled into reception, carrying a large brown cardboard box. She looked very business-like, dressed in a coffee-coloured tailored suit. Her camel cashmere coat rested on her shoulders.

"Tell us about what?" she asked.

273

"Free's turned up and Dermot's rearrested Emmet O'Connell," Grace said. "So I suppose he must have got new evidence." She reached for the phone but there was no reply from Poppy's number.

"She's probably at the cop shop with Free," Phoebe speculated.

Grace tried Harcourt Terrace. Kate Grady told her that she'd briefly interviewed Free.

"And she told me that O'Connell's wife, Carenza, had a holiday cottage near Kilternan. O'Connell was holding her there," she said. "She's convinced he was going to kill her. Lucky for her she escaped."

"Pity Dermot jumped the gun," Grace said. "O'Connell would probably have led him there the other night."

"Who's to say?" said Kate. "Anyway, I've got to go. I'm off out there with the technical team."

"Is Free still there?"

"No," Kate replied. "Her mother collected her. I think they're on their way home. Dermot's going there later, after she's had a rest, to take a detailed statement."

"Thanks, Kate. Talk to you later." Grace hung up the phone.

"Well?" Phoebe said.

"He was holding Free in his holiday cottage out in Kilternan," she explained. "But this is really weird. Kate says that Free's convinced

O'Connell was going to kill her. So what was he waiting for? Why didn't he just finish her off like Luke?"

"Who knows how a psycho's mind works?" Phoebe said.

"And I agree with you about Brian Drummond. I just don't buy it that he killed Carenza. So that means that O'Connell probably did. And if he killed her, he probably killed Anabell too, which makes him a serial killer, as near as damn it. Maybe he was getting some sadistic pleasure out of dragging out the agony with Free."

"I wouldn't put it past him," said Grace. "He strikes me as a control freak. What d'you think, Xin?"

Xin didn't reply. She was lolling on the sofa, mouth open, snoring quietly. Phoebe got up and covered the sleeping Ninja with her coat.

"Of course you realise what this means?" she asked Grace.

"What what means?"

"If Dermot's arrested O'Connell, we're out of a job."

"Oh well," said Grace, sounding less than confident. "I'm sure we'll pick up some work soon."

"It's a good job one of us is looking ahead," Phoebe said. "I bumped into my Polish friend again yesterday."

"And?"

"And he called me back this morning and I got us some undercover work."

"I thought you said he was a Pole you wouldn't touch with a barge?" Grace said.

"I reconsidered," Phoebe said. "I only agreed to help him after laying down some ground rules."

"I don't understand?" Grace said. "Why would you lay down ground rules?"

"You don't know Milo," Phoebe said. "He expected me to be part of the deal, but I soon put him straight. Anyway, you'll be doing what you're good at. You'll be doing undercover work for him."

Something about Phoebe's tone made Grace suspicious.

"What kind of undercover work?"

"Milo has a chain of fast-food joints. You must have seen them. The Chucklin' Chookie?"

Grace nodded. "Isn't that the place where the waitresses have to dress up like eejits in stupid chicken suits?"

"Yes. Anyway, Milo thinks one of his managers is ripping him off. So you're going in undercover to catch him in the act." She tipped the uniform out onto the desk.

Grace picked it up. It was a lurid yellow sort of padded dungarees thing, with the outline of feathers and wings printed on the fabric in equally lurid orange. It came complete with matching orange T-shirt. A red cockscomb head dress and chicken-feet shoes completed the ensemble.

"You're joking, right?"

Phoebe shook her head.

"Why do I have to be the one undercover?"

"Because you're the best qualified for the job," Phoebe said.

"You could do it."

Phoebe looked incredulous. "Don't be silly, Grace. No one would believe I was really a waitress. Besides, yellow's your colour."

* * *

Whilst searching O'Connell's holiday cottage with the technical team, Kate Grady came across the body of Cassie Drummond. She was lying on her back on the stone floor of the pantry. Her hands were tied behind her back and an angry purple mark around her slim white throat strongly suggested that she had been strangled.

Chapter Twenty-Five

"Well that's that," Dermot said. "We've charged your uncle."

He was standing by the window of Free's sitting room in Raglan Road. The decor was in total contrast to Poppy's room. It was bright and airy and uncluttered. A shaft of winter sun showed between the muslin drapes.

"With murder?"

"Just abduction and false imprisonment at the moment," Dermot said.

"But what about Cassie Drummond? Aren't you going to charge him with her murder as well?" Free sounded anxious.

Dermot smiled. He patted her arm.

"All in good time," he said. "As soon as we get the forensic evidence. Now, I'd like to go over your statement with you again, just in case there's anything else that you've remembered."

Free sat down on the windowseat. She looked

frail and vulnerable. "Where do you want me to start?"

"At the beginning," Dermot said. "Just take your time. There's no rush."

Free nodded. "Well, Luke and I stopped for a drink at The Wayside Inn. We'd been for a long walk, you see, and needed to warm up." She stared wistfully out of the window.

After a while Dermot said, "what then? What happened then?"

"I phoned Mother to tell her that I wouldn't be home for dinner, and then we left. I drove. Then we got a puncture, so Luke changed the tyre. I was holding the torch and this car stopped about ten or twelve yards behind us with the headlamps full on." She paused and bit her lip. "Anyway, Luke looked round and walked back to see what the problem was. That's when the car revved up and drove straight at him." She buried her head in her hands and started to cry. Dermot waited patiently. She blew her nose and wiped her eyes. "I was rooted to the spot. It all happened so fast I didn't know what to do. He hit Luke and drove right over him, then reversed and drove at him again. Poor, poor Luke . . . It was awful."

"Yes," Dermot said. "What happened then?"

"I ran down the road, trying to get away. But I heard the car rev up again and he came after me. I only got a few yards before he caught up. He grabbed me and I struggled and . . ."

"Who grabbed you?"

"Emmet, of course. Emmet grabbed me."

"But it was dark. How did you know it was Emmet?"

"The headlamps. He left the headlamps on."

"So what happened next?"

"If you'd stop interrupting I'll tell you," she snapped. "He put something over my mouth and nose. The next thing I knew I woke up in the cellar with a screaming headache."

"And what did you do?"

"I tried the door but it was locked. I yelled and yelled. After a while I realised there was no point. No one could hear me out there."

"How did you know that?" Dermot asked.

Free looked puzzled. "How do you mean?"

"How did you know no one could hear you? How did you know where you were?"

"I know Aunt Carenza's house well. I've often stayed there with her," said Free. "Why? Don't you believe me?"

"Of course," Dermot said. "But these are things O'Connell's defence will ask you." Free relaxed and smiled at him.

"I'm sorry," she said. "All this has been such a strain."

"I understand. Don't worry about it. What happened then?"

Free took a deep breath and stared into the distance. "I seemed to be there for ages. I was freezing cold and hungry. I must have fallen asleep, then he woke me up."

"When was this?" Dermot asked.

"I'm not sure. There's no window in the cellar. My watch said one-thirty. I don't know if it was am or pm." She fingered her watch as she spoke. "He said, 'Drink this', and handed me a cup of coffee. I was so thirsty I scalded my mouth. I was shivering. He threw a blanket at me."

"Did he say anything else?"

"I asked him, why? He said I had it coming to me for turning Carenza against him. But that's not true. I never tried to turn Aunt Carenza against him." She stood up and grabbed hold of the lapels of Dermot's jacket. "He did it himself. He was so cruel to her."

Dermot eased her fingers open. She looked embarrassed when she realised what she was doing. She sat down again.

"Then I passed out. I think he must have drugged the coffee."

"How did you get away?"

"I don't know how long I was unconscious. I sort of drifted in and out. Finally my head cleared and I heard him moving about in the house. Then he came down to the cellar and told me he'd killed Cassie."

"Why?"

"Why what?"

"Why did he kill Cassie?" Dermot asked. He had his own theories but he wondered what O'Connell's story was.

"I don't know," Free said. "He didn't say. He just said that I was next."

"Didn't you ask him?"

She frowned. "No," she said. "I didn't bloody ask him. I was too worried about saving my own skin."

"OK. Fine," Dermot said. "Carry on. What happened then?"

"I tried to humour him. I told him I wouldn't say a word if he'd just let me go. I said I'd make over Aunt Carenza's estate to him. That I never wanted her money."

"What did he say to that?"

"He just laughed."

"What happened then?"

"He was laughing. He thought it was really funny. He went back upstairs. I think he's mad. He went back upstairs. It was only after a short while that I realised I hadn't heard him slip the bolt. I crawled upstairs. I felt very weak. I tried the door. It was open. I couldn't believe my luck. I was afraid it was some sort of game he was playing. You know, cat and mouse?" Dermot nodded. "Anyway, I crept through the house, but there was no sign of him. The back door was locked so I climbed up on the draining board and smashed the window."

"Weren't you afraid he'd hear you?"

Free didn't seem to hear him. She went on, "It was only when I was outside that I realised that I hadn't my shoes on. It was pouring with rain. I ran around the house and saw that he'd parked my car by the garage. The keys weren't in it, but I keep a spare taped under the bumper."

"How did he get your car back to the cottage?" asked Dermot.

"I haven't a clue," said Free. She stood up and walked over to the fireplace, where she threw another log onto the fire. Sparks exploded up the chimney.

"Why did you drive home? Why didn't you go to a garda station?" Dermot asked.

Free shook her head. "I was in a panic," she said. "I wanted to get as far away from there as possible. And all the time poor Cassie was lying dead . . . " She couldn't finish the sentence. She took out a hanky and blew her nose. "I hope they throw away the key. Four murders. The man's a monster."

"Only one that we know for sure," Dermot corrected. "But that's enough to send him away for a long time."

Free looked puzzled. "Two then. Cassie and poor Luke."

"Oh God. I'm sorry," Dermot said. "I thought you knew."

"Knew what?"

Dermot grinned. "Luke isn't dead. He's in a bad way, but the medics are fairly confident he'll pull through."

Free looked stunned. "Alive? But how could he be?"

Dermot was still grinning. "I know. He must have the proverbial nine lives."

Free gave a strained smile. "Do you mind if we finish this another day? I'm really tired."

"No problem," Dermot said. "And I'm glad that at least I could cheer you up a bit, after all you've been through."

"Cheer me up? . . . Oh yes. Thank you." She walked towards the door. Dermot followed. She saw him to the front door and stood on the steps as he walked to his car.

"Inspector?" Dermot looked back. "What hospital is Luke in? I'd like to go and see him."

"He's in Vincent's," Dermot said. "But I'm afraid there's a no-visitors rule at the moment."

"Maybe I'll send him some flowers then," she said.

She watched Dermot drive away.

* * *

Panic gripped her. How could he be alive? She went back to her sitting-room and curled up in the armchair by the fire. Pictures flooded her memory. Luke leaning into the boot. Reaching in and picking up the brooch. The blessed wheat-sheaf brooch. She saw herself raising the jack and smashing it down on the back of his head. He staggered, holding his hands over the wound. He half-turned. She smashed down the jack again as hard as she could. He fell and hit his head on the edge of the boot. The awful crunch as his head hit the road. She drove the car forward and reversed over him. Bump, bump. Then into first. Forward with her foot to the floor. Bump, bump. Then back again, then forward. She was crying. "It's all right", she kept telling herself. "It'll be all right. I'll get away from here. I need time to think."

Aunt Carenza's cottage was only a couple of miles down the road. Poor Aunt Carenza. Silly Aunt Carenza. Why did people have to be so fickle. Luke. Carenza.

She'd promised to leave her everything. It was easy to persuade the stupid old bat after they'd spent that time together in the cottage. She'd managed to get Carenza to cut Emmet out of the will. Then Brian Drummond had sweet-talked the old bat with his pathetic sob story. She was going to lend *him* what was rightfully *hers*. She hadn't meant to lose her temper with Carenza. They were in the garage. She'd finally talked Carenza into leaving Emmet. She'd dictated the note for her. They'd laughed about that. Carenza had said that it would really hurt him. The thought that she could love someone other than him! What a joke. She was about to get into the car when she dropped the bombshell. Matter-of-factly. As if it was of no importance. "I'm going to lend poor Brian a hundred and fifty thousand", she'd said. As if it was nothing. *Her* money going to bail out that moron. She felt the anger rising in her chest. The hammer was in her hand. She walloped her really hard a few times, until her anger was spent. The next moment Carenza was lying at her feet, blood gushing from her head. It was obvious she was dead. Her eyes were open and staring. She couldn't have known what hit her.

Suddenly she was calm. Time to be practical. She was splattered with blood. She took off her shoes and went up to the bathroom to shower. Then she rooted in Carenza's wardrobe and found a loose sweater-dress to wear. Her own clothes she carefully put in a carrier bag to launder when she got home.

She'd drive Carenza's car out to the Ballycoyle estate and leave the keys in it. That should guarantee it'd never be seen again. Later, she checked round the house to make sure that everything looked normal. She couldn't believe how heavy Carenza was as she tried to lift her. She looked so frail but she was a dead weight. Free smiled to herself. Yes. A dead weight! With a good deal of effort she'd heaved the body into the boot of the Volvo. Then she drove straight to Ballycoyle woods and unloaded her grisly cargo. She was worried that someone might happen along. So she dragged her out and dumped her at the edge of the woods, rolling her over and over like a log until she was hidden by the long grass. Then fled the scene as quickly as possible. When she got back to the house, she tripped over Carenza's case in the garage. Shit! She picked it up and dumped it at the end of the garden in the shrubbery. She took great care to wipe her fingerprints from the handle.

Killing Cassie had been easy. The bitch was against her too. She'd never liked her. And what better way to implicate Emmet? Dermot McEvoy was convinced he'd killed Anabell and Carenza, thanks to Mother. One more would cement the blame firmly on Emmet. Poor stupid Cassie. She was so gullible. No one saw her arrive at the house in the darkness. It was easy to persuade Cassie to lock up the monster dog. She'd had a story ready in case Cassie had heard that she was missing, but that wasn't necessary. The silly cow had even offered her coffee. Then it was only a matter of slipping the cord around her neck from behind and twisting it until she stopped struggling. It had to be the wicked Emmet. How could it be her, when she was so cruelly held captive in Aunt Carenza's cottage? She laughed out loud as she remembered her masterstroke. Sending Emmet the fax. There were bound to be witnesses who saw him at the hotel in Kilternan. Then she remembered the brooch.

It was only when she was dumping Carenza's body in the woods that she realised that the wheat-sheaf brooch was missing. She was certain that Carenza had been wearing it. The bloody elusive wheat-sheaf brooch. It had disappeared again after she finished off Luke. She didn't have time to search. What if someone came along? Still, there was nothing to tie her in with the brooch and Carenza's death, even if they found it on the road. Except of course Luke. Suddenly she knew what she had to do.

Chapter Twenty-Six

"I'll have a double chucklin' chookie burger and large fries."

"Piss off, Dermot!"

"Love the suit."

"What d'you want?"

"I told you. A double chucklin' . . ."

"What d'you *want*, Dermot?"

Dermot sniggered.

"Don't you dare laugh, Dermot! I'm warning you."

He straightened his face. "Sorry," he said. "I called your office and Phoebe told me you were here."

"Oh *did* she?"

"Hmmm. Anyway, I thought I'd drop in and tell you the news in person," he said. The corners of his mouth puckered, but he managed to control it. "We charged O'Connell with abduction and false imprisonment."

"Excuse me?" A young man in biker's

leathers and a courier's satchel tapped Dermot on the shoulder. "D'you mind if I go first? I've a delivery to make."

Dermot stood back and swept his hand towards the counter. "Be my guest," he said, grinning. Grace glared at him.

"I'll have nine chunky chucklin' chookie dippers with tangy curry dippin' sauce, please," said the courier. "No gherkin."

"Tangy curry dippin' sauce and no gherkin." Grace repeated as she got the order together. The young man hurried down the counter to the till. "Have a chucklin' good day!" she said self consciously to his retreating back. She gave Dermot a warning look.

"And if you say one word . . ."

Dermot pointed at his chest. "Me, make fun of you when you're at the cutting edge of an investigation?"

Grace relented and grinned back at him. "OK. So I look a prat, but those are the breaks. I have to earn a crust now that Poppy isn't footing the bill."

"What's in that stuff?" Dermot asked, indicating the hatch through to the preparation area.

"God knows," Grace said. "Minced salmonella gromits probably. If they cook too many at a time, they nuke them in the microwave to reheat them."

"On second thoughts, cancel the double chucklin' chookie burger."

"So how's Luke?" she asked.

"Getting there," Dermot said. "He's off all the life-support stuff and he's drifting in and out of conciousness. The quacks say that's hopeful."

Grace brightened up. "That's good news. And how's Free?"

"I'd say she's been better," Dermot said. "You know she was a witness when O'Connell ran over Luke?"

"That must've been pretty horrifying," Grace said. "How come forensic didn't find anything on O'Connell's car?"

Dermot shrugged. "Search me. Unless he used a different car. Free couldn't make it out because of the glare of the headlamps. Maybe he did kill Carenza. Maybe he used her car. It hasn't turned up yet."

"What does he say?"

"Nothing. He's alternating between staring at the wall keeping his mouth shut, and protesting his innocence. But then he would, wouldn't he?"

They stood in silence for a minute, each lost in their own thoughts. Suddenly Grace said, "How did she get away?"

"Who? Free?" Grace nodded. "O'Connell forgot to lock the cellar door. You should have seen the state she was in this morning when got to Harcourt Terrace."

"What time was that?" Grace asked.

"About eight am. Why?"

"So, let's get this straight. You had O'Connell in custody until what time?"

"We chucked him out at around two-thirty, two-forty-five. Why?"

"So when did he go out to Kilternan to Carenza's place?"

"He must have gone more or less as soon as we let him go."

Grace frowned. "But he couldn't have."

"He must have. Free escaped as soon as he left the cottage. So he must have been there between he left here and about six-thirty, because she got back to Raglan Road at about half-seven."

"But I'm telling you, he couldn't have. Xin was on his tail from the moment he left Harcourt Terrace and he went straight home. He stayed there until the cavalry arrived to cart him back to the cop shop."

Dermot looked stunned. "Are you sure? When I asked Mungo how long he'd been outside O'Connell's, he said since seven am."

"That's right. But he took over from Xin. She might look a bit weird, but she's all there. She knows what she saw," Grace said. "But why would Free lie?"

Dermot was deep in thought. "OK. You last saw Luke drive off with Free?"

"Yes. I followed them from Lorenzo's to Stephen's Green, and they drove off in Free's Volvo."

"So who was watching O'Connell?"

"I was supposed to be, but I followed Luke and Free instead." Dermot opened his mouth to say something.

"Don't even ask," Grace warned.

Dermot shrugged. "OK. So O'Connell's no alibi. But he didn't leave Lorenzo's for, what, about fifteen minutes after Luke and Free?"

"About that," Grace said.

"So how did he know where they'd be four hours later?"

"Did Free definitely identify O'Connell as the attacker?" Grace asked.

"Positive ID," replied Dermot. "So she must be lying. But why, for God's sake?"

"What if it was her? What if she attacked Luke and left him for dead?"

"But why would she do that?" Dermot asked.

Grace leaned her elbows on the counter. "Phoebe had a theory that maybe a jealous lover zapped Luke."

"Jealous lover? . . . Well that puts you well and truly in the frame," Dermot said, grinning. "Where were you?"

"Shut up, Dermot," Grace said. "Stop being

an asshole. I mean a jealous lover of Free's. Anyway, we asked Poppy about that but she knocked it on the head. You see, apparently, about three years ago, Free had a breakdown over this guy that she fell for. The way Poppy put it, Free was crazy about him, but he didn't feel the same way. She said that Free's inclined to be very obsessive. She believed the chap was equally mad about her. The upshot was that he dumped her. She wouldn't let it go though and kept phoning him and hassling him. Virtually stalking him, in fact. In the end she cracked up and had a breakdown."

"So where's this leading?"

"Don't be so thick, Dermot. She obviously took a shine to Luke. What if she made a pass at him and he turned her down? Maybe she snapped."

"It's a thought," said Dermot. "But the only one who knows for sure is Luke."

"Does Free know Luke's still alive?"

"Yes," said Dermot. "Come to think of it, though, she seemed pretty shaken when I told her. At the time I thought it was relief. Now I'm not so sure."

"Is there a guard on his door at Vincent's?" Grace asked, anxiously.

Dermot shook his head.

"I'm taking my break now, Alison," Grace yelled at a miserable looking girl who was picking at her nails as she sat at the till. Then she and Dermot made a run for the door.

On the way to Vincent's, Dermot called Harcourt Terrace.

They abandoned the car at the hospital entrance, leaving the door swinging open. Grace ran ahead of Dermot down the crowded corridor, shoving past anyone who got in the way. She took the stairs two at a time and made it to intensive care, breathless and panting. She made a mental note to start visiting the gym again. A skinny orderly stopped her.

"Sorry, you can't go in there," he said, feebly trying to block her way. She was so out of breath, she couldn't explain. Instead she barged past him into the corridor. Luke's bed was empty. The ward sister heard the commotion and hurried out of her office.

"What's going on?"

Grace leaned against the wall and pointed at Luke's empty bed. "Luke Ryan?" she gasped.

"He's on a side ward," the sister said. "Why? Who are you?"

"Which side ward?" Grace demanded.

The woman stared at her open-mouthed and didn't answer. But then she'd never been confronted by a five-foot-seven chicken before. Grace grabbed her shoulders.

"Please. It's important. A matter of life and death. Which side ward?"

"Second on the right, through the double doors."

Grace set off again at a run and skidded through Luke's door. Thankfully he was alone. He looked quite peaceful with only a couple of drips running into his arm, compared with the last time she'd seen him attached to all the life-support paraphernalia. She heaved a sigh of relief as she stood at the end of the bed. A couple of seconds later two burly security men rushed into the room followed by the ward sister.

"This is the . . ." she hesitated, " . . . the person." One of the security man grabbed her by the arm.

"It's all right!" Dermot staggered into the room, red-faced and sweating. He was holding up his ID. "Inspector McEvoy. Harcourt Terrace," he gasped. "The chicken's with me."

Chapter Twenty-Seven

Unaware that half of Harcourt Terrace were looking for her, Free sat alone in Herbert Park, making plans.

Dermot meanwhile was driving Grace back to the Pembroke Street branch of The Chucklin' Chookie. When they stopped at the lights on Merrion Road, Grace said, "Why don't we stop off at Raglan Road and take a crafty look at Free's car."

"But she's not there," Dermot said. "Molloy called me just before we left the hospital."

"Well, let's look all the same. It's on our way."

The lights changed. Dermot shifted into gear and signalled left. "If she's not there, she must be in her car." Dermot said, almost to himself.

"Humour me, Dermot."

As they pulled into the drive, Dermot said, "There, see. No car."

"Try around the side," said Grace.

Dermot drove round and stopped in front of

the double doors of a garage. Grace jumped out of the car. Dermot hesitated. "Come on," she said, irritated by his reluctance.

She cupped her hands against the glass panel at the side of the door and peered into the dimly-lit interior.

"It's here," she hissed. "Come on."

Dermot got out of the car and followed her.

"You realise we don't have a warrant," he said.

"You're worried about Free's state of mind, Dermot? You're afraid she might have harmed herself, aren't you? So you're checking her car."

She knelt down and looked under the front of the Volvo.

"The number plate's pretty bent," she said. Dermot leaned over and looked. Grace went round to the boot. It wasn't locked. "Have you a torch?"

"Not on me," Dermot said. "I've one in the car. I'll get it."

While he was gone, Grace opened the boot. In the poor light, she could make out the spare wheel and the jack. It looked as if they'd been thrown in, willy-nilly. She leant in, supporting herself by holding onto the edge of the boot. She couldn't see anything else. Dermot came back with the torch. He directed it at the wheel and the jack.

"That looks like blood." He looked around.

"Find me a screwdriver or a piece of rag to pick this up with," he said. Grace walked over to an old chest of drawers by the back wall and grabbed what looked like an old curtain. She handed it to Dermot. He gingerly picked up the jack.

"That's dried blood all right," he said. Then, "What's that on your hand?"

Grace looked down. Her hand was covered in dark red, almost black, half-congealed goo. "Ugh!" She held it out in front of her, then grabbed the rag from Dermot's hands.

"No! Dermot snapped. "That's evidence. Here." He took a clean hanky out of his pocket. "Wipe it on this."

Grace feverishly rubbed her hand with the hanky. She felt like immersing her hand in boiling water for twenty minutes. Whose blood was it? *Take your pick,* she told herself, *Carenza's? Luke's? Cassie's? No Cassie was strangled, it couldn't be hers.*

Dermot hurried out to his car and came back with a couple of big plastic evidence bags. Grace stuffed the hanky in the bag and handed it back to Dermot.

"I called the office," Dermot said. "Jack's coming down with the technical team. Let's see what Poppy has to say."

Poppy was not at home. In fact, no one answered the bell. Dermot got on the phone again and ordered a search warrant for the house and garage.

"I should get back to the chicken factory," Grace said. "Can you give me a lift?" She couldn't face meeting the team from Harcourt Terrace, dressed in her chicken gear. Dermot took pity on her.

"OK," he said. "Why don't you wait in the car."

When Jack Molloy swung into the drive, Grace sank down in the passenger seat and tried to be invisible. As he was talking to Dermot he kept giving her sidelong glances and smirking.

Oh God. I'll never live this down, she thought, sinking even lower in the seat, until she was almost lying on the floor.

"What's the matter with you? Dermot asked as he climbed back into the driver's seat.

"Nothing at all," Grace said sarcastically. "Apart from having my street cred washed down the toilet."

"What street cred?" Dermot asked, smirking.

He started the engine and drove out onto Raglan Road.

"What's the job?" Dermot asked as they resumed their journey.

"Job? Oh yes. The owner thinks Chuck, his manager,is ripping him off."

"And is *Chuck* ripping him off?"

"Yes," Grace said. "He's buying in stuff on the

quiet and taking the profits from that for himself."

"Good God! You didn't waste any time. How did you work that out so fast? You've only been there a couple of hours."

"Brilliant detective work," Grace said.

"No. I mean, really?"

"OK. So I asked Alison. You know, the miserable-looking cashier? She grassed him up. He used to share her nest until he dumped her for a younger chookie."

Dermot sniggered. "What d'you expect. I mean, she's no spring chicken, is she?"

"Very funny, Dermot."

He pulled into the kerb. "So why are you coming back here if you've rumbled the manager?"

"I'm going to string it out for another week." Dermot raised his eyebrows. "Don't get sanctimonious on me, Dermot," Grace said, as she slid out of the passenger seat. "I'm living in the real world now and we need the money. Besides, I need to get photos and stuff. You know, proof?"

"Ah, yes," Dermot said wistfully. "Proof. It's a bugger, isn't it?"

* * *

Free wrapped her coat tightly round her body

301

and leaned into the wind. It was growing dusk and the rush-hour traffic was thickening up. Everything was clear in her mind now. Luke Ryan had to die. She couldn't afford to take the risk that he might regain conciousness. It was his own fault. He shouldn't have let her down. Cheating on her with that bitch, Grace de Rossa. They'd all let her down. Tim, Carenza, Luke. Even Mother.

Why did people have to be like that? She'd loved Tim. He told her he was crazy about her. But people in love should want to be together all the time. Then he said they should cool it. That she was suffocating him. Suffocating him? How can you be suffocated by someone you're supposed to be in love with? She'd begged him. Bombarded him with phone calls, but it was no good. She couldn't convince him. She knew he was only fooling himself. He loved her. Someone must have poisoned his mind against her.

She stopped abruptly as she rounded the corner into Raglan Road. Parked outside her gate she could clearly see two police vans, one with the blue light still flashing. Two uniformed gardai stood like sentries on either side of the gate. This wouldn't do. This wouldn't do at all.

She turned around and hurriedly retraced her steps back towards Merrion Road.

Poppy Dalglish-Stuart barged into reception ranting and raving incoherently and waving her arms about. Phoebe's first thought was that she looked like Medusa on a bad hair day.

"Poppy. I don't know what you're talking about," she said, but Poppy was in no mood to listen.

"What am I paying you for? That's what I ask myself." She leant over Phoebe, who was sitting on the low leather sofa. Phoebe felt trapped. She tried to get up. Poppy turned her attention to Xin. "And take that silly smirk off your face, you stupid girl."

As she paused for breath, Phoebe struggled to her feet.

"Poppy. Please slow down and start again. I haven't a clue what you're on about."

"It's Emmet O'Connell. They've released him. The evil man has slithered out of it again."

Phoebe and Xin were equally dumbfounded.

"Are yeh sure?" Xin blurted out. Poppy gave her a look that would shrivel a lesser person than a trained Ninja.

"Poppy, I swear to you, we know nothing about this," Phoebe said as she reached for the phone. "I'll call Dermot McEvoy. There must be some mistake."

"There most certainly *is* some mistake. A bloody big one. And don't bother trying to get hold of McEvoy, he's tearing my house apart as we speak."

"Your house! But why?"

"He came out with some drivel about Free. But you must know this. He mentioned something in passing about Grace finding evidence against her. So don't try and pull the wool over my eyes. It's as plain as day. Emmet is at liberty and my daughter is missing again. Doesn't that strike you as something of a coincidence?"

"I know nothing about it, I swear to you, Poppy." Phoebe looked over at Xin. "Did Grace call in? D'you have any idea what all this is about?"

Xin shook her head. "Not a clue."

Suddenly Poppy seemed to run out of steam. She sat down heavily on the sofa and buried her head in her hands. Phoebe felt sorry for her. She walked over and awkwardly put her hand on the older woman's shoulder.

"Start at the beginning, Poppy."

Poppy didn't move for a moment, then she slowly sat very upright and took a deep breath.

"Dermot McEvoy has released Emmet O'Connell. He tells me that Emmet could not have abducted my daughter because he has some sort of alibi. He also tells me that the body of Cassie Drummond was found in Carenza's summer house out in Kilternan. And it seems Grace was poking around my garage this morning and has come up with some cock-and-bull story about Free."

"Good grief!" Phoebe said. "But I can't see that's right. Why would Grace do that? When Free was kidnapped, we weren't watching . . . em . . . I mean, Emmet had given us the slip. He definitely didn't have an alibi."

"That's exactly what I told McEvoy. But would he listen? No. And it gets even more preposterous. He even claims that Free's the guilty party."

Phoebe furrowed her brow. "This doesn't sound right at all."

"O'Connell was ou' in Kilternan," Xin said. "If yeh remember, Mungo folled him ou' there."

"There, you see," Phoebe said. "There's bound to be a perfectly reasonable explanation. Grace is sure to have the right story." Phoebe walked behind the reception desk and sat down.

"And just where *is* Grace?" Poppy demanded.

"She's ou' on a job," Xin said.

"Then get her back here. I demand an explanation."

Poppy's attitude was getting right up Phoebe's nose.

"Look, Poppy. I can't contact Grace till later. She's undercover on a job. Why don't you go home and get some rest. I'll ring you as soon as she gets back."

Poppy drew herself up to her full height and adopted her most imperious expression. "Don't patronise me, young woman. I insist that you contact Grace. I demand it. I would remind you that *I* am paying the piper. So *I* call the tune." She leaned over the desk, her face only inches from Phoebe's. Phoebe sat back in her chair and glared back. Impasse.

Xin cleared her throat. "I think I migh' be able t'get holda Grace."

Phoebe turned her glare on Xin. She hated to think that the likes of Poppy could get the better of her. Xin ignored her and said, "She's goin' to visit her folks in Vincent's as soon as she finishes her shift. I could go along an' get her. She'll be finished any time now."

Poppy threw her hands in the air. "Eureka! At last someone with a bit of intelligence. Run along, dear. Run along and get her."

Xin looked at Phoebe. Phoebe gritted her teeth and said, "Oh, go on then. Go to Vincent's. See what she has to say."

Xin didn't move.

"What's the matter now?" Phoebe snapped.

306

"I'll need yer car. The brakes on mine 're knackered."

Phoebe threw her the keys. "And if there's even one little scratch . . ."

"As if?" Xin said grinning. She gave Phoebe a broad wink behind Poppy's back. "Youse can have a nice little chat an' I'll be back before yeh know it!"

Chapter Twenty-Eight

Grace felt as if every pore in her body was oozing stale chicken grease. She peered at her reflection in the cracked mirror of the staff toilets. Her hair was plastered to her head. She could almost feel the pimples waiting to erupt from her chin. God! How did people do this job all the time? Her feet were killing her and her vertebrae felt is if they were all compacted together. She leaned forward and pushed her arms against the wall, stretching her spine.

A picture of her father flashed across her mind. It was so foreign to her to see him helpless. What would happen to him now? How would he handle life in a wheelchair? And what about Mother? What about Luke? Had Free really tried to kill him? Would he even remember?

She hung up her dungarees in the locker provided (with key. Staff, for the use of) and pulled on her jeans. She wondered idly if Dermot had caught up with Free yet.

Alison stuck her head around the door. "You off then?" she asked.

Grace nodded. "Yes," she said as she tied the laces of her Reeboks.

"Fancy going for a jar?"

"Sorry. I have to go and visit my folks. They're both in hospital."

Alison leaned against the door-jamb. "Oh dear. Not too serious I hope?"

Grace smiled at her. "Oh, they're on the mend," she said.

"Old, are they?"

"Sorry?"

"Old. Your parents?" Grace stared blankly at her. "I thought with them both being in hospital, they must be elderly or something," Alison explained.

"No. It was a car crash," Grace said, miffed that Alison should think she looked old enough to have elderly parents.

"Tough luck," said the younger girl. "Oh well, I'll see you tomorrow." She turned to leave, then stopped.

"About what I told you . . . About Chuck.

"Yes?"

"You wouldn't say anything to anyone else about it, would you?"

Grace pulled an imaginary zip across her lips. "My lips are sealed," She said.

"Cos I wouldn't want to get him into no trouble," Alison said.

Grace was mildly surprised. "Why ever not?"

Alison gave a shy smile. "Well he's not the worst. And I think he might be going off yer woman."

"You're not serious?" Grace said.

Alison grinned. "Yes. So that means he might come home."

"No," Grace said shocked. "I meant, you wouldn't take him back after the way he treated you, surely?"

"You know yourself," replied the girl. "Better the devil you know . . . Anyway. See you tomorrow." The door swung shut behind her.

Grace threw on her coat and headed for the fire exit. As she neared the foot of the fire stairs, she saw the brave Chuck talking to another man. The man handed him a large cardboard carton and Chuck in turn handed the man a couple of bank notes. Grace rummaged in her bag for her camera, then took a couple of frames. *Great,* she told herself. *One day less to spend in the Chucklin' Chookie factory.*

* * *

Free hurried through the doors of the shopping mall. After-work shoppers jostled each other, each intent on picking up something for dinner, or collecting the dry cleaning they forgot at lunch-time. Christmas carols jingled over the canned music system and a not-quite-fat-enough Santa sat in his grotto.

"Ho ho ho," he said as she passed by.

As she made her way through the automatic doors of the supermarket, her eyes scanned the overhead signs, looking for the household section. A feeling of irritation overcame her. Why couldn't they sign things clearly? They should have a clear sign directing people to the extremely poisonous household substances section. She laughed aloud, prompting a few puzzled looks. *Pull yourself together,* she told herself. *This is serious.* Eventually, frustrated, she asked a young boy stacking biscuits on shelves.

"The detergent's over there." He pointed to the back of the store. "Just past the do-it-yourself section."

She felt hysteria rising in her chest. She wanted to laugh again. How appropriate. Do-it-yourself! She took a deep breath and hurried off. Her eyes scanned the shelves. Ah, Jeyes Fluid. Good old reliable Jeyes Fluid. Fifty mils down a vein should do the job. She picked up the narrow rectangular tin and joined the line of impatient shoppers at the check-out.

* * *

Alice de Rossa lay, unstirring, in a deep sedated sleep. Her head was swathed in bandages and a drip fed into her wrist. She looked so frail. Her skin so pale. A nurse came into the room, fiddled with the drip, and then took readings from the monitors. She smiled at Grace. Faith stood at the other side of he bed.

"She looks so small," Grace said. "She'll hate it that they've shaved her head."

"Maybe I'll get her a wig tomorrow," Faith said. "It'll make her feel more like herself once they take the bandages off."

"Have you spoken to Charles?" Grace asked.

Faith nodded. "He seems quite happy with her progress."

"But what are we going to do, Faith? How will she cope with Daddy?"

Faith sat down on the edge of the bed and took hold of her mother's hand. "We'll have to cross that bridge when we come to it," she said. "But Charity said she'd look after Mummy when they let her out. And you know how good she is with Mummy. Daddy's another matter, of course."

"You can say that again," Grace said. "He'll be impossible."

"I think you might be misjudging him, you know, Grace. This business seems to have changed him."

"Of course it's bloody changed him!" Grace

312

burst out, then lowered her voice as she realised she was almost shouting. "Of course it's bloody changed him. He'll be totally dependent for the first time since he was a child."

"Have you spoken to him lately?" Faith asked.

Grace shook her head. "Not for a couple of days."

"Then go and see him. You'll be surprised."

"I doubt that," Grace said. "But I was going up to see him anyway."

"How's Luke? Or is that a taboo subject?"

"Why would Luke be a taboo subject?" Grace said, on the defensive.

Faith looked embarrassed. "I thought he'd . . . eh . . . cheated on you with your client's daughter or something."

"For God's sake, Faith! You shouldn't jump to conclusions," Grace snapped. "He might not've been. Anyway, I'm giving him the benefit of the doubt."

Faith threw up her hands in mock surrender. "Fine by me," she said. "I was just asking."

Alice stirred slightly. Both women looked down at her.

Grace said, "Faith, does Mother make you feel guilty?"

"What about?"

Grace shrugged. "Everything."

Faith shook her head. "I don't know what you mean."

Grace sighed. "There's my answer," she said.

She bent down and kissed her mother lightly on the cheek. "I'll go up and see Daddy."

* * *

The garda car passed her slowly. It wasn't until it had gone by that Free recognised it as such. Her heart skipped a beat. She pulled the collar of her coat up round her face, and paused to see where it was going. The car slowed down and stopped by the main entrance, engine running. A cop got out, then leaned his head in through the passenger door. He slammed the door shut and walked in through the glass doors. The garda car drove forward a few yards and parked by the no parking sign. Free put her head down and hurried through the doors, without looking back.

The entrance hall was busy with visitors coming and going. They were laden with flowers or plastic carrier bags full of biscuits and Lucozade and copies of *Woman's Own* or *Hello!* magazine. Ways to pass the time. Chewing gum for the brain.

The cop was ahead of her, standing by the lift. She stopped and looked at a notice board, half turning her body away from him. He punched the call button, impatiently. Then that girl, the strange little fat one who worked for Grace de Rossa, hurried past. Free hid behind a pillar and peered round. The girl stood by the lift. It was definitely her. What on earth was she doing here? A bell pinged and the doors opened. They both disappeared inside.

Grace was surprised to see her father sitting up in bed when she walked into his room. He still had the cage contraption over his head and shoulders. Michael was leaning against the radiator under the window, arms folded. They were both laughing.

"Hello, Grace," Paul de Rossa said to his daughter. "You look serious."

"You look better," she said.

"Yes. I'm a lot better, thank God."

Grace had never heard her father thank the almighty before. "I was down with Mummy," she said. "Charles says he's happy with her progress."

"Yes. I spoke to him myself a while ago," her father said. "She'll need a long convalescence."

Michael picked up his jacket. "I think I'll go and get a bite to eat, as long as you're here," he said, making for the door.

"Oh . . . I can't stay long," Grace said anxiously. Afraid that she'd have to stay alone and make conversation with her father. "I have to . . ."

Paul de Rossa held out his hand. "It's OK, Grace. I don't need a baby-sitter. You don't have to stay. You can go as soon as you like."

"It's not that. I mean, it's not that I don't

315

want to stay," she babbled. Then, "you moved your arm!"

"Yes," he said. "God's seen fit to give a sinner another chance in life."

He smiled at her. The smile had warmth. She blushed.

"Come and sit here," he said. He patted the edge of the bed. "And tell me what's bothering you."

She hesitated, then sat next to him. "I'm worried about you," she said, "You and Mummy. What'll happen when they discharge you? How will you cope?"

"You mean, how will your mother cope with me?"

She smiled at his candour. "Well, yes."

"I'm not the ogre you make me out to be, you know, Grace." She opened her mouth to speak but he stopped her. "I know I haven't always treated your mother well." He caught her look. "All right," he conceded, "I know I've often treated your mother downright badly, but a brush with death can change the way people look at their lives. Their values. God has shown me the error of my ways. He's given me another chance." He paused as if waiting for her to speak.

Grace said "Are you on medication? D'you know what you're saying?"

"Of course I'm on medication, but it has nothing to do with the truth of what I'm telling

316

you," he went on. "I know you may not believe me, you know that I haven't always been faithful to your mother, Grace. But I promise you I'll make sure she gets the very best care. Whatever the cost, God willing. She's precious to me."

"You're right," Grace said. "I *don't* believe you."

"Then all I can do is hope and pray to God that my actions will speak louder than my words, Grace. I dearly love your mother, and I'll prove it to you."

"Don't prove it to me," Grace said, "Prove it to her."

He smiled benignly at her. "I'll do just that, Grace. With the help of God."

"I have to go now." Grace backed towards the door. "I'll pop in again tomorrow."

"Goodbye, darling. God bless you."

Grace pulled the door closed behind her and leaned her back against the wall. She saw Faith walking down the corridor towards her.

"Well?" Faith said.

"I'm not sure. When did he find God? I never heard him mention Him before."

"Don't be so cynical, Grace."

Grace snorted. "D'you blame me? I'm not sure I can cope with Daddy as a born-again Christian."

"He's not. And give him a break. He's been through a lot. It has changed him."

"We'll see," said an unforgiving, sceptical Grace.

Chapter Twenty-Nine

The cop was standing outside Luke's room. *Shit!* Free hurried back down the corridor into the ladies toilet and locked herself in a cubical. She wanted to be sick. What if he blabbed before she could get to him. *Calm down,* she told herself. *That won't happen.* She concentrated on breathing. Deep breaths to slow her heart rate. The panic receded. She left the cubicle and ran her wrists under the cold tap, then splashed her face with cold water. That felt better. Now to business. She had to find a way to get into Luke's room and a syringe by which to administer the fatal dose. Where was the best place to find syringes lying about?

Accident and Emergency perhaps. She set off once again for the ground floor.

Xin was annoyed. When she got to Alice de Rossa's room, the nurse told her that she'd just missed Grace. Then she took ages to find Paul de Rossa's whereabouts. She was sent from pillar to post, eventually discovering him in a private room, sitting up in bed saying the rosary. Her hasty retreat was thwarted however when she identified herself as a colleague of Grace's. He insisted she stay and join him in a decade. She didn't know how to refuse and half heartedly made the holy-mary-motherofgod-prayferussinners responses, finally escaping when Michael came back and took pity on her. The next logical place to try was Luke Ryan's ward. She headed for the lift and Intensive Care.

Grace walked as far as the main entrance with Faith.

"I'll call you tomorrow," she promised as they embraced. She watched Faith disappear into the shadows of the car park. She was half-jealous of her younger sister. Not of her lifestyle, but of the way she handled all her relationships. She was totally content in her marriage. She had no difficulty relating to her parents or siblings. She accepted them as they were, without judgement.

Grace heaved a heavy sigh and set off again to see Luke. Phoebe was right. If she wasn't careful she'd alienate him completely with her mindless insecurity. She knew it was stupid to judge all men by Andrew's standards. Heaven forbid.

The lift door opened and she filed in after a nurse, an elderly man and a young woman with a toddler balanced on her hip. Ping. The lift rose. Ping. It stopped at the first floor and the nurse got out. They all stood staring straight ahead, as you do. The doors started to close. Suddenly Grace snapped wide awake. Free Dalglish-Stuart, wearing a white doctor's coat hurried across her line of vision. It took her three seconds too long to react. The door slid closed and the lift continued its journey ever upwards. At the pace of a crippled snail Grace frantically stabbed the second floor button. The lift glided to a halt. After an age the doors opened and she rushed out, bumping straight into Xin.

"There yeh are. I've been on a bleedin' tour'a this rotten place lookin' fer yeh."

Grace grabbed her arm and dragged her towards the stairs.

"Quickly! I've just seen Free."

Xin bobbed along beside her. "So?"

"We have to find her. She's going to try and finish Luke off."

"Wha?"

"Don't ask," Grace said. "Trust me. We have to stop her." They reached the stairwell. Grace clattered down two at a time. Xin followed closely behind.

"Why're we goin' down here?"

"I saw her on the floor below when the lift doors opened."

Xin stopped dead and grabbed Grace's arm.

"Hold on. This is daft. If she goin' t' try an' kill yer man, she'll be goin up to the third floor."

"Shit! I wasn't thinking," Grace said. They did an about turn and ran back up the stairs, erupting on the third floor, almost knocking a nurse, wheeling the drugs trolley, for six.

"There's a cop guarding his door," Grace gasped. Xin overtook her on the outside and skidded round the corner.

"No there isn't," she yelled over her shoulder. Grace rounded the corner seconds after Xin. She was right. No cop on the door. What was Dermot thinking about?

Xin thundered through Luke's door. Through the opening Grace saw Free, standing by the bed. As she ran through the doorway, Free plunged a syringe into the fluid bag attached to the intravenous drip in Luke's wrist. The clear fluid turned cloudy.

Xin, defying gravity, spun on the ball of her right foot and aimed a straight-legged kick with the heel of the other foot at Free's chest. At the same moment Grace ripped the drip from Luke's arm. Winded, Free let out an *oooph* sound as all the air left her lungs. She dropped to the floor like a sack of sand. Then all hell broke loose.

Within seconds the same two burly security men who had attempted to eject her earlier in the day appeared, followed closely by a very red-faced garda Joe Bean, who had slipped off for a sly smoke.

Free screamed and ranted like a mad woman as he cuffed her. She cursed Grace, Emmet O'Connell and whoever else, and cast doubt on Joe Bean's parentage. Xin had to use the Vulcan death grip to stop her flailing arms. After Free had been subdued, Dermot, who looked close to a heart attack, lumbered down the corridor accompanied by half of Harcourt Terrace who carted Free off.

Joe sidled up to Grace.

"Sure you won't tell Dermot I went for a smoke?" he said.

Grace glared at him. "She could've killed Luke, Joe. You were bloody lucky Xin and I were here to bail you out."

"Ah . . . you know yourself . . ."

Grace was disgusted. "Ah, nothing." She turned away.

"So what's the story?" Xin said.

Grace told her what had happened earlier in the day, when she and Dermot searched Free's garage.

"So if it wasn't fer me followin' yer man, he wouldn't've had an alibi, an yer woman would'a got away with her story about him kidnappin' her, an tryin' t'kill Luke?"

"Yes," Grace said.

Xin beamed with pleasure "Well how abou' tha'?"

"Why were you looking for me?"

"Oh yeh. Poppy's back at Baggot Stree'. She came in rantin' and ravin' abou' you and Dermot. We didn't know wha' the story was. I mean, yeh didn't call in or anything. Did yeh?"

"I didn't have time," Grace said. "I had to get back to the other job at the Chucklin salmonella joint."

"She's not goin' t'be too thrilled abou' yer woman bein' carted off, is she?"

"Maybe I'll phone in and let Phoebe break the news," Grace said, thinking aloud.

Xin agreed. "Hmmm. Good move."

Dermot joined them. "Fair play to you," he said, looking Xin up and down. "For a pint-sizer, you pack a punch."

Xin sniffed dismissivly. "All in a day's work," she said.

Grace waited around until the doctor had checked Luke over.

"You did the right thing pulling the drip from his arm like that," she said. "You probably saved his life."

"Will he be OK?" Grace asked.

The doctor nodded. "He'll be just fine," she said, "relatively speaking."

"What d'you mean, relatively speaking?"

"Well, apart from the broken leg, the broken wrist, collar bone and . . ."

Grace heaved a sigh of relief. "Nothing actually life-threatening then?"

"No. Nothing life-threatening. Though don't be surprised if he can't remember anything about the accident."

Oh well, Grace thought. *Every cloud and all that. With a bit of luck, if he ever fancied Free, he'll have fogotten.*

Chapter Thirty

"What was she trying to inject him with?" Phoebe asked.

"The nurse said it smelled like Jeyes Fluid," said Grace.

"That would've cleared his arteries for him," remarked Phoebe.

It was well after seven and Poppy had long gone. She'd thundered down to Harcourt Terrace shouting the odds and accusing Sleuths of gross disloyalty as soon as she'd heard the news about Free's arrest. But that was Dermot's problem. Poppy had paid her sizeable bill as soon as Emmet O'Connell had been arrested the previous day.

Phoebe, Grace and Xin were sitting round a roaring fire in Grace's flat. Phoebe and Grace were drinking from steaming mugs of coffee, liberally laced with Bushmills. Xin stuck to plain coffee. What with her body being a temple and all.

"You should've seen Xin," Grace said. "She was amazing. Gravity-defying in fact."

"It was nothin'," Xin said, embarrassed. "It's my mission in life t'see good triumphs over evil."

Phoebe handed Xin a box in a plastic carrier bag.

"What's this?" Xin asked warily.

"Open it and see," said Phoebe.

Xin struggled with the carrier. "Wow! Me own mobile."

Phoebe grinned at her. "It'll help in the fight against evil."

"Dermot said that they'd found traces of Carenza's blood in the boot of Free's Volvo," Grace said. "I wonder if she knew about the will all along?"

"She must've," Xin said. "Bit radicle, killin' the auld wan, though. I mean, she could'a waited 'til she snuffed it of her own accord. Carenza wasn't exactly in the first flusha youth, was she?"

"Maybe Carenza told her about Brian Drummond," said Grace. "Remember the unsigned loan agreement we found after he killed himself?"

The doorbell buzzed. Grace went down to answer it.

"Yeh wouldn't think butter'd melt in her mouth t'look at her, would yeh?" Xin said, as she rummaged in the box for the phone's operating instruction book.

"Whose mouth?"

"Free's. D'yeh think Luke was givin' her one?"

Phoebe shrugged. "I don't know. I hope not. It's time Grace had a bit of luck with men."

Grace returned accompanied by Dermot. He walked over to the fire and warmed his hands, rubbing them together. Phoebe, who was sitting closest to him, could feel the cold radiating from his overcoat. She stood up. "Sit here," she said. "You must be freezing." He hesitated for a second. then sat down. Grace handed him a mug of coffee. He cupped his hands around it.

"Thanks."

"What's happening back at the ranch?" Grace asked.

Dermot took a swig of coffee. "Free's been charged with attempted murder for starters, though I expect once we get all the forensic stuff back we'll get her for Carenza and probably Cassie Drummond too."

"She has to be crazy," Phoebe observed.

"Clinically mad," agreed Dermot. "Mind you, it wasn't from the wind she got it."

"Why d'you think she tried to kill Luke?" Grace asked, tentatively.

He stared into the fire and shook his head. "Your guess is as good as mine. He was probably in the wrong place at the wrong time. By the way, Pattie Doyle found the brooch. You know the diamond one that was missing?"

"The one like a wheat-sheaf?"

Dermot nodded.

"Where?"

"Inside the spare wheel in the boot of the Volvo," said Dermot.

"So what has Free said up to now?" Phoebe asked.

"Not a lot," Dermot replied. "She was in such a state the doctor put her under sedation. I'll interview her properly tomorrow."

"And what about Poppy?" Xin asked. "How's she takin' it?"

Dermot exhaled loudly. "I've kept out of her way up to now," he said. "Jack Molloy got to talk to her."

"Couldn't happen to a nicer guy," Grace said, smirking.

They all sat in silence staring at the fire. After a while, Dermot knocked back the last of his coffee, and stood up. "Well. I'm off," he said. He looked over at Grace and grinned. "I only came over to let you know Luke's conscious. He was asking for you."

"Why didn't you say so before!" Grace said as she grabbed her coat and rushed through the door, leaving it swinging open.

Phoebe, Xin and Dermot stared at the empty doorway.

"Fer wan who was accusin' him of all sorts, she isn't wastin' any time gettin' down there," Xin wryly observed.

Luke was a little on the groggy side by the time Grace got over to Vincent's. After giving a promise to stay only a few minutes, the night sister allowed Grace in to see him. His eyes were closed when she entered his room. She stood at the foot of the bed and stared at him. After a minute he opened his eyes. When he recognised her, he flashed his lop-sided grin at her.

"Hello," she said.

"Hello, yourself," he replied.

"How d'you feel?"

"How do I look?"

"Terrible."

"Thanks," he said. "Dermot said you and Xin saved me from a death worse than fate."

Grace laughed. "Something like that," she said. "For some reason, Free was trying to pump you full of Jeyes Fluid. What can you remember?"

"Not a lot," he said. He frowned. "I remember having lunch with her." He saw Grace's expression. "And before you kick up a fuss, I couldn't avoid it. She was upset so I went for a drive with her. Then I remember leaving the pub. I was anxious to get back to town to meet you. But that's it. After that, it's all a blank."

"We think Free ran over you and left you for dead."

"So Dermot said. But I don't remember," he said.

"They found traces of Carenza's blood in the boot of Free's car. So it looks as if she's implicated in that murder, as well as poor Cassie Drummond's."

"Why?" Luke pondered. "Why would she kill Cassie?"

She walked round the bed and sat on the edge beside him, holding his hand. "Who knows? I think she's probably mad. As Dermot said, 'It wasn't from the wind she got it'."

Luke smiled at the remark. "That's true. Though I like Poppy. She's a nice harmless old biddy. She'll be devastated about Free."

"Hmmm," said Grace. Luke's eyelids started to droop. She got off the bed.

"Don't go yet," he said.

She sat down again and took his hand.

"This hospital visiting thing's getting to be a habit," she said. "My folks are in here."

"Both of them?"

Grace nodded. "They had a car smash."

"How are they doing?" he asked, concerned.

Grace shrugged. "They're getting there. My father seems to have turned into a religious fanatic. He even cornered poor Xin into saying a decade of the rosary the other day!"

"And her a card-carrying Ninja!" Luke said, giving her a sleepy grin.

Grace laughed again. "It must be all the drugs they're pumping into him."

"It could be the medication," said Luke. "I don't know what they're giving me, but I think it's making me have hallucinations."

"Really?"

"Yes. At one point I could've sworn I saw a huge yellow chicken standing at the end of my bed."

"Good Grief! Are you serious?" Grace asked, stifling a snigger.

"Deadly serious," he said.